LYEL

Mail-Order Brides of Crakair, Book 6

AVA ROSS

LYEL

**An alien warrior seeking redemption
meets a captured Earth woman
being treated as a pet.
Will their love survive in a hostile world?**

Kidnapped by four-armed, blue skinned aliens, Isabelle "Isi" is sold to the head of the Al'kieern kidnapping operation. Isi has accepted she'll live and die as a songbird pet to the queen. If nothing else, performing for the Al'kieern beats being sold as a breeder. But a Crakairian warlord storms the Al'kieern compound, determined to destroy everything and everyone in his path. When he's captured, Isi offers to free him if he helps her get away.

Scorned by Crakairian society after his father tried to murder a respected military commander, Lyel is willing to die to redeem his family name. He takes on a suicide mission to destroy the Al'kieern kidnapping operation on the moon, Mara. But as he's about to blow the place to heille, he sees Isi. As she sings, a symbol appears on his palm, telling him she's his destined mate. He'll do anything to free her, but to escape, they must cross a grueling wasteland filled with deadly traps and with the Al'kieern hot on their heels. Will their growing love survive this challenge?

Lyel is Book 6 and the final book in the Mail-Order Brides of Crakair Series. This standalone, full-length romance has on-the-page heat, aliens who look and act alien, a guaranteed happily ever after, no cheating, and no cliffhanger. You can find the rest of the series here.

ONE

Lyel

L yel crawled through the long-abandoned tunnel beneath the Al'kieern stronghold on Crakair's moon, Mara, evading the hairy vister bugs dangling from the tunnel ceiling. A vister's wispy appendages secreted toxin. When the toxin makes contact with the person's skin, it stuns them. While the victim lay twitching, the mother vister descends and wraps her victim in a sticky mesh. Dragging the cocooned body to her nest, she leaves them as a tasty treat for her hatching children.

Lyel's death would not be at the claws of a vister bug. He was not afraid to die—he expected such an outcome today—but destroying the cursed Al'kieern kidnapping operation had to come first. He welcomed passing through the veil, where he would reunite with his deceased mother and little sister.

Stopping, he opened the pouch he dragged with him and pulled out a dynatem device filled with explosives. After nudging it carefully into a crack in the crumbling wall, he attached the detonate harness micro-linked to his com. Leaving the dynatem, he pulled himself farther down the passage, stopping periodically to plant more dynatems. When he reached the end of the channel, he crawled up the rung ladder leading to a tiny hidden cave below the first floor of the stronghold.

The only thing left to do was ensure the heads of the Al'kieern kidnapping ring gathered together in the great hall. Crakairian intelligence learned the covert group's leaders would meet tonight to discuss their new plan to take ships to Earth to kidnap females they'd sell to breeders. An army of Al'kieern would remain on Earth. They intended to build a complex to facilitate ongoing capture and transfer of Earth breeders throughout the galaxy. Any Earthlings who did not fit breeder criteria would be killed.

After their failure on the jungle planet, Yarris, where the compound was destroyed by a lizzer army, plus the destruction of their space station, the kidnappers were getting desperate. They had to know the Crakairians were on to them. If their Intel was as sophisticated as that of the Crakairians, they knew the Crakairians would do everything they could to stop the project.

Once Lyel did his part this daela, the organization would be decimated. The galaxy could rest easy for the foreseeable future.

Checking his com and seeing he was ahead of schedule, he settled on the ground. Before he activated the dynatems, he'd leave his hiding spot dressed in a holosuit that would project an Al'kieern image and infiltrate the great room where the organization's top generals planned to meet. Once he assured himself they were all present, he'd block the exits, activate the sequence on his com, and run, hoping to get far enough from the location before the dynatems deployed. The explosion would eliminate the compound and those plotting to take over Earth.

If completing this task meant his death, so be it. At

least he would die restoring his family's honor. Not long ago, his father, Piersag, declared a vengeance against Lyel's childhood friend Vork, intending to steal Vork's Earthling bride. Lyel was forced to fight in his father's place, but he could not find the will to kill his friend. His father was wrong. The vengeance was wrong. Lyel allowed Vork to win, and in a rage, Piersag tried to kill Vork himself. His father died from his efforts.

Lyel watched a centitrillion approach a tiny fly that landed on the stone wall opposite where he leaned. The centitrillion pounced, eating the fly with one gulp. It stared at him, its antennas twitching, before scurrying into the gloom.

To think it had come to this, spending his last minars beneath the ground on the Al'kieern moon, Mara. Alone other than for random insects. An ache filled Lyel's chest. No, he did not need to spend this time alone. He lifted his wrist and typed on his com. He needed a good memory. Pulling up the holoimage of his little sister, he projected it in front of him.

While Therena dipped and swayed, her gown dancing across her ankles, Lyel's lips twitched and slowly rose to a pain-filled smile. During happier days, as he walked through the estate's gardens, he heard his sister's laughter. Moving closer, he saw her dancing and paused to catch the image and store it. She was unaware he watched, he never had a chance to tell her. She and their mother died three weeks after the image was taken, when the plague swept through the galaxy, killing most of our females.

Watching his sister this daela hurt, but it felt fitting.

"Soon," he murmured. "I will restore our honor, Therena, and we will be together again."

He missed her. His ma, too. His father? Turbulent emotions jumbled together inside Lyel. His memories of a father, who handed him a youngling-sized kalina and taught him the ancient khatalm fighter ways, battled with flashes of a hard, cruel father who drank too much and cut everyone around him with his hands and words. Lyel and his father lost the people they loved during the sickness, while his father spiraled into anger, Lyel clung to his humanity.

A soft chime from his com told him it was time. Opening the bag on his lap, he tugged out the sheer, skin-tight holosuit that would fool even the most discerning eye. He tugged it over his clothing, careful to tuck his naanans beneath the membranous hood. After adding an Al'kieern laser pistol to his belt, he stuffed the bag into a depression in the wall. He closed his eyes and sent out a wish that this would go as it should. It was never easy taking a life—let alone multiple lives—but this act would save others.

Carefully edging up the secret hatch overhead, he listened, ensuring his location had not been revealed. It took the Crakairians many likars and more dinars to locate this rumored passage and secure it. When they made plans to send in a single operative, Lyel volunteered.

"If you are captured, they will kill you," Vork said through gritted teeth when Lyel stepped forward to give himself for this role.

"I am aware of this," Lyel said dryly.

"We cannot allow it."

"You cannot stop me." He rose from his chair and paced across Vork's office, pausing to stare out the window at the Ikeline Mountains. Turning, he faced his old friend. They'd only spoken twice since they fought the vengeance, first when Lyel approached Vork with a formal apology and the second, via com, when Lyel contacted Vork two likars ago to volunteer for this mission. Vork told him to come in to discuss it. "This is something I need to do. You know that."

Vork raked his hands across his naanans. "I do. But…"

From Council papers Lyel found in his father's desk while tidying the estate, he learned about the government's plan to stop the kidnapping operation. He knew then what he must do.

Vork grumbled, but Lyel could see he relented. His protest was a mere formality. He rose and came around his desk. "We appreciate your offer to do this."

"What kind of support can you provide?"

"The Al'kieern airspace missile system will not allow a craft to land outside the Mara capital, and we need to place you beyond the wasteland. We have a new cloaked transfer system we have used with some success. Complications experienced by a friend have been corrected. We can get you to the edge of the wasteland, but we will not be able to extract you after. You will need to escape Mara on your own."

Assuming Lyel lived. They both knew the odds of that were slim. After this, no one would say the Sastray family lacked courage or honor.

"If you are successful, get to the city and send word. We will do our best to extract you."

Lyel dipped his head. "Thank you."

"Be aware. Any attempt to use your com beyond basic functions will not pass through their atmosphere. Until you reach the city, you will be on your own." Vork's grim gaze met Lyel's. "There are other ways. We can still—"

"Nothing this certain, am I correct?"

"You are," Vork's naanans flared out in agitation. "I do not like this."

"It is for the best." In his heart, Lyel knew this. Only by going in himself could Lyel make the galaxy safe again.

"All the yaros since our fathers argued," Vork said, steepling his fingers beneath his chin. His probing gaze met Lyel's. "We have not spoken."

"I regret this," Lyel said, emotion clogging his voice. "I missed you, old friend."

"Yet you did not communicate."

"I honored my father's wishes to cut all ties between us." Why had he let Piersag dictate this? Yaros ago, Lyel's father attempted to steal a military appointment offered to Vork's father. When he lost, he slunk to his estates and plotted, determined to seek what he saw as revenge. And he had. Rumor had it Piersag killed Vork's father. But that was not enough to satisfy Piersag. When Vork was matched with an Earthling bride, Lyel's father tried to claim the woman. Piersag declared the vengeance and forced Lyel to fight but paid the price with his life.

Some males would retreat to their estate and avoid showing their face in society again, but not Lyel. He had to make this right, even if he also paid the final price.

Lyel closed the hatch, masking the entrance to the hidden tunnel from view. As he was told to expect, he found himself in a small closet. Moving around brooms and buckets of murky water, he cracked open the door, listened, and peered into the stone hall, noting the passages leading to sleeping chambers, droid service areas, and the main function room where the Al'kieern kidnapping operation's leaders would gather—directly above the explosives Lyel planted.

After engaging his holoimage, Lyel strode out into the corridor, shutting the door behind him. He squared his shoulders and ensured his laser pistol would slip easily from its sheath.

"Halt," a guard barked from farther down the hall.

Lyel stiffened. His spine twitched, and his heart thrust

up into his throat while he waited for a laser blow, for the Al'kieern to call for guards, or for him to see through Lyel's disguise. When nothing happened, he turned, his fingers twitching near his pistol.

"Were you speaking to me?" Lyel frowned at the Al'kieern guard striding toward him.

"Why are you in this area of the compound?" The male returned Lyel's scowl. "You should be with the others."

"I was using the facilities, and I became…lost." Lyel studied the Al'kieern, waiting for an aggressive move, but the male didn't twitch.

"This is not a valid excuse."

Sweat trickled down Lyel's neck, and he controlled his breathing. One wrong move and this would fall apart.

"You dare to question me? Do you know who I am?" It was time to test the holosuit, so he moved out of the shadows. Lyel should appear as an Al'kieern general, but what if the suit failed? "I am tempted to take your name and rank and report you."

"Oh, no, Sir," the guard sputtered, his attention dropping to the floor. "Please do not. You are right, Sir. I…I misspoke."

"Good," Lyel barked. "Now direct me back to the main hall and go about your business."

The Al'kieern bowed. "Straight ahead and then a left at the intersection, Sir. You will see—and hear—the hall from there."

Lyel tilted his head in acknowledgement and strode away from the guard, maintaining an even stride and projecting a confidence he did not feel. Inside, he heaved a big sigh. His suit worked. However, the mission wasn't over yet.

Worst case, if he was caught, he'd detonate the

dynatem wherever he was, but he wanted to ensure the head of the operation was inside the room before doing so. Intel suggested Fedeema, the self-appointed queen of the group, would not arrive until the last minar. Removing her would set the organization back yaros, giving the Crakairian government time to secure Earth's airspace and keep the Al'kieerns from interfering. The kidnapping operation would be left in tatters.

Rumor had it, the Al'kieern government had appointed a new leader in the capital, and it was hoped this person would step in and prevent this from happening again.

The scent of roasted meat and sickly sweet rutlar hit his sinuses when he hit the intersection. Once a bottle of rutlar was opened, the heady aroma of the hallucinogenic wine filled the air. They were drinking, which would make it easier for Lyel to avoid detection. His holosuit held enough power to maintain his Al'kieern holoimage for thirty minars. After that, he'd be exposed.

He strode up to the open archway and carefully assessed the situation. At least one hundred Al'kieern pirates sat at long tables set up in rows throughout the room, their boisterous conversation filling the air. Huge platters of food sat in the middle of the rustic wooden tables, and the hands of the almost-exclusively male Al'kieern reached in and scooped out meat and tubers. They ate directly from the community trenches, washing the food down with big mugs of rutlar.

Good. Lyel recognized faces from the intel vids the Crakairian military sent him. Fedeema was not present, but that was expected.

He slipped into the room and settled on the end of a bench, close to the others but not near enough to touch. If someone made contact, his holosuit would chew through the power caps quickly, and the energy needed to maintain his false image would fail. Eating was not an option either, but he doubted anyone around him would notice. To be safe, he hefted a glass of rutlar and toasted, placing the glass against his lips without drinking.

A horn sounded and silence swept through the room, leaving only harsh breathing and a rare burp breaking the pall. An arched door in the back of the room opened. Lyel, like everyone else, watched raptly. Behind him, the doors in the front of the room closed, and guards secured them with wooden bars, making Lyel's task easier.

From the back door, Fedeema strode into the room, her long, silver gown swishing around her ankles. Her bald head gleamed in the lamplight and her eyeridge spikes whipped back and forth. Her height was enhanced by spiky heels, and she'd glossed her wings with something to make them sparkle. As she strode toward the head table mounted on a dais, her four arms swinging freely, Lyel sucked in a breath and ensured his com was ready. Once she sat, he would act.

"Therena… Sister. I will be with you soon," he said softly.

The queen dropped into her seat and waved for a mug of rutler. Her gaze surveyed the room, thankfully skipping over Lyel without pausing. She sipped her drink and held up her hand.

Lyel's finger hovered of the detonation switch on his com.

It was time.

His belly lurched.

Three… Two…

The door behind the queen banged open again, and a winged Al'kieern strode into the room, a leash clutched in one of his four hands. He yanked on the chain, and someone stumbled out from the shadows.

An Earth female dressed in a pale pink gauze gown was hauled over to stand beside Fedeema. Fasteners on the female's leather collar winked in the low lights as the Al'kieern guard handed the leash to the queen.

Fedeema tugged, dragging the woman down close to speak in a voice too low for Lyel to hear.

How could an Earthling female be here? The Crakairian intel had not indicated such a thing was possible.

The woman shook her head, making her pink and golden...not naanans, but...flares. Yes, that was the term. *Flares.* The flares on her head swirled across her shoulders, prettier than a sunset. Was the color natural? Lyel had not paid much attention to reports about Earthling females, feeling unworthy of applying for the Selection after his family's dishonor, but he swore none of the women he saw had flares like this on their heads.

The queen paused, and her nose twitched. Her gaze scanned the room, studying each face, but she skimmed over Lyel.

His heart started beating again. For a mina... No, the suit would hold.

As if nothing had happened, Fedeema shoved the woman and barked out a command.

With a shudder, the female straightened and stiffened her shoulders. She climbed up a short flight of steps to stand on a raised platform mounted at the front of the dais. Her lips trembled, and she closed her eyes a minar before opening them to stare dully into the room.

Lyel leaned forward, unable to drag his attention away from her.

Her teal-colored eyes met Lyel's, and she blinked in confusion.

She wrenched her gaze from his and took a deep

breath. As she released it, hush descended across the room. With a tilt of her head, she met Lyel's gaze again and began to sing, her voice pure and sultry and unlike anything Lyel had heard in his life. It reached deep inside, speaking to an untouched part of him.

"I want to be where the people are," she sang in a lilting tone. "I want to see, want to see them…"

He couldn't look away and neither could the rest of the room. Everyone watched her, eager to hear what she'd sing next. Like a majestic songbird perched on a tree tweeting joyously to the world, she held the room bespelled. Lyel was equally mesmerized.

Her voice rose, and a few Al'kieern sobbed into their rutler mugs, overcome with the emotions she stirred in them all.

Even Fedeema seemed enthralled. Other than speaking quickly to a guard who inched along the side of the room toward the entrance, the queen stared at the woman.

Her voice fell as she sang the last bit of her song. "Part of that…world…"

She finished to roars of approval from the audience. Fedeema, surveying the room, released a sharp smile. She lifted an arm, and something banged behind Lyel.

It was time. The Earthling woman's gaze met Lyel's again, and his hand twitched on his lap. No matter how hard he tried, he couldn't make himself touch his com.

Heat burned across his palm. Flipping his hand over, he stared down in amazement and horror.

A matebond symbol.

Unable to drag his attention off his hand, he didn't look up until a shadow passed over him and held.

The queen stood across the table from him, and a force of Al'kieern crowded behind Lyel.

"I smelled you the minar I entered the room," she said

pleasantly. "How could you, a lowly Crakairian male, hope to escape my notice?" Her hand lifted. "Toss him into a holding cell. I shall deal with him later."

Lyel surged to his feet, reaching for his kalina, the spear he carried with him from Crakair. The Al'kieern hollered battle cries.

He released a guttural yell and jumping up onto a table, sliced out with the blade mounted on the tip of his kalina, severing the windpipe of the first Al'kieern to come at him. While others tried to grab his arms, he flipped up and backward, landing on the floor in a crouch. He stabbed an Al'kieern in the chest and raced for the door. If he could lift the bar… Others flew after him, landing on his back and shoving him forward. He stumbled, righted himself and pivoted, his kalina whistling through the air, eliminating two more Al'kieern. So many. In a battle with seven or eight, Lyel stood a chance, but against nearly a hundred? He was doomed. But he would take down as many as possible before he was captured.

Despite the combat, his gaze sliced through the air, seeking *her*. His mate. Fedeema held the woman's chain. With a yank, she hauled the Earthling in, wrapping the leash around her hand. The woman clutched the collar, pulling it away from her throat.

She looked toward Lyel, where he fought two Al'kieern at once, and the sorrow in her eyes cut deeply.

Winged Al'kieern flew up and over Lyel to flank him. They flapped toward him while others challenged his front. Surrounding him, they closed in, sneering.

While he bellowed and sliced his kalina at another Al'kieern, the others used numbers to overcome him. One ripped his spear from his grip while others pinned his arms behind his back. They threw his kalina across the room and it clattered on the floor.

Tossing Lyel down, they bound his hands and feet and dragged him across the room.

As he was wrenched through a side door, he looked up, seeking her again.

They'd already taken her away.

TWO

Isi

———

Lifting the chain pinning her to the foot of the Al'kieern queen's bed, Isabelle—Isi to her friends— shifted her hips across the thin cushion on the floor where she slept each night. On the bed above her, a snort rang out. As far as Isi knew, Fedeema, who referred to herself as the queen, didn't snore, but both of the two four-armed guys she slept with each night did.

Isi had remained awake for hours, waiting for them to finish wearing each other out and go to freakin' sleep. Lying here while they did it made her want to gag, but at least she hadn't been forced to join them. Fedeema didn't share.

Leaning close to the post attached to her chain, Isi care- fully stuffed a tiny metal poker into the lock and wiggled it back and forth. She'd stolen it from the meal hall her first night here and had initially kept it hidden in a crack between the floorboards to use as a weapon, paltry as it was. A week ago, she discovered it made an awesome tool.

Someone moved on the bed, and a groan cut through

the silence. Isi froze. Sweat trickled down her spine, and her fingers slipped. The metal tool fell from her hand and clinked when it hit the floor. Awesome. Just awesome. Her back flinched, anticipating a blow that thankfully, did not come. Counting to a thousand, she waited with a solid knot in her belly until one of the Al'kieern rolled over and started snoring again.

Her mouth dry, she lifted the pick and carefully slipped it into the lock. After twisting it and biting back multiple unvoiced swears, it clicked and opened. With her heart in her throat, she tugged the bracket away from the bedpost and lowered it to the floor beside her pallet. She coiled the chain connecting to her collar around her palm, making sure the links didn't bang together. After hiding her pick, she rose to a crouch and counted to one thousand once more.

When the room remained quiet, other than the threesome snoring, she held her breath and tiptoed to the door, inching it open to peek out.

As usual, the guard sat on the floor on the other side of the hall with his head tipped back and his eyes closed.

Perfect. She wasn't eager to try one of the karate moves she learned while growing up on Earth.

She bit her lower lip and watched while counting, but he didn't move. Some people would have said the risk was too great and crept back inside, relocked themselves to the bedpost, and tried to get some sleep.

Not Isabelle Clara Wadsworth. While daring was a word no one had ever used to describe her before, she wasn't chicken shit. She knew just enough self-defense to be dangerous. Tonight of all nights, she needed to take the risk.

This wasn't the first time she slipped from the room at

night, and it wouldn't be her last, though she made a few mistakes after they brought her here.

Six months ago, Isi worked for a well-respected accounting firm. When she noticed some improprieties in one of her regular accounts, she brought it to the big boss's attention. The account was taken from her, and she was told to forget what she saw. Leave it to her to log in after work and go through the account one last time, only to discover they were laundering money.

That was mistake number one.

Her second was sneaking onto a Crakairian starship docked at the spaceport. But really, did she have a choice? It was her only way off Earth. She either bailed on her home world or let someone put a bullet in her head.

Isi eased past the sleeping guard, keeping her footsteps light. Once she reached the end of the hall, she darted to the right, moving as quickly as she could. She was on a vital mission, but if she was caught…

It would be best not to think about what happened when they found her struggling with the front door handle the night after she arrived. The scab lines on her back had just passed the itching stage. Another beating would not only reopen the wounds, but it might also result in her death.

It hurt, being hit like that, but it had almost been worth it. She came *so* close to escaping.

Try again, Fedeema taunted as she secured the collar around Isi's throat, *and you'll see my full wrath. I can buy another songbird.*

Songbird—the name Fedeema gave her after she purchased Isi from the guys who kidnapped her off the Crakairian ship. Fedeema didn't ask Isi her real name, and Isi wouldn't give it. Names were a piece of a person's soul,

Isi's grannie told her before she died. After Grannie passed on, Isi moved into foster care.

Isi darted into the great hall and…yes. They'd ignored the warrior's spear lying against the wall. She crossed on light feet, snatching it up. Staring down at it, she contemplated keeping it. It would serve as a better weapon than her pick, and she knew how to use it.

But no. She had a plan and intended to follow it. Leaving the great hall, she crept down an eerily empty hallway and reached the stairs. She took them as fast as she could while her skin crawled with fear. She hit the ground floor and bolted across the open lobby toward the hallway leading to the kitchen. Hunger gnawed on her bones. As usual, the queen forgot to call for Isi's tray when they reached the room earlier. Fedeema was too interested in talking about what she'd do with the Crakairian male she caught. Isi's needs came last.

After they'd left the great hall, Fedeema stomped back and forth in the room, gnashing her fangs. "How dare he sneak into my compound. What does he want?" she shrilled at Isi, who shrugged. "The Crakairian government is involved, that is for sure, but they will not get away with it."

"What will you do?" Isi asked, rubbing her aching belly. Singing for her supper was all well and good until no supper appeared. Did she dare ask Fedeema to send for a tray?

Fedeema glared at Isi. "Why do you ask?"

Isi shrugged. She didn't care. Not too much. But something about him… She'd be stupid to care. He'd be dead soon.

"I was only curious about what you plan to do to him," Isi said.

"Because I am willing to satisfy your curiosity—this

time—I will tell you. Soon, I will throw him into the Orcal."

Isi's limbs froze. From what she overheard, the Orcal was a grueling race across the desert with creatures hunting whoever was thrown into the "game". To make it interesting, the Al'kieern set traps along the route. One person made it through the course, but whispers suggested they weren't the same after.

"When do you plan to do that?" Isi asked, tracing her finger along her leather collar.

"The newly appointed Al'kieern leader arrives in two days and I need a distraction from…"

Her organization. From what Isi gleaned, the Al'kieern government recently lost their leader to a suspicious death and this person's daughter assumed command. Fedeema told the original head of the Al'kieern government she was working on a solar and sale extraction project in the desert. While Isi was unaware of what the queen was doing instead, it was clear no one was extracting salt, let alone setting up solar panels.

"The Orcal will please her."

Why would Fedeema need to distract the new leader?

"Tricardi! Fitzwit," Fedeema cried. The door opened and her latest boy toys strode into the room wearing matching grins. Fedeema took them to bed. At least the males wore Fedeema out. As long as she slept, Isi could set her plan into place…

Creeping through the sleeping building at night reminded her of when she tiptoed through the Crakairian starship after she snuck on board. A girl needed to eat and wash her face every now and then. If only Isi hadn't chosen that particular moment to leave her hiding spot in an unused supply closet and venture into the main part of the craft. And if only she hadn't run into the Al'kieern pirates who boarded the ship to steal women. They didn't care that she wasn't an official bride. She was an Earthling and female, that was all that mattered.

They sold her to Fedeema who asked if she had skills. Isi mentioned singing, and after a quick demonstration, Fedeema took her to this compound. Isi performed each night. It was getting tough, though, as she was running out of Disney songs. Next, she'd sing the 2010's greatest hits. Her Grannie had been a singer, playing in clubs when Isi was little, and Isi inherited Grannie's voice.

As she swept through the kitchen, Isi snatched a loaf of bread off a wooden platter and bit off a hunk. Bread was a loose term. The Al'kieern enjoyed something similar to a pita pocket made with what Isi hoped were black beans. She didn't look closely at the inky flecks peppering the "bread".

Ducking across the room, she hurried down a back hall and creaked open the door on the end. During one of her late-night forays to the kitchen, she snooped and found this led to a dark, dingy basement full of enormous cobwebs, bugs she chose not to examine too closely, and empty holding cells. A dungeon, she supposed, though this was a fortress in the middle of a vast desert.

The one time she took the stairs to the bottom, she only walked down one hall flanked with empty cells before scurrying back upstairs. What she heard was enough. Wind howled through cracks in the stone foundation, a ghoulish sound that haunted her sleep for nights. Ghosts resided down there.

At the bottom of the rickety wooden stairs, she paused to listen. Glowing blobs encased inside half globes mounted on the wall oozed around the inside of the glass. Were they creatures or something else? Standing on tiptoe, she squinted at the blob. It flung itself forward, plastering itself against the glass. Four rows of razor-sharp teeth scraped along the surface and clawed the sides.

Isi reeled backward and gasped when she became entangled in a big spider web. The urge to rush back up the stairs overwhelmed her, but she shoved it away along with the web. Raking the sticky mess aside with the warrior's spear, she bolted down the hall, her bare feet smacking on the hard-packed dirt floor.

At the end of the hall, she came to another running perpendicular to the first and halted. Right or left? With a shake of her head, she went right, scurrying past more empty cells. Halfway down, she found the one holding the Crakairian.

He lay on a bunk with his back facing her. While she couldn't see his features, from behind he looked different than when she last saw him—watched him—in the great hall. Then, she saw his image waver from Al'kieern to Crakairian while he battled. Whatever covering or costume he used was gone. His skin was no longer Al'kieern blue but a dark, mossy green like a forest cloaked in misty dawn. Nearly naked, he wore only a small scrap of cloth wrapped around his waist.

As if he sensed her attention, he rolled over. His eyes met hers as she gripped the bars and pinched her face between them.

Rising, he limped toward her. She chomped back her growl. She didn't like that her heart ached to see they hurt him. She didn't know this guy. Why should she care about his injuries more than any other alien being held in these cells?

But she did, and she needed to stop that emotion right now. She took in ten deep breaths while he moved toward her, the action helping her regain control of her emotions.

"Name, have you?" he asked, stopping a few feet away from her.

She took in his numerous muscles and thighs like tree trunks. Small scales covered his body, though there were larger, pointy ones spanning his shoulders. No hair, just… she wasn't sure what his thick dreadlock-appearing things were called, but they moved like arms, reaching toward her.

She took a step backward while her heart rushed around faster than it should.

"I'm Isi." Her name came out easily, considering her protestations about following Grannie's rules for not sharing a piece of her soul.

"Eeee-see," he said softly.

She also shouldn't like how he pronounced her nickname, but damn, she did.

He dipped forward in a jagged bow, his rough movement telling her it hurt to move. "Dreafillar."

"Is that a greeting on Crakair?"

"Yes. Someone special it is for."

He couldn't know her plan. Why did he think she was special?

She bowed. When in Rome… "Drea…fillar." She hoped she got that right. First impressions could make all the difference, Grannie always said.

"Music you make…" His lips quirked up on one side—much too sexy—and he bared two-inch fangs, causing her lungs to freeze. Would he bite? "Beautiful, you like."

You like… Oh, *like you.*

His gaze—black pupils ringed with blue of a stormy sea—met hers. He tapped his chest. "Lyel Tair'im Iradran Sastray." He bowed again. "Dreafillar."

"Drea…" She snagged a strand of pink and gold hair

and yanked on it. "I'd say nice to meet you, Lyel, but the circumstances are awful."

"Here you are, why?" he asked. His gaze took in the empty hall. "Unsafe, it is."

"Partly for this." She poked the blunt end of the spear through the bars.

Hissing, he took it. "Welcome, this is." Hefting it, he tested the weight. "Harmed it is not."

"Good. Good." She had no idea why he was talking like Yoda, but who cared? That wasn't why she was here.

Back to business, Isi.

"I wanted to talk with you," she said. At least she could understand him, unlike some of the species she met. Although, they wouldn't be together long enough for it to matter.

Back on Earth, when she read the women traveling to Crakair had translators implanted behind their ears, Isi paid a guy named Tito a lot of money for an implant. While Isi might be stupid for snooping into the accounting files, and for stealing aboard a Crakairian spaceship to escape Earth, she wasn't completely clueless. To survive on Crakair, she needed to fit in. Understanding the language could make all the difference. "I suppose I should get right down to business. I'm here to get you out."

"No. Flee, you must."

"That's a problem. Fedeema will kill me if I'm caught."

"Flee, you must."

"As I said, that's the idea, but I have a few conditions before we take this further."

"Tell me, you must." His gaze drifted down her front and with any other guy, the gesture would make her twitchy. For some reason, coming from this seven-foot-tall, scaly alien, it felt like a caress. She needed to watch out. This guy was dangerous.

"Condition number one," she said, her voice shakier than she liked. He was too close. Too naked. Too…male. "I want you to take me with you."

"Nothing else, I would do."

That was easy. "Good. Good. Condition number two. I want you to get me off this planet and to Crakair."

"A mate, you do not have?"

He said it like a question, but it must be a statement. "Yeah, that's an issue, but I plan to find my way around it. I won't be returning to Earth."

"Agree, I do."

Again, that was easy. Too easy?

Creeping closer and pressing her face between the bars, she held up her hand. "Hold on a second there, dude."

He leaned forward, and his lips captured hers. Whoa.

She should be jerking back. He could be anyone. He could have…alien herpes! Instead of backing away, she reached through the bars and clutched his muscular arms. Damn, who would have thought a guy with fangs could be such a good kisser?

It didn't last long enough. He backed away and dipped forward again in a bow. "Courtship. Marriage. Fucking."

"Slow down there. No courtship. No marriage. No fucking."

"Like fucking, you will."

"This is not why I came here," she fumed. He unsettled her and made her want…something she couldn't define. It was vital she regain control of the conversation, assuming she'd been in control. "You kissed me without my permission."

"Ask me, you did."

She huffed. "In no way, shape, or form did I ask you to kiss me. "

"This." He lifted his hand. "Gesture kiss you made."

"You actually think I wanted you to kiss me because I did this?" She lifted her hand but slapped it back down by her side. What if he was right? She wouldn't use his secret Crakairian kissy signal again. "We're going to shove that aside, though your *gesture* is timely and relates to my third condition."

"Condition is?"

"Assuming we can escape, it won't be a friends with benefits situation. Despite the kiss."

"Like my kiss, you did."

"It doesn't matter if I liked it or not." She had, damn her.

"Like, you did."

She growled. "I'm not going to admit it."

"Fair, that is." The scales on his face stood out starkly in the low light and he bared his fangs. Some women would've found his fang-baring thing frightening. On him, it only enhanced his appeal. Which irritated her. She wasn't here for sex.

She stormed up to the bars. "Why do you look smug?"

His arms lifted out at his sides, and she paused to admire the view. Damn guy had too many muscles. "Smug?"

"Cocky."

His hands went to the scrap of cloth covering something bigger than it should be. "If cock, you wish to see——"

"No!" After glancing around to make sure no one was running in their direction after she essentially shouted, she lowered her voice. "No. I don't want to see your…cock."

"Fair, that is. Soon, you will."

"You're pretty confident, aren't you?" Of course, if she was as gorgeous as him, she'd be confident, too.

"Mean, what do you friends benefits?" he asked.

"It means, if I go with you, there will be no sex. No kissing. No inappropriate touch. This is a business deal. I'll get you out of this cell and you'll take me to Crakair. But you leave me alone in between then."

"Unless beg you do."

"Excuse me?" Her eyebrows flew up. "Why the hell would I beg?"

"Mate, you are."

"I just told you, I don't have a mate on Crakair."

He cocked his head. "How here, did you arrive?"

"I was kidnapped. Purchased." She shuddered at the memory, "I was brought to this fortress when they heard me sing."

"Free soon."

"I hope so."

"Go, we will." His attention fell to her hands gripping the bars. "Key, you have?"

"Key?"

"To door." He pointed to the lock.

"Not yet."

"No key."

She had to hand it to him, he didn't sigh.

"I only came here to negotiate. Tomorrow, we'll get you out. Fedeema told me the new Al'kieern leader's arriving soon, and she's planning to throw you into the Orcal as a distraction."

"New leader?" He growled.

"The old one recently died and was replaced with his daughter."

"We… Get out of here I must do." He shifted his arm as if looking for a watch. "Com, I must find."

"Com?"

"Communicator."

"Who would you communicate with?"

"Government my own. And controls dynatem, it does."

She had no idea what dynatem was and doubted it mattered. "We need to get you out of here before she puts you in the Orcal. I'll find the key and come back tomorrow night. As a consolation prize, I brought you your spear and this," she thrust her hand between the bars with the bread.

"Thank you." Taking it from her, he shifted it around, studying it.

She, of course, cringed because it was obvious from the hunk missing on one end, she'd been gnawing on it. "I was hungry."

"Understand, I do." Lifting it, he bit where she had.

Why did that not gross her out? Instead, it made heat swirl through her, as if he put his mouth on hers.

No. She shouldn't be thinking about how awesome his kiss was. He was nothing but a way out of this hellhole. He'd drop her on Crakair and say *see ya' later*, just like Isi's mom did when Isi was ten.

He carefully ate the bread, finishing it. She watched, wishing she'd brought a second loaf.

"I can get more," she said, realizing he must be as starved as she was most of the time.

"Good, this was. Enough."

"You're sure? The kitchen is—"

"Fine I am," he said softly. "Feed me, you have, before garlong, I wear. Worry not, someday, also zinters."

Lots of alien terms in his statement, but they could talk about them later.

"All right, then." She stiffened her spine. "Do we have a deal?"

"If key you get, yes. Escape together, we will do. Conditions, I will try to meet."

"Try?"

"Try."

She supposed she couldn't ask for more than that. "As long as you put in a good effort."

"Effort, I will do. Yet, condition, I also must offer." His scaled face gave nothing away.

"What's your condition?"

"Persuasion, you will allow."

This conversation shouldn't be a turn-on. Why was her heart thumping behind her ribcage like a herd of giraffes were galloping through? She was scared, that was it. Worried about being caught. If only she could convince herself of that.

"What kind of persuasion?"

"Touch simple."

"What does touch simple mean?"

"Court you, I must."

"Don't sound too excited about it, there."

His lips twisted, but his eyes sparkled. "Tease, I shall. Simple touch, I will do."

Okay, she got that. He wanted permission to *persuade* her into giving him more. Hot, he was. Hold herself back, she could do. "What if I tell you to stop?"

"Stop, I will."

There had to be a trick here somewhere. She couldn't figure it out, but she knew herself. He could turn on the charm, but she'd be able to resist him like she did everyone else. "I accept your condition."

He dipped his head forward. "Dreafillar, mate. Courtship. Marriage. Fucking."

"Getting ahead of yourself a bit with the courtship, marriage, and fucking, aren't you, dude?"

"See, you shall."

She grunted, which was not agreement. "Why are you talking about all that? As far as I'm concerned, we'll get to

Crakair and say goodbye. You'll go on with your life, and I'll build mine."

Moving closer, he tapped her hands gripping the bars. "Hands, see?"

Another odd ritual? If so, there was no harm in this one. She flipped them over, baring them to him.

She wasn't sure what his wince meant, but it hardly mattered. He was the means to an end. Nothing more. She could control her attraction to him until they reached Crakair. After that, she'd be the one saying *see ya' later*.

Holding out his hand, he showed her a tattoo on his palm, a swirling symbol that compelled her to touch. Reaching out, she traced her fingertip along it. He hissed, and his gaze met hers, searching…

"What feel you do?" he asked, his voice husky.

"Feel? I don't know what you mean. What am I supposed to feel?" Nothing, right?

Keep lying to yourself.

Shut up.

And now she was carrying on a conversation with herself. A snarl slipped past her lips. This was silly. Flustered for no apparent reason, she snatched her hand back and latched onto the bars to hold her body up. Why did he unsettle her? He was a green-skinned, scaly alien. Sure, he was hot, but so were a thousand other guys. She needed him, and he needed her. This was a business exchange, nothing else.

"All right, then. We're good." She backed away from the bars. His closeness…unsettled her. She was hyped up, strung out, and nervous about the situation. Not him. Never him.

"Good, we are." Turning, he walked slowly to the concrete bunk and sat, facing her. There was no missing the creases on his face. His gaze darted to the hall behind her. "Hide, you must do, before—"

Something banged, coming from the stairs. Shit. Isi spun in that direction, but didn't see anything. Yet. Voices echoed. Someone was coming!

"Go," he said, standing and moving toward her with the stealth of a panther. "Hide." The urgency in his voice made her heart flip.

"I'll find a way to free you tomorrow. Watch for me." The voices behind her grew louder. "They chain me at night, but during the day I have a bit more…freedom." A relative term, but at least she wasn't secured to the bedpost 24/7.

"Go. Catch you, they will."

Beat her, they would.

No thanks.

"Go!' The concern in his voice hit her in the solar plexus, stealing her breath.

With a jerk of her head, she ran down the hall, hoping to loop around and approach the stairs from a different direction.

Somehow, she evaded the guards.

Slipping up the stairs, she raced back the way she'd come. With shaky fingers, she eased open the door to Fedeema's room.

A few more steps, and she'd be secure on her tiny bed. She'd lock herself to the bedpost and…

Lights flared in the room.

Fedeema stood in the middle of the room, glaring. Her guys had left.

"Guards," Fedeema yelled. "Grab her!"

THREE

Lyel

E asy—he loved her name. She was beautiful, from the pink and golden striped flares on her head, to her lush frame, to her teal eyes.

That kiss…

It kept him tossing on the stone bed. That, and worry she had not gotten away. But the guards had merely strolled past his cell, ensuring he remained inside. No shouts and no cries told him she could be safe.

Easy. Such an unusual name.

While he hadn't applied to the Selection, he still mate-bonded with an Earthling female. Who would believe this was possible?

She did not carry a matebond mark, but he knew she was his fated mate. He only needed to convince her. This presented a dilemma. He had not come here to find a mate. Death had been his expectation. His plan was in tatters.

Finding a mate here of all places…

She made it clear he was not to touch her. It would be

wrong to push her for something she did not ask for, but she agreed to his persuasion.

His matebond to her would not drive his behavior. A warrior, he was stronger than that. When she sang, his matebond blood surged, overwhelming him. The moment she reached this floor of the compound, it rushed through him again, telling him she was near. Her sweet scent hit him before she stood in front of his cell.

It burned that he waited here, unable to protect his mate, while she secured his freedom.

Grumbling, he lay down on his bunk and plotted how he could locate his com so he could finish his mission. His mind kept drifting to Easy. That kiss…

Somehow, he slept, waking to footsteps in the corridor outside his cell. Rising, he stretched the kinks from his spine and crossed his arms on his chest, waiting for whatever came next.

A mass of Al'kieern crowded against his cell, Fedeema in the front of the group.

"Today, we will celebrate," she said.

"Anything in particular?" he asked, fearing what she might say. When they captured him, they took his com. He failed his mission. But it wasn't over yet. He still had hope for eliminating the operation. This time, instead of remaining here to die, he would escape with Easy. He would choose honor with life, not death.

"Our plan is in position," Fedeema said rubbing her four hands together. "Soon we, the underappreciated Al'kieerns, will have the respect of our brethen."

"I do not know what you speak of."

"Do not play with me, Crakairian. I know who you are. Lyel Tair'im Iradran Sastray, son of Piersag, formerly of the Crakairian High Council."

Dread froze his lungs.

"You are mistaken," he said, grateful his voice did not shake. "I am a lowly Crakairian named Takir Ai'terren."

"Do you lie to me, Lyel?"

"I do not come from a noble family." This was true. His father dishonored the Sastray name.

She pressed up close to the bars. "Why are you here in my compound, you lying Crakairian?"

He bowed. "I am a lowly scientist, here on Mara to study the desert and its creatures."

She gripped the bars tight, her fingers blanching pale blue. "Tell me!"

"I have. Release me. My financiers will be disappointed if I do not relay information about my research to them soon."

"You persist in this silly tale," she said with a twist of her full, deep blue lips. The fine scales on her face glistened with her secretions. "A scientist has no reason to enter this compound."

"I sought respite from the sun."

"Another lie! Tell me the truth, and I may consider releasing you."

"You have no interest in releasing me. Tell me what you plan to do to me instead."

"I need answers."

"Which you will not receive from me."

Her ridged brows flickered, and the hairs spiked forward, dripping with toxin. "I have ways of obtaining information. You would be wise to tell me."

Even under torture, he would protect his country, but this was no longer about him alone. His mate was here, bound with a collar and owned by the Al'kieern pirate queen. How could he manipulate this to save them both?

"I am a lowly Crakairian here to do research," he repeated.

Her fangs snapped together. "Enough." Turning, she strode through the opening created by her blue-skinned, winged entourage, but she stopped after a few steps down the hall and returned to the cage. "Since you refuse my offer of leniency, I have a plan you will enjoy."

His gaze never left her face, watching in case she revealed something.

Her chest rose and fell with her sigh. "It is boring here. But the newly appointed Al'kieern leader will arrive soon. She… needs to be entertained."

She needed to be distracted, the queen meant. The leader would not be pleased if she learned what Fedeema planned. If only he could contact Vork. Then the Crakairians could work with the new head of the government. Perhaps she would not approve of this awful plan.

Had the pirate ships left for Earth yet? He thought… No, he was told if he eliminated Fedeema and her sycophants, the project was over.

"I am afraid I do not understand," he said, aiming to look thoughtful yet knowing he could not pull it off. Lyel was no actor. *Your face shows everything*, his sister used to say.

Therena. He had looked forward to seeing her face again in the afterworld, but he could not leave now.

"*You* do not understand?" Fedeema mocked. "I do not need to explain this to you, Lyel Tair'im Iradran Sastray." She turned to the winged Al'kieern beside her. "Prepare the course."

"Yes, the course," the Al'kieern she spoke to keened, his arms fluttering. "Which items shall I make ready?"

Fedeema studied Lyel. "All of them. It will be more interesting that way. Allow him…one sinar of water and two trungeons." Her wings stretched before retracting to her body. "We will release him in the Orcal and the new

Al'kieern leader will enjoy the game. She will leave, unaware of what we…" Snarling, she shut her mouth.

Lyel's suspicions were confirmed. The new Al'kieern leader was unaware of Fedeema's plan and would not approve. If he could get word to Vork, his government could reach out to the new leader. Perhaps they would end the kidnapping operation themselves.

As for the Orcal, he read about the gruesome game they played with prisoners. The Al'kieern dropped the person into a vast wasteland filled with venomous, hunting creatures. While they tried to cross the wasteland—and most did not make it—the Al'kieern flew ahead and set up traps. If the person made it to the end, they still needed to find a way around an electrified fence. Beyond that, lay the capital. There, Lyel could contact Vork.

Failure… Lyel did not wish to think of this.

"You would put a research scientist in the Orcal?" he asked, continuing his ruse. "How do you expect me to survive? I am no warrior."

"Yet you managed to kill many of my guards when you were captured."

He shrugged; grateful he'd hidden his spear underneath his bed. "That was luck."

"Do not play me for a fool, Crakairian. Few fight with a kalina."

"If you must do this, give me my com," he said as politely as possible. "Surely I can have that back before I run the Orcal." If she came close, he would wrap his fingers around her neck and squeeze until the smirk left her face. "It has sentimental value to me."

Her brow spikes drew together. "I do not know where it is."

One of the other Al'kieern dangled it in the air, and she snatched it from him. She stared down at it lying on her palm before lifting her gaze to Lyel. With a sly smile, she dropped it onto the floor. Her foot came down on it, crushing it.

She pivoted and strode down the hall, calling over her shoulder. "Prepare this male for the Orcal. Our glorious new leader will arrive soon, and I would like the game to begin." Her gaze met his. "As for you, *Lyel*, I have a surprise. Someone will join you in the field."

An opponent?

"My songbird is determined to take flight. It appears she needs to learn a permanent lesson."

Sweat broke out on Lyel's forehead. Fuck. Songbird was Lyel's mate, Easy.

Wings fluttering and clawed feet scrambling on the floor, the other Al'kieern followed her down the hall. A door banged shut, and the click of a lock rang out.

Lyel burst forward, skidding onto his knees. He thrust his arm between the bars and straining, reaching his com. He dragged it toward him and lifted it, hoping…

Triple fuck.

He stared down at the mangled fragments in horror.

When she crushed his com, she activated the detonation sequence.

Lyel had three denjars to escape his cell, find Easy, and get out of the compound before it blew up.

FOUR

Isi

When Isi arrived back at the room, still buzzing from her conversation with Lyel—never mind that kiss! — Fedeema was waiting.

She snatched Isi by the hair and dragged her from the room and down the hall to what she called the punishment room.

Isi attacked the moment the Al'kieern let go, striking out at his throat, but he winged backward, snickering. Two more leaped on her, driving her to the floor. While she struggled to catch her breath, she was tied to the wall with her arms stretched overhead.

Standing on her toes, Isi clung to bindings wrapped around her wrists. Closing her eyes, she tried to put her mind somewhere else.

When the first blow hit her back, she flinched and stifled her groan.

Each time Fedeema hit Isi, a scream rose in her throat. She clamped her lips tightly together to hold it back. She focused on Lyel, trapped in the basement. Moss found only in the most beautiful forest; that's the color she'd use to describe his skin. Scales the size of nickels. And warm eyes filled with trust, a novelty for Isi. He believed she'd find a way to free him.

She would hold strong. This would end soon. Then she could plot. If she didn't get him out of the compound soon, Fedeema would throw him into the Orcal, where he'd die.

Anyone would have sympathy for someone forced to run the Orcal, but it was more than that for Isi. Her chest ached when she thought of Lyel struggling to make it across the wasteland while the Al'kieern hunted him. Would he know what the game entailed? Locating water and food would be a challenge.

She was amazed by how Lyel battled the Al'kieern in the dining hall, but against the Orcal, he didn't stand a chance.

After her first beating, within days of arriving here, Isi's wounds became infected. Her fever raged, and she nearly died. Fedeema brought in an elderly, blue-skinned alien who coated Isi's skin with an ointment that cleared the infection and accelerated healing. After, he rubbed her arm and told her to behave in a gruff, kind voice.

"I told you not to try this again," Fedeema growled behind Isi. She smacked out with a strap, hitting Isi's back another time.

Her throat aflame, Isi closed her eyes and held in her tears.

Lyel's scales had a silvery sheen that… Pain burst through her brain, making it difficult to focus.

Silvery scales… Silvery scales!

After two more hits, Fedeema tossed aside the weapon. "Coat her back with the potion," she said. "I want her to heal quickly, in time for…" Her voice devolved into a whispered conversation Isi couldn't—and didn't care to—hear. The alien witch strode to the door. "Take her to my room. I will send for her shortly." She tossed something at Isi. It hit her shoulder and fell, clattering on the floor. The pick she used to release her binding to the bed; the pick she planned to use to open the lock on Lyel's cell. Defeat filled her, but she shoved it away. She'd make a new plan.

After applying the ointment, an Al'kieern loosened the bindings keeping Isi upright and when she would've slumped to the floor, he caught her. He steadied her on her feet and guided her to the door, making her take the steps rather than carry her.

Her back on fire, she stumbled, her vision wavering. Only six blows, but still. Her shoulders and spine screamed with each step she took. Sucking in a breath stretched the skin. Her head pounded.

At the door to Fedeema's room, the Al'kieern shoved Isi inside. The panel banged shut while Isi swayed, trying to remain upright. The world spun, and darkness crowded across her vision. She forced herself to walk to her thin pallet, each step a living nightmare. Moaning would do her no good.

"I…" she mumbled. "I have to get out of here before they finish me off. But I need to…rest." She dropped to her knees and slumped onto her side, pressing her cheek against the thin folds of fabric. Now that she was alone, she let her tears flow. She crushed her sobs with her fist, refusing to release the guttural cries. This took her to the brink. Her mind wanted to tumble down the other side, where oblivion waited. She wanted to give up. The ointment helped; she could feel her skin knitting together already, but wounds to the soul never sealed shut.

She might've passed out, though she wasn't sure. All

she knew was she woke up and her back felt better. Her mouth tasted like a herd of horses had galloped through it. Groaning, she got to her feet and staggered to the low cabinet set along one wall holding a pitcher with water and mugs. Nothing felt better than the brackish liquid sliding down her throat. She drank her fill, until it sloshed around in her belly.

She pivoted to return to her simple bed, but her attention was snagged by something gleaming on the floor near one of the tall, wooden armoires. Hobbling in that direction, she leaned forward very carefully and picked it up. A knife?

Awesome.

Hope bloomed in her heart, but she told herself not to get too excited. If they found it on her, they'd take it. But damn, it felt good to have some sort of defense, even if it was a puny, two-inch blade.

There was no guarantee it could be used to pick open cell doors, but she was going to try. No better time than the present.

She shuffled to the door. Her legs ached, and her back twitched, but her skin was not broken this time.

She twisted the knob, but it wouldn't open. "Locked," she groaned. Stooping down, she inserted the knife tip into the lock. But after wiggling it around, the door wouldn't open. Heaving a sigh, she returned to her bed and sat, leaning her side against the bedframe.

The doorknob jangling woke her, and Fedeema strode into the room.

"Get up," she said, kicking out at Isi.

Isi moved as fast as she could, scrambling to her feet and backing away before another blow hit. Her thigh hurt, but she wouldn't give the Al'kieern fiend the satisfaction of seeing Isi rubbing the fresh wound.

"It is time." Pivoting on her heel, Fedeema strode to the door. "Come."

What now? She carefully tucked the knife into her pocket, grateful she'd been allowed to keep the jeans she arrived in. They dressed her for singing but left her alone otherwise, and her Earth stuff comforted her. Her jeans, that is.

Her t-shirt was long gone, torn by the elderly alien when he treated her wounds. Fedeema tossed Isi one of her own stained tunics. Having four sleeves made it fit oddly, and the gaps in the back for wings let in cool air when she huddled on her thin bed each night, but it beat striding around naked.

Three winged Al'kieern ushered Isi to the door, one prodding her back. Each poke made Isi wince. They took the stairs to the ground floor and pushed her around to the back, toward a door she tried to open once when she crept through the compound. An Al'kieern unlocked the panel and swung it wide, and Fedeema swept onto a landing with Isi following. Globes with glowing nasty creatures lined the stairwell.

Fedeema skipped off the top step and floated down to the bottom, her gown fluttering behind her.

Isi took the stairs as fast as she could and rushed out into the hall behind Fedeema. She kept pace with her all the way to the Crakairian's cell.

He must've heard them coming because he stood in the center of the stone floor, his arms crossed on his broad chest, a scowl on his forbidding face. Being in such a dire situation should keep Isi from seeing anything but Fedeema and her henchmen, but she noted how broad Lyel's shoulders were and how they led to a muscular chest and a narrow waist. How would his silvery scales feel beneath her fingers?

No, no, no. She'd made a deal. No friends with benefits. Why was she regretting her decision already? It was stupid. Fedeema hadn't brought her down here to gawk at Lyel. She was pissed off at Isi for sneaking out again, and her warning from last time rang out in Isi's mind. Mess with her once but never twice. What did she plan to do to Isi now?

"Are you ready for some light entertainment, Crakairian?" she asked.

Isi doubted Fedeema understood the real meaning of entertainment.

Lyel's watched Isi and ignored Fedeema.

"Crakairian?" Fedeema shrieked. Really, she was a walking cliché. After she arrived here, Isi kept looking for a soft spot in Fedeema, something she could use to her own benefit. So far, she hadn't found it. The queen didn't have a pet she adored, though she seemed fond of the guys parading through her bedroom on a regular basis.

Lyel sighed. "Yes?" He dragged his gaze from Isi.

She waved her hand toward the door. "Open it and bind him."

Once the barred door swung open, five Al'kieern flew into the cell, piling onto Lyel, and driving him to the ground. He got a few blows in, sending one of the winged aliens smacking against the wall, and he scrambled to retrieve his spear from beneath the bed, but he was dragged to the floor and trussed up like a pig for slaughter.

With anxiety making her shake, Isi bit her bottom lip until it stung. It was all she could do not to run into the cell and smack the aliens.

"How did you obtain this?" the queen asked, lifting the spear with two fingers. She reeled on Isi, who cowered. "No matter. We will allow you to keep it, as it will add to the fun. Bring him upstairs." She flounced down the hall, calling out to Isi over her shoulder. "Come, Songbird."

They took the stairs to the main entrance and walked into the council room, where the queen sat on her throne. Yeah, she had a real throne, complete with silver gilt and red cushions. Tacky as far as Isi was concerned.

She sat and drummed her clawed fingers on the cushioned arm. With a flick of her hand, she indicated Isi should sit by her feet. No singing today, then?

Fear made Isi's knees quake. Fedeema punished her, but if Isi knew the witch, she was planning a new way to make Isi pay further.

Winged Al'kieern carried Lyel into the room and dropped him on the floor in front of the throne, close to Isi. If she leaned forward, she could touch him, but Fedeema had the chain wrapped around her hand, and Isi wasn't eager to choke.

He remained silent, but his gaze met Isi's, and she swore she read panic there.

She shrugged to show she had no idea what might come next, but a dark suspicion was growing inside her. Naming it might make it come true, so she didn't.

Eight or ten Al'kieern entered the room and stood milling together in the back.

"Today we will enjoy some fun, boys," Fedeema said grandly. "We have a Crakairian eager to play."

Damn, did she mean the Orcal? It was too soon! Isi still hoped to find a way to free them both.

The Al'kieern jeered, jostling each other and releasing gut-rolling chortles, their version of laughter. They sounded like they were trying to hurl, but what did Isi know about Al'kieerns?

"I thought we should sweeten the game," Fedeema said.

Of course. She'd never pass up a chance to add a twist.

Her gaze darted to Isi. "Do you think the male will fight harder if more than one life is at stake?"

There was no denying what she was saying. Goosebumps peppered Isi's skin, and she cringed when the queen spoke again.

"We will throw them into the Orcal together!"

FIVE

Lyel

C heers erupted in the room.

Lyel watched his mate's eyes widen. She knew what this meant, then.

"Give the Crakairian his kalina. A research scientist." Fedeema sneered. "Do you think me stupid to believe that?"

He hoped. Believed? No. She would not have risen this high in the organization if she wasn't clever.

Why give him his kalina, though?

He would not complain. Armed, he could defend them. They needed every possible advantage if they were going to survive the upcoming challenge.

From his internal clock, they had twenty, thirty minars at most to escape the compound before it blew all to heille. He had to get them out of here. If that meant through the Orcal, then so be it.

"You tease," he said, goading Fedeema, hoping she would become angry and move faster. "You will not go through with this. You do not dare."

Growling, the queen stood. "You think not?" Her glare

fell on Easy. "You, Songbird, will not be able to sing your way out of this."

If Easy pleaded, Fedeema might change her mind, but she didn't. She stood stoic; her attention trained on the floor. She wished to escape the compound, but surely she knew their odds of surviving the Orcal were slim?

"Take them to the course," Fedeema said. "I will follow." Her attention drilled into Lyel. "We will see what you are made of, Crakairian. Will you abandon the Songbird or fight to protect her?"

He'd guard her with his life, but he refused to give Fedeema that weapon. She already had the advantage. Once they entered the course, there was no way out other than dubious sanctuary on the opposite side of the wasteland. If they reached the city, they could hide until he arranged transportation off the moon.

"What are the conditions?" he asked, well-aware of the stakes but hoping to gain some concessions.

"Why do you believe I will give you an advantage?" Her lips curled, and she coiled her four arms together. "Because I am generous and because I have enjoyed my Songbird if only for a short time, I will give you your kalina and one flask of water."

"Two."

"This is not a bargaining opportunity. Do not test me."

He grumbled but said nothing.

"You will have a fifteen minar start and then I will follow."

That would not do. If he could find a way to keep her here while he and Easy were removed from the compound, this might work the way it should. Best case scenario, they would be on this side of the fence when the place blew up. Worst case, they'd be inside the course. After that, there was no choice but to cross the wasteland, but their odds of survival would improve if they didn't have Al'kieern flying overhead, laying traps, and stirring up beasts living in the desert.

Fedeema waved her hand. "Take them outside."

Easy's gaze met his, and her lips twitched before she turned to the queen. She gripped the collar snug around her throat. "Remove this."

"You do not make demands," Fedeema said, shoving past Lyel's mate. "I like the idea of you trying to survive with a chain dragging behind you. It will teach you to listen."

"My role has never been to listen."

Fedeema snorted. "You have no role. You sang because I gave you a voice. Now you will play this game because I thrust you into the course."

"My voice is my own, and I do not play games."

"I do not expect your cooperation in this." Fedeema started across the room, but stopped, not turning back. "If I know the Orcal and the wasteland, you will die quickly."

Not if Lyel had anything to say about it. But the collar and chain posed a problem. Perhaps, with his kalina…

Four Al'kieern lifted Lyel off the floor and flew toward the broad double doors while others grabbed Easy. She winced and shook off their arms, choosing to lift her chin and follow Lyel on her own. He admired her strength of will and her courage. It would serve her well in the upcoming challenge.

They continued through the front door, and the sun hit his face, making his eyes sting. Lifting him higher, the Al'kieern flew across the scrubby surface, aiming for a three-story fence surrounding the property. The compound did not fence in the wasteland; the Al'kieern fenced themselves off for protection. Their ability to fly allowed them to travel short distances, but they needed frequent rest. For longer travel, they used shuttles like everyone else, and star ships for interplanetary distances.

"I'm going," Easy shouted. "Stop pushing me. You know that hurts."

They were hurting her? A growl rumbled in his chest, and the Al'kieern carrying him gulped. Lyel tried to yank free but all that did was make him bleed when his bonds cut into his flesh.

They soared up over the fence and dropped quickly, tossing him to the ground. His kalina and the flask of water landed in the sand beside him.

Two Al'kieern lifted his mate up over the fence and lowered her nearby. Diving forward, she grabbed his kalina off the sand and stood over him, glaring at the encircling Al'kieern. She slashed the weapon as if she knew how to use it, impressing Lyel.

"Back off, assholes," she snarled. "You don't want to deal with me."

The Al'kieern sneered but maintained their distance, flying around them in a widening arc.

Stopping near the other side of the fence, the queen snickered. "I am looking forward to this. Two unique beings facing adversity together. Will one aid the other or turn and slash their throat? One skin of water will not last long."

Lyel's mate stood over him with his spear in hand. She would protect him. Fight for him. And he would do the same.

This was it. A fifteen minar lead was not much. If they weren't picked off by creatures living in the wasteland, Fedeema would kill them from above.

"Bindings, will you cut?" he said, sitting up and holding out his hands to his mate.

"Oh, yes, sorry." She stooped down beside him and

carefully sliced through the ropes they used to pin his hands.

Once free, he took his kalina from her and cut through the bindings at his ankles. He stood, grabbed the water pouch off the ground and slung it over his shoulder, and held his hand out to Easy.

"The Orcal begins," Fedeema said with death in her voice. She held up her hand and an Al'kieern standing at the top of a tower along the wall lifted a trundar, the instrument's golden surface gleaming in the sunlight. The Al'kieern pressed his mouth to the instrument and a long, mournful call echoed in the air.

The ground rumbled.

"Run, can you?" Lyel asked. Fuck. The beasts heard the call and knew the game had begun. They would swarm the area.

Easy's wide gaze met Lyel's. "Tell me what to do. We have to cross the desert, but there must be some way to win this. Where can we go?" Scanning the desert around them, she shivered. "I've heard about the Orcal. We won't make it fifteen steps before we're eaten."

"Trust, you must have."

"In what?" Panic heightened her voice.

"Me." He tugged her away from the fence and into the desert. Ahead, big, sandy hills loomed in the distance, a few scruffy trees spotted the landscape. The sooner they put distance between them and the compound, the better. There wasn't much time left.

"I'll try to trust you, but I can't offer much more than that," she said. "I don't trust easily." She picked up her pace to a jog, and he was grateful she wore pants and a tunic. Her unusual footwear appeared to have decent tread and looked sturdy. He hoped they held up. "And I don't know you."

He loved how she challenged him, how she stood her ground. "No worries, mate. Soon, you will know and trust me."

"Mate?" She pried her hand from his. "Don't get any ideas."

"Court you, I will. Marry you. Fucking after."

"Confident of your charms still, Lyel?" She paced beside him, unwinded.

As he moved, he dipped forward in a short bow. "Courted you will be, mate."

"Mate, mate, mate," she panted. "You saying it doesn't make it so."

He bared his fangs. "See, you will."

"Sure, sure. This isn't what I call persuasion." She continued up a hill beside him. Would she be able to run far? He could carry her, though he had a feeling she would balk at the suggestion. "Where did you say we were going?"

He hadn't because he wasn't sure himself. Away from the compound before it exploded. Across the wasteland. Those were the goals. "Faster, you must run."

"Got it." She sped up, the compound growing smaller behind them. "When are you going to talk normally?" she panted. "I like Star Wars as much…as the next person, but don't you think it's…overkill?"

"Translator training. Talking, eventually we will do. Improvement, you will see."

"You're saying this isn't permanent."

"No."

Her face cleared. "Good…good. Any…time, now, would be nice."

They crested a hill, and he stopped to look around and to give her a short break. From what little he read about Mara, the wasteland continued for many kleks, but he grew up hiking the mountains, surviving on his wits and his will. He would see them through this.

His internal clock told him the time was nearly out.

"Faster," he grunted, pulling Easy behind him down the hill.

"Are they coming?" She shot a look over her shoulder. "They're picking something up. I'm not sure what it is, but it's long, thin, and gray."

"A net."

"They'll trap us?"

"Pin us down so beasts can more easily find us."

She darted past him, her gaze alight. "I'm running. Keep up, Lyel!"

Savoring her humor, he raced with her until the ground twitched beneath his feet.

A soft woof was followed by an ear-shattering series of bangs.

Lyel leaped onto his mate and grabbing her, carried her to the ground.

SIX

Isi

As the world exploded around them, Lyel protected Isi's body with his own.

Hunks of blue and pink flesh rained down along with stones and hunks of metal.

Her ears rang, and she caught a smell she remembered from when she was a kid and a house a few blocks over from Grannie's place burned. Sharp and musty, it hit her sinuses hard. Like old, dead things were smoldering.

Lyel climbed off her and tugged her up to her feet. His arms went around her, and he spoke, but she couldn't make out what he said over the ringing in her ears.

"What was that?" she hollered.

He cupped her face, holding it steady, and his gaze met hers. "Compound gone."

Halleluiah. If they were lucky, the explosion took out all the Al'kieern with it.

He kissed her forehead, and she hated that he smelled so good. What did they call this mix of cedar, fresh air, and sunshine? This guy was a lust-inspiring hunk of pure alien male, and he was wreaking havoc with her resolve.

As he pressed himself against her, she noticed a few things. Most of them, like the warmth of his arms and the feel of his hair-thingies caressing her shoulders, she could dismiss. One unforgettable thing stood out, the sizeable mass beneath the scrap of cloth wrapped around his waist. It didn't feel erect, just…big. Why the hell was she thinking about his cock size at a time like this?

She stepped out of his embrace before she gave into her overwhelming urge to taste his lips. This wasn't like her. She was a boring accountant who was equally boring in bed. All her ex-boyfriends said so.

He bared his fangs and for whatever reason, it made her want to dance around, grinning. He made the same gesture before. The first time, she was hit with a mix of this-guy-is-hot and why-am-I-not-scared? Now his fang-baring made her knees weaken.

No. His version of a smile wasn't making her feel dreamy. That was from the explosion.

Right. Right. Just keep telling yourself that and you won't try to ditch one of your conditions.

Only now did she fully understand the temptation of friends with benefits.

Beyond the fence, smoke billowed into the sky.

"It's all gone?" she yelled, knowing she was speaking louder than she needed to, but unable to hear herself without raising her voice. She sort of heard herself, in her mind, at least.

He shrugged. "Perhaps."

Fedeema took flight and rose from the smoke and up over the fence. But when it seemed she'd fly toward them and take revenge, she turned and flew toward the remains of the compound.

Perhaps the leader had arrived and Fedeema needed to scramble up some answers to some pertinent questions.

"A vengeance, she will seek," Lyel said. Taking Isi's hand, he nudged his head toward the desert, indicating they should keep going. "Go, we must."

She wanted to live but at the moment she had to wonder what the point of running was. The queen would rally her surviving troops and come after them in seconds, lobbing nets and dropping rocks on them from above. Or simply blowing them to pieces with laser pistols. Her henchmen would fly with her. They wouldn't stop until Isi and Lyel were dead.

Her foot hit something hard. A rock? She kept running, pushing for speed, but it was tough. Her back stung from the movement, and her feet bogged down in the sand. And the collar… It made deep breathing a challenge. She kept a tight grip on the coiled- up chain.

When a jagged piece of metal stabbed up in front of her, she leaped sideways to avoid running into it. Another spear shot from the ground, almost impaling her. Around her, metal rods thrust up from the ground like pokers.

Lyel's fear-filled gaze met hers, and he lifted her off her feet. Flinging her over his shoulder, he jumped, shooting into the air at least fifteen feet. He came down hard and rolled, somehow avoiding crushing her. Flinging himself to his feet, he bolted with her over his shoulder. Behind them, the spear forest disappeared into the sand.

He ran for what felt like an hour before he slowed and lowered her feet to the ground.

"For once," she huffed. "I'm not going to complain about being manhandled."

"What handle of the male is this?"

Her gaze shot to his groin before she dragged it away.

"Earthlings a cock man handle called?" He chuckled.

She snorted. "Not to my face, but I'm sure they use the term in private. They have all kinds of words for it."

"Cock I prefer."

"You can call it whatever you please." Peering toward the sky, she didn't see anyone following them. "Do you think they'll give up? Fedeema must be busy sorting through the compound after the explosion and fire."

"Fedeema angry is."

"She's fuckin' pissed."

"Like this term, I do."

"It fits, doesn't it?"

He took the chain from her hand and dropped it. Lifting his spear, he tucked his hand beneath her collar. "Still, you will hold."

"Or impaled, I will be?"

He flashed his fangs, and her insides warmed up fast.

A quick slice and her collar parted. It fell to the ground, and she kicked it.

"Glad that's gone."

He nodded and frowned as he studied her neck. It had to be red. The damn thing rubbed. A growl rumbled through him, and he shot a glare back in the direction they came from. "Walk we shall."

She stepped forward carefully. "Do you think we'll come across more spears?" If so, could she dart to the side before she was impaled?

"Know I do not. Dangers many await."

"Awesome."

A shadow passed overhead, and she gaped up as a large bird swooped past them.

"Predator alert," she said, jerking her head toward the sandy colored bird. She'd never seen one with six wings before.

Lyel lifted his sword. "Touch us, it will not."

"I hope you're right."

Passing a scraggly tree, she avoided the thorn-encrusted

branches. A smaller bird, about the size of a thin chicken with four clawed legs, peeked around the trunk. Its gray-blue feathers gleamed in the fading sunshine. Where had the day gone? Oh, yeah, she'd spent some of it sleeping off her beating. Her back felt…okay. Not wonderful, especially after the jarring she took while lying on Lyel's shoulder, but she'd live. Trying not to be obvious about it, she carefully stretched, testing the skin. It stung, but it was more a dull ache than the sharp, mind-numbing pain she felt immediately after.

"Where are we going?" she asked.

Lyel pointed to a pile of rocks ahead, to their right. "Shelter we will seek there."

It looked as good as any other place to hide. But how long could they stay among the rocks? Fedeema would track them down and drive them out into the desert, where she could pick them off. She'd expose them to the elements and whatever Hunger Games trap she had in store for them next. Especially after the compound blew up.

Hold on. Isi's pace slowed, and Lyel looked back at her, his ridge brows lifted. "I don't suppose you had anything to do with that explosion?" He told Fedeema he was a scientist, and Isi found that cutely nerdy and appealing. Scientists could build bombs, but it sounded like he was someone who did research, not work as a secret agent sent to destroy the Al'kieern compound.

Flashing his fangs, he nodded. "Effective, am I not?"

"Very. I can't believe it." She sped up, passing him, aiming for the rocks. "How did you do it?" How had they randomly escaped being blown to pieces along with the building? It was horrifying to realize they were inside a few minutes before.

"Explosives beneath compound, I planted, setting to

detonate at command of mine, but Fedeema my com crushed, putting into motion the sequence."

"We barely escaped."

He nodded grimly.

"Are you truly a scientist?"

"No."

"A secret agent, then?"

"What this agent of secrets is?"

"Like a cop or someone who works for the government, a la, James Bond. A secret agent takes on impossible tasks knowing they might die, but they're willing to do so for the betterment of others."

"Ah. Agent of secrets, I am."

"No way," she said, studying him further, but he didn't look any different than the Crakairians she saw on TV. "You're really a secret agent?"

"Yes. Good, this is?"

She swore she heard glee in his voice. "It's cool. We can call you… What's your last name?"

"Lyel Tair'im Iradran Sastray."

That would take time to learn. Why did she think they'd be together long enough for her to memorize his full name? "Do all Crakairians have long names?"

"Length normal this is."

"All right, then. You're Sastray. Lyel Sastray, double-oh…one. I think you should be number one."

He bared his fangs. "Always, I am your number one agent of secrets."

She grinned, enjoying how he twisted her language. She'll miss it once her translator caught up.

They reached the edge of the rock pile the size of a house, and Lyel paused to study it. He strode to their right and stooped down, stretching his arm into a gap between two large boulders. Turning her way, he waved, urging her near.

Behind her, something shifted across the desert floor but when she spun to look, she didn't find anything other than endless sand. The sun hovered near the horizon, preparing to dip from view. Did creatures hunt the desert at night?

She hurried over to Lyel, he tugged her down between his thick thighs, and nudged her onto her hands and knees.

Well. This was an interesting position.

And she needed to forget about how little clothing he wore.

While she contemplated what she shouldn't, he tapped her butt. He leaned over her, much like he would if they were naked and doing it doggie style. How could she be thinking of crap like that at a time like this? They were being hunted. Fedeema would be lobbing bombs or rockets at them soon, and all Isi could think about was the rod he sported between his legs.

He pressed closer.

Hell, he had an erection. She guessed she wasn't the only one distracted by the position.

Fortunately, she saw where he was urging her to go. Not onto her knees for a humping but forward, into a wide crack in the rock pile.

She inched inside and was enveloped in shadows. Lyel's hand stayed on her butt, pressing her to go deeper into the crevice.

Crawling, she came to a small opening. Muted light entered from overheard, like the little area had a moon roof. Sand covered the floor, and a circle of boulders rose around them like turrets on a castle.

"Here," Lyel said, tapping her butt again. "We wait."

Sitting, he patted his lap, urging her to climb onto his broad thighs. "Rest, Easy."

"Easy?"

"Name, you. Eee-see."

"It's Izz-ee."

"Ah. Not Easy."

She smirked. "Not always."

He patted his lap again. "Sit. Izz-ee."

"If I did that, you could definitely call me easy." A girl only has so much willpower. She dropped down onto a scrap of ground beside him.

He huffed, but them's the breaks. If—and that was a big IF—she changed her mind and decided she might consider a few of the sizeable benefits he had to offer, it would be on her terms. No more hugging and smooching until she could keep her brain from spinning at his touch.

"Eaten today, have you?" he asked.

"Last night, same as you."

"Sorry, I am. Poor mate, I am not to provide food."

"We're in a desert, man. No worries. I'm sure there's a bug or snake around we can eat if we get too hungry."

"Snake, you would eat?" he asked.

"If I had to. Beats nothing, right?" She'd never eaten snake, but she had tried a Cajun scorpion once. Crunchy. Spicy. Like fishy beef jerky.

"Snake, I will find." Pressing his fist to his chest, he leaned back to look down at her. Damn, even sitting, he was big. At five-four, she had to crick her head back to see his face. Standing, her eyeballs were a little below his nipple line. He didn't have nipples, but that was the general area. Sitting, they were a bit more even than when standing, though the top of her head hit level with his neck. And broad! He could be a linebacker.

"Do you play football on Crakair?" she asked.

"Think so, I do not." His gaze glided down her legs. "Food I will find and serve you, I will. Emulse your feet, we must, but no boodler, do I have."

"I'm not sure what that has to do with football. And what do you want to do with my feet again?" She tucked them underneath her butt to protect them because…boodler?

"Courtship. Marriage. Fucking."

"Sounds lovely, but we're in a desert. The Al'kieern are hunting us. I doubt there will be opportunities for courtship, let alone the other two items on your very specific agenda."

"Rest, we will. Running, we must do."

"I get it. We need to run across the desert, but what then?"

"Safety, we will find."

"Is there another compound on the opposite side of the desert? A village? Hell, will we find an airport?" Then she could go back to Earth. She could get a fake I.D. and hide from the mob. They'd lost her scent by now, right?

He wrapped his arm around her and tugged her close. "Rest."

Her gasp slipped out because it hurt when he touched her back.

His brow ridges drew together as he looked down at her. "Pain where is?"

She flicked her hand and steadied her breathing. "Oh, it's nothing."

"Something it is. Show?"

"Really. It's nothing. Fedeema was pissed off about me sneaking out of the room. She…hit me."

Stiffening, his throat rumbled. "Where?"

Isi squirmed at the intensity in his gaze. "It doesn't matter. It's over. We got out. She won't do it again."

"Please. Show."

Scooting around, she faced away from him and lifted her tunic. "See? It's nothing."

His breath hissed, and he carefully traced his finger down her back. "Kill her, I will."

"I appreciate that, but as long as we get away, I'm happy."

"Happy, I am not." His breath eased out. "Sorry, I am. Protect you, I did not."

"How could you? You didn't know I was there."

"Protect you, I would have."

That was sweet. "Thanks."

He eased her shirt back down and tugged her onto his lap. "Rest. Protect you now, I will."

"Mmm," she mumbled into his chest. It did feel good sitting here. He was warm. Not soft, but she'd be the last to complain about his muscles. "I will."

How was she expected sleep with this guy wrapped around her?

Start by closing your eyes.

Easily said, but then her other senses kicked in. She could hear the wind whistling through the rocks, a good thing because it meant her hearing was returning. Lyel smelled awesome when he shouldn't. He'd been locked in a cell and should reek from sweat or smell like three-day-old cooked cabbage.

She probably smelled like three-day-old cooked cabbage. Fedeema was as generous with bathwater as she was with food.

What other senses were there? Eyes closed meant no vision.

Touch. His scales were scratchy against her cheek, but his warmth cupped her like a heated blanket on a chilly day. She felt secure with him. Safe.

Taste.

It would be unwise to taste Lyel, though she was tempted.

Why was she tempted?

He was hot, but it was so much more than that. When he fought off the Al'kieern yesterday, she was amazed. And today, he again showed them who was boss.

Things could be worse. She could be facing this alone instead of with an alien who could fill in for a full SWAT team.

Her agent of secrets.

What else? He… She yawned.

Stress from hiding on the ship jumbled together with the gut-wrenching fear she lived with since her capture. The two smacked together and dragged her down…

She woke to silence and warmth. Snuggling into the heat, she nuzzled the neck of the guy she…

Hold on. Guy. Neck.

Warmth beneath her.

Lyel shifted, and his arms tightened around her. She soon found herself lying under an awake but sleepy hot dude with his thick, dreadlock-like appendages draping around her shoulders. One teased her jawline while she swore another traced the side of her breast. That couldn't be happening; they were hair!

Groaning, he nuzzled her collar bone and traced his tongue along her jawline to her ear. He bit down, his fangs pinching the tender flesh. While she quaked and desire flooded her, his mouth moved down the column of her neck to her shoulder, where he bit again, not hard enough to break the skin, but firmly enough to mark her and send exquisite pleasure through her body.

Damn, she was going to have alien hickeys.

She should buck him off. Tell him to climb off her and

leave her alone. Remind him of their no-friends-with-benefits agreement.

Maybe later…

She wove her fingers into his hair and the strands responded to her touch, entwining around her hands and teasing down her arms.

Lyel fanged the top of her tunic and tugged it aside, exposing one of her breasts. She'd long since lost her bra, and sultry air hit her skin like honey. Lyel's hot breath followed.

He lifted his head, but a band of his hair teased the side of her breast. "These…"

"Breasts?"

"Breasts," he breathed. "Lovely." His mouth trailed down her skin, and he paused over the nipple. It peaked from the change in air temperature and plain old anticipation.

She arched her spine, seeking something she'd never felt before. Lyel could give it to her.

His tongue slipped out, long, thick, and forked on the end, and he licked her nipple.

A moan jumped from her throat.

"This is not pain," he said as if he needed confirmation.

"It feels good."

His fangs flashed, and he straddled her hips and leaned closer. Cupping her nipple with his lips, he tugged it into his mouth. His tongue swirled across it, his forked tip entwining around the nub, teasing and pulling.

Shockwaves flashed to her groin, and she shifted beneath him in blissful agitation. Fuck the no friends with benefits idea.

Keeping his mouth on her breast, he shifted backward

to let his fingers trail down her belly and lower, cupping her through her clothing.

She groaned, unable to bear how wonderful his mouth felt on her breast. His hair stroked her other breast, which wasn't physically possible, and something vibrated against her nipple, the sensation roaring through her like an inferno.

He rubbed between her legs, his big hand teasing and stroking. She bucked beneath him, wanting more.

Her hands shot down to her pants to undo them. She didn't care about the world. About Fedeema. About needing to cross a freakin' desert.

She needed him pumping inside her.

He shifted down, kissing her belly while his hand rubbed harder.

Light flickered overhead as if something passed over the roof opening. The throaty roar of a large bird was followed by a squeak.

A creature plunged toward her; its claws extended.

SEVEN

Lyel

His senses might be dulled by lust for his mate, but the blood of warriors ran through Lyel's veins. Tumbling off Easy—Isi—he rolled with her secure in his arms. He flipped up to a crouch and nudged her behind him. His kalina lay on the ground, and he grabbed and brandished it.

"What was that?" Isi asked, peeking around his side. Her hands held onto his hips as her body pressed against his spine. He liked her there, but he enjoyed her beneath him even more.

Straightening, Lyel lowered his kalina. "A charlong." The creature sat in the center of the room, and he watched the palm-sized being for sudden moves, though he believed it was no threat. It appeared unable to bear weight on one of its legs.

"What's a charlong?" Anticipation rang in her voice. Did she hope to eat the creature?

He pulled his kalina again and stomped toward the small beast. "It is wounded. I will kill it. Tonight, I will roast it and serve it as an offering to you while wearing this modified version of the traditional garlong."

"It's hurt?" She leaped around him and stretched out her arms, blocking his access to the charlong. "Hold on. There's a lot of stuff going on here. First, you're talking normally."

"Our translators have synced." He flashed his fangs as he remembered her moans while he touched her. "As have we." Grabbing her hand, he flipped it over and sighed. No matebond symbol, but deep inside, it was clear she was his true mate.

Courtship, he reminded himself. She would not be able to resist him if he courted her in the proper Crakairian ways. This was the honorable thing to do.

The thin lines above her eyes lifted. "What we did a few seconds ago," her hand flipped toward the sandy floor, "was a momentary aberration on my part. Trust me, it won't happen again."

"We shall see, mate."

"No, we won't, *mate*."

"I like that you call me mate. As you should."

"I was being sarcastic. I was not calling you mate."

"You were." He eased her to the side. "Remain here, and I will kill for you." When she jumped ahead of him again, he straightened with a huff. "The creature is wounded. Allow me to slit its throat. I will skin it and cook it, and you will be happy with my courtship."

"Leave it to a male to think a woman will swoon because a mighty hunter slayed a defenseless bird-like crea-ture." Her lips twisted. "You have a lot to learn about Earth women."

His shoulders drooped. "This is the way to win a female's affection. Courtship. Marriage. Fucking."

"You keep mentioning those three items in that order. I don't understand why, but I imagine you have a reason."

"Traditional Crakairian courtship rituals will please you."

"Why do you think murdering a little creature will please me?"

"Because you will be fed. This is also our way."

"I get it. Courtship. Then comes marriage and," her gaze slanted to where they'd been entwined in the sand. "All that other stuff, which we're not doing. Remember? We had a deal."

Mostly. He would not force this, but that did not mean he wasn't above teasing a response out of her. He bowed in acknowledgement of her words, choosing not to remind her of what she had also agreed to. His persuasion was working.

"Keep that in mind at all times, and we'll do well together." She turned toward the charlong. "Is it deadly?"

"I do not believe so. Some Crakariains tame creatures such as this for pets."

"You mean like a parrot or a pet crow?"

He did not know those terms, but he nodded to the word pet.

A shadow passed over the air vent above, and Isi looked up. "Aw, I bet that big predator bird attacked the little one. That's why it's hurt." She raked her flares off her face and secured them up with something that stretched. Interesting material. He would examine it later to see if it would serve as a weapon. For now, he could only stare at her glorious cascade of pink and gold flares dangling from her head. Infinitely desirable. When she lay beneath him, why had he not buried his face in it as he wished to do the minar they met? Oh, yes. He had been fascinated by the soft, lush mounds on her chest—breasts.

Lyel was not completely naïve about Earthling females. He read a booklet about them. They used these mounds to nurse their younglings, unlike Crakairian females who projected a fleshy tube from their abdomen to deliver nutrients. He doubted Crakairian females moaned when their fleshy tube was caressed. Isi's response to him touching her breasts was unusual and appealing.

"For now," she said. "I'm ignoring most of what you said about slitting throats and skinning the poor creature, because ew. No thanks. I don't want you doing anything like that on my behalf."

"It is tradition to provide a courtship meal."

"The way to a girl's heart is through her stomach, huh?" She tapped her chest. "Not this girl. We'll find something else to eat."

"If I cannot kill and cook the charlong or emulse your feet, you must tell me how to court you in the Earth manner."

She cocked her head. "I must, huh?"

Perhaps he was too demanding, but he ached to show her what he could offer. "If you are willing," he added with a sigh.

"That sounds more like it. We can talk about ways to win an Earth woman later. Right now, I have to help this little guy." Turning, she dropped to her heels and extended her hand.

He stepped forward, his kalina lifting. "Your fingers…"

"Are fine. You poor thing. Your leg looks sore." She tipped her head back to look up at Lyel. "We need to help him."

"Him?"

"Or her." She faced the charlong. "It doesn't matter, does it, baby? How can we help you?" Scooting down onto her ass, she stretched out her legs.

The charlong hopped closer, avoiding using its wounded leg.

"My grannie had a pet parakeet when I was little," Isi said. "It was super old, like twenty, and it died when I was twelve, but I loved that bird to smithereens."

"What is a smithereen?" Let alone a para-tweet. He stooped down onto his heels beside her, keeping his weapon ready if the charlong became aggressive.

"Smithereens is a saying. For example, you blew the compound to smithereens."

"I like this word smithereens. I will find new ways to use it."

"Go for it." She shifted closer, keeping her hand outstretched. The charlong twirped, and she laughed. "Do you have a home, little charlong?"

"Charlongs do not need homes." He moved forward along with Isi, ready to protect her with his life.

"This one does, don't you?" she cooed. "Look at it. It's so sweet! I love its four, clawed legs like a chicken's, and pretty, grayish-blue feathers. And that beak. Would you look at that? I've never seen a bird with a purple beak before, let alone fangs. And wings. Those clawed tips look like they could do some serious damage."

"It is a charlong. They all look the same."

Isi stretched out her hand and the charlong hopped backward, evading her touch.

"I won't hurt you, but you're shy, aren't you?" Isi asked. "You come near when you feel safe, baby. I'm patient." She grinned at Lyel to share the moment, her smile hitting him in the chest like a rapitire. "I think it likes me. I'm going to hang out here for a while and see if I can get it to trust me. Do we have time?"

He'd stay here forever if she granted him another smile.

The charlong edged closer, pausing by her foot. Cocking its head, it examined her clothing before moving up to her outstretched hand. It squinted at her fingers but didn't attack.

Feeling foolish, Lyel lowered his kalina. He was disappointed he could not prove his bravery to Isi by slaying the creature. She was bonding with it when she should, instead, be bonding with Lyel.

He was not jealous. Not too much. He was…Heille, he did not know what he was. Wild, untamed emotions raged around inside him. Lust for his mate who had so exquisitely responded to his touch. Protectiveness. Anger at Fedeema for hitting her. It hurt to think of anything causing her harm, even this puny charlong. And a growing affection for this tiny Earthling female who teased him like no one had before. He didn't know what to make of it or of her.

Isi cooed to the charlong, coaxing it closer. It took one hop in her direction before skittering back to the wall. Its twirp showed it was relenting, however. If she kept at this, she would tame the heart of the tiny beast as easily as she was taming Lyel's beastly heart.

"Do you have family, Lyel?" she asked.

"Not any longer."

"I'm sorry. What happened to them?"

For the first time, he wanted to share his history with another—with Isi. "My father—Piersag, as he insisted I call him—often said, 'without regular blows, one will spoil a youngling'."

She flashed him a concerned look. "What are you saying?"

"I loved my father—for many years."

"I'm sure you did. I hear a but in your statement."

Her hand remained extended, but she stilled as if she didn't want to miss a single word Lyel spoke.

"As I aged, I started to see more than the image I created in my mind. Piersag was not a kind, caring person. He was not a good parent. What started as occasional blows became more frequent, especially when Piersag drank vintip. This was why my mother retreated to her own estate, taking my sister along with her." He closed his eyes as memories surged through him, blocking out everything else. "I suspect Piersag extended those blows to Therena and my mother, too, not just the youngling son he was determined to control. It guts me to think I did not protect them."

"How old were you when your mother left?"

"They visited." The last time only weeks before they died.

"Not an answer. How old were you?"

"Old enough."

"Lyel." Her voice dropped off to almost nothing. "Tell me?"

"Twelve yaros."

"A boy."

He opened his eyes and the sadness in hers burned through him. "Big enough to protect a mother and younger sister."

"You have a sister?"

"They both died when the disease swept through."

"I'm sorry. But you weren't big enough to protect anyone from an adult, not even yourself."

And that was true. "Again, I had no honor."

"Honor has nothing to do with it."

"It has everything to do with it. My father destroyed our honor."

"When he hit you."

"That and when he…"

"What?"

He could not meet her eye. "He forced me to battle in his place in a vengeance."

"I don't know what a vengeance is, but he shouldn't have forced you to do anything. You didn't owe him."

"I owed our family. Our name. And when I threw the battle—I was unable to kill my former friend—my father's rage ignited. He…"

She waited in the hush that followed.

"He died, as he should. And that is why I am here. I am no agent of secrets. I came here to destroy the Al'kieern organization and restore my honor."

"You expected to die, didn't you?"

He could only nod.

Her shoulders slumped. "You're already honorable."

"I am not."

"You succeeded."

"Fedeema lives."

"She's defeated."

He sighed. "I wish that were so, but I must still kill her."

"I'm all for that, but not if it means your life."

"You do not understand."

She cocked one brow ridge. "Are you sure?"

He crossed his arms on his chest. It ached in there and he did not know why. "I do not wish to discuss this further."

"I feel bad for you. Your mother left you," she said softly. "Why didn't she take you with her?" Bitterness came through in her voice, but he did not know why.

"She did try."

Her lips compressed. "In that, you were lucky."

Luck had nothing to do with it. "Piersag refused,

stating a youngling male needed to be raised by his father. Rather than face his wrath, my mother relented."

What would it have been like to grow up under his mother's kind, caring touch, instead of his father's heavy hand? Lyel soon learned to lock down his emotions because showing them—especially fear or sadness—only incited his father's rage and made the lesson worse.

The charlong twirped and tilted its head, watching Isi.

She blinked fast, and her eyes shimmered. "I'm sorry, Lyel. I… I know what it's like."

Did she?

Before he could ask more, her sigh leaked out and she turned back to the charlong. "Come on, baby. I won't," she swallowed hard, "I won't hurt you."

It tiptoed over to her and tapped her foot with its beak. Isi released a surprised huff and held her palm out. "Hop on, buddy. I'll check out your leg and find you something to eat." She looked up at Lyel and sniffed. Sorrow still creased her face, and it touched him that she cared about this, if nothing else. "What do charlongs eat?"

"I do not know. Insects?"

"Sounds about right. Looks like I'll need to go hunting." She looked around and plucked a cricorn beetle off the wall and held it toward the charlong. "How about this, little guy? You hungry?"

The charlong snatched it from her and tipping its head back, swallowed the insect whole.

"Whoa. You're starved. Let me see if I can find you more food."

When Lyel approached Vork with an apology, Vork asked Lyel why he'd fought for his father. Lyel had not been able to give Vork an answer.

Perhaps, now, he knew.

He did it to protect Vork. By allowing the defeat, he

was able to break free. He showed Piersag he was his own male, not one dominated by the whims of an abusive father.

Piersag died before he saw the person Lyel was, a male of honor. His final curses still rang in Lyel's ears. His anger, even while dying, would haunt Lyel for many yaros.

He thought of sharing this with Isi, too, but his emotions felt too raw to reveal. They were getting to know each other. He did not wish to frighten her away.

Perhaps Lyel was no better than his father. After all, he obeyed his father's wishes regarding a good friend. He fought Vork in the vengeance instead of refusing.

"Abuse can haunt a kid," Isi said, not looking up from the charlong who hopped forward and stopped close to her, looking up. It twirped.

"Kid?"

"Youngling, I think you call young Crakairians, but you know what I'm saying."

Did he? He waited to see if she would speak more.

"Do you want to be my friend, little alien bird?" she cooed, holding out another beetle, which the bird snatched from her and ate. "You can't walk, but I can carry you around." She tilted her head, and he knew she spoke to Lyel now. "I imagine you blame yourself for how he treated you."

"It is proper to discipline a youngling."

"Discipline? What did you do wrong?"

"Nothing specific, just everything."

"Ah, Lyel," she sighed. "I doubt you ever did anything bad enough to deserve being hit."

"I…"

"What?"

"One does not carry a charlong," he said, focusing on

the words she had spoken to the charlong. She was wrong. Piersag's punishment had been appropriate.

Hadn't it?

He suppressed a growl. Throughout his childhood, he'd tried his best to be the youngling Piersag demanded. Sometimes, though, he wanted to be himself. To run and yell like the other younglings. To push the limits and be rewarded for taking chances. Watching Isi lure the charlong closer made his throat hurt, and he rubbed it. He didn't envy how kindly she treated the creature, did he?

"There's no harm in carrying the poor thing, is there?" she said.

The weak are abandoned—his father's words. Only now did Lyel see how harsh, how cruel they were. "A charlong flies or runs across the desert floor," he said weakly. He could barely focus on the charlong. His mind remained locked in the past.

Piersag had been wrong about many things, but mostly about Lyel.

"My grannie's parakeet rode on her shoulder," Isi said. "Do you think charlongs can be taught to repeat words? Our parakeet was a heck of a lot of fun."

He loved how Isi distracted him, how she pulled him forward, dragging his mind from a past that could not be changed and into a future where anything was possible. "What would you teach the charlong?"

"I don't know. Ahoy matey? People teach that phrase to parrots, but I bet a charlong could learn it, too." She dropped forward, putting her face within striking range of the creature. Lyel held his breath, but the charlong did not attack. "Ahoy, matey! Can you say that little guy? Ahoy, matey."

Lyel's breath eased out, and his fingers twitched on the hilt of his kalina.

"Hello!" Isi chirped. "Try that instead, little bird. Hello! Hello!"

Lyel swore the bird was as puzzled as him. Its tiny brow feathers scrunched together.

"We should leave." Lyel peered up. Night had fallen while she coaxed the bird. It would be difficult for Fedeema to track them in the dark. While Crakairians saw well at night, Al'kieerns did not.

"All right," Isi said but she did not get up off the ground. "Is hello too hard to say, little bird? We have lots of other words and phrases we can try, don't we? Thar she blows! How about that? Can you say thar she blows?"

The charlong cocked its head. Lyel felt like doing so himself.

"You need a name if you're going to join the family," she said.

"Family?" The word popped out of Lyel.

"Figuratively speaking." While her words reinforced her caution, the smile she shot him warmed his insides to boiling. "No reason our charlong friend can't come with us, right?"

They might die, and if the charlong was with them, it could die as well, but he chose not to say that. "It…could."

"Awesome."

The charlong hopped close enough so Isi could carefully touch its wounded leg.

"It doesn't appear cut, just banged. Maybe it has a bruise, and it hurts to put weight on it. No matter." Standing, she scooped up the bird as if it wasn't a threat under normal circumstances and dropped it on her shoulder. It wavered, but its small claws dug into her tunic to maintain balance. "How do you like things up there, Buccaneer? And just like that, he has a name. Buccaneer. Bucko, for short."

Lyel expected the creature to rake her throat, and he hefted his kalina, but the bird only glared his way. He glared back in warning. The creature needed to behave. It was not too late to find itself on a plate as Lyel's courtship meal.

Cooing, the charlong—Booko—rubbed its face against Isi's cheek, making her laugh.

"I think we're ready, right Bucko?" she said.

"Ahoy!" the bird cried.

Turning toward the narrow tunnel, Lyel sighed.

EIGHT

Isi

W hen Isi emerged from their hiding spot and out into the desert, a hoarse, barking cry echoed in the distance. She scrambled to her feet, almost unsettling Bucko clinging to her shoulder.

"Watch the claws, buddy," she hissed, prying them away from her skin one by one.

The barking cry repeated, and her mouth snapped shut. Her skin peppered over with goosebumps, she pulled her knife, but nothing rushed their way.

"What is this?" Lyel asked, pointing to the blade.

She showed it to him. "I stole it from Fedeema."

"Smart," he said. "You do not need anyone to save you."

"I'm trying."

"Doing."

Heat flooded her cheeks. She shouldn't be embarrassed by his compliments. She'd gotten them before, though not from a hot guy. "Thanks."

He dipped his head. "You are a worthy mate."

Her lips twisted. Why tie this into his belief they were destined mates? "Thanks?"

"The question is, am I worthy of you?"

That popped her irritation balloon. "Aw, Lyel." Her emotions had been screwing with her since they met. After he shared his past… What she felt was not pity; it was something she could hold onto. But she was a stubborn person who hated to back down, and she… Okay, she worried if she trusted him, he'd hurt her like her mom did when she left.

Foolish, but there it was.

"You have so much to offer a woman," she said.

"What about you?"

"I…" She shook her head. "Me, too."

"That is enough for now."

Overcome with her new, raw feelings, she strode out into the desert and stopped, letting the night enclose her. To hide her before he saw something she wasn't yet ready to reveal.

Inky blackness coated the land, and a desolate aloneness sunk claws into her skin. If Lyel wasn't here with her, Isi would crawl back into the tiny hideout among the boulders and stay there for the next month or so. What did tonight hold for them? Would they survive until morning?

"Hello!" Bucko called beside her ear, making her jump.

Yips resounded across the desert, followed by the barking cry. It reached through the darkness, making Isi shiver.

As much as she loved how quickly Bucko was learning to speak, now was a good time to keep quiet. She stroked his long, sharp beak. "Shh, there matey. If you keep that up, we'll be cast to the fishies."

Joining her, Lyel's brow ridges scrunched together. "Fishies?"

"It's a saying that means we'll be dead," she whispered.

"The cry was a woosterine. It hunts but it is not moving in our direction."

How could he tell?

"That's a relief." Not really. Girding herself, she stared around. Two moons shone down from overhead, one tannish gray, as if the planet was made up of sand, but that would be wrong, because that was her view of Mara. The other moon's minty green color reminded her of leaves in the spring. And Crakair…whoa. She could make out lights on the surface. A city? Lyel's home world was huge.

Would she ever reach there safely? If so, how would she survive in a strange culture and among people she didn't know? Maybe she could get an accounting job. Numbers were numbers, right?

Except…her translator worked for oral language, but it was unclear if written would translate the same.

Lyel would help her settle in on Crakair if she asked, wouldn't he?

She watched as Lyel surveyed the area, his hand tight on his weapon. He moved with the cunning of a warrior yet when he spoke, she could tell he was well educated. He used his spear with a skill that suggested years of training. His scrap of material fluttered in the light breeze, and his scales gleamed in the moonlight.

So gorgeous, it almost hurt to look at him.

Her gaze flashed to his sizeable groin. The two times they kissed, she felt him—it—but the beginning of a stiffy pressed against a person wasn't the same as seeing and holding an erect cock in her hands.

Was he scaled there, too? Interesting that was she eager to find out because she hadn't felt that way initially. The more she got to know him, the more he worked his way beyond her barriers. She shouldn't be thinking of him in a sexy way, though it was clear he thought of *her* that way.

She huffed. As tempted as she was to see where this took them, they needed to pay attention to their surroundings. If the woosterine came after them, she could be dead before she had time to gasp.

But Lyel spoke to her, to the person she was inside, and she wasn't sure she could let that go.

Taking his hand, she linked their fingers. "I feel a bit overwhelmed."

"By me."

"By everything, but especially by the feelings you stir inside me. I don't know where it's going, and I know this isn't the time to figure it out."

"We have time."

"Do we?"

He nodded slowly. "I will not pressure you, mate."

"Just try to persuade me, right?" she teased.

"Can you blame me?"

"Actually, no, I can't."

"This is enough."

For now—the thought was left unspoken. One of these days, he'd bring this conversation back. Would she be ready for more by then? Only time would tell.

"We must leave," he said, his attention trained on the direction the howl had come from.

"I'm ready. You, too, Bucko?"

The bird fluffed its feathers but remained quiet.

She walked with Lyel around the boulders, and out into the desert.

She welcomed the distraction of moving. Everything in this world was big, from Lyel to the wasteland to the creatures around her. She couldn't process it, maybe because she was sore and tired or maybe because, for the first time in her life, she was with someone who unsettled her. He drew her out from behind the wall she built for protection and showed her things could be different.

"We will walk at night and find shelter during the day," he said.

"Shelter from Fedeema."

"And her army."

"How long will it take to cross the desert?"

"Many daelas, but we can do it."

She loved how confident he sounded, but she'd wait and see.

"What are the moons called?" she asked softly. Her sneakers shifted on the sand, making each step a challenge. If she was looking for a workout, she would get it. Sadly, they had a long way to go before they could find safety.

He tipped his head back, and she noted he kept his sword ready, as if he expected something to attack them.

Her spine tingled, as if something watched, and she kept her knife ready.

It came in a whoosh.

Bucko shrieked as something smacked into Isi's back, driving her onto her knees. She spun and swiped out, hitting whatever it was.

It flopped on the ground while Bucko cowered against her neck.

With an angry screech, the predator bird she saw earlier took off. It soared at a crooked angle, favoring one wing.

"Will it be back?" Isi asked.

"We will watch for it. You…amaze me." He shook his head, his hair lifting up and around his face. One of the thicker bands reached toward her.

"Why does it do that?" she asked, keeping her eye on the speck of bird limply flying away from them.

"Why does what do what?"

Jumping up, she tapped the end of the band of hair that reached for her cheek. "If this was a horror film, I'd be shrieking it's alive."

"It *is* alive."

"You know what I mean."

"My naanans are like my arms. They move independently."

"You're saying you don't have hair."

"Hair?" He huffed. "I am mistaken. I thought…" His laughter snorted out as they started walking again. "I thought your beautiful tresses were called flares."

"My hair is brightly colored, but it's plain old hair. It's not alive. Truly." She tweaked the tip of a longer naanan, making Lyel shiver. "Does that hurt? If so, I'm sorry."

"My naanans enjoy attention."

"Ah." She nodded slowly. "Sexual attention?"

"That, too."

"And they have minds of their own?" They must since he didn't seem to control them.

"Not usually."

"Which isn't exactly an answer, dude."

"I can direct them but sometimes…"

"They direct themselves?"

"Yes. They feel the matebond and respond."

Huh.

"About the moons," he said, she assumed he must want to steer her attention away from his naanans. Did they give him away? "Mia is the smallest and is made up of wasteland."

"From our surroundings, I thought Mara was the only wasteland moon in the neighborhood."

"Only this part of the planet. A good part is covered with city, and there are vast oceans beyond that."

"And the other moon?"

"Tress. A vacation paradise for Crakairians."

"Maybe someday, I'll go there. I could work at a resort, assuming they have any. You know, sing for my supper."

"How long have you been a singer?"

"Most of my life. My mom and Grannie…" It hurt to remember her mother, because she bailed on Isi, but… "I used to sing with my mom when I was really little, then with Grannie. Sometimes, Mom and I would harmonize together. She taught me how to control my voice." Until she left.

"A good memory. Does your mother still live?"

"I don't know. She abandoned me when I was a child. I was raised by my grandmother until she died, then foster parents. They were decent, but they had four other kids and with full time jobs, they were busy."

"I am sorry about your mother and grandmother."

"Grannie was the best." She missed the fun they had together. "After Grannie died, the state looked for Mom, but couldn't find her. When I aged out of foster care, I didn't look for her myself."

"Why not?" He studied her face. What did she reveal?

"Because I cut her from my life when I was ten."

"Perhaps she had a reason to stay away."

"She bailed and she didn't come back. There's no reason in that."

"Sometimes people need to disappear."

Like Isi? She paused but started walking again. Stomping, that is. Isi and her mother were nothing alike. But she couldn't dismiss Lyel's question. What if Mom needed to hide? She may have left Isi behind to protect her, knowing Grannie could give a world of love to her grandchild.

Isi would never know, but Lyel's comment made her think of this from another angle. They started across a long stretch of smooth sand peppered with rocks the size of grapefruits. "Mom's reasons no longer matter. I'm not going back to Earth."

"That is right. You will be a singer on Tress." He stared forward, but if he saw anything in particular, his loose posture suggested it didn't concern him. "When I heard you sing, it stilled something inside me."

His words stilled her. Her steps faltered, and she halted beside one of the black rocks. "Thank you."

"Your song shared a slice of you."

"I'm not quite sure that's true. A song is just words and a melody." Disconcerted, she started walking again, stepping over a rock. They climbed a small hill and Lyel paused at the top to survey the area. With a grunt, he started down the other side, she kept pace with him, her feet sliding in the soft sand. Bucko rode along, swaying with her movements, his head dipping back and forth as he studied their surroundings. At least the predator bird hadn't returned. Yet. Isi's back loosened, and she was grateful she avoided an infection this time. Her ointment had blown up with the compound. Where would she find treatment in the wasteland?

"What did you hear in my song?" Why was she asking? It would be easier to let this go, to suppress…feelings. Whatever he said would make her turbulent emotions rise to the surface all over again. Caring was to be avoided at all costs.

He was a means to an end, someone to share defense with until they escaped this planet.

But she did care. No harm in admitting it to herself. From the brief time she'd known him, Lyel had impressed her and not only with his fighting abilities. He was sweet if reserved, protective of her and, if she was honest with herself, he sparked something inside her no one else had.

Her footsteps slowed. Emotions. Damn things were crap. Who needed them?

Maybe…Isi did.

No. She didn't. *She didn't dare.* Catching up, she kept pace with Lyel, moving around another black rock.

"In your song, I sensed longing for something beyond your touch," he said.

Huh. That was too close for comfort. "The words say that, how the girl feels like she's on the outside looking in, longing to be part of something she's never known. They were her words, not mine." Liar.

"It is true words can be statements unrelated to feelings. But when you sang, you put your heart into your words. I felt it," he pressed his fist against his chest, "here." His hand dropped to his side. "But that wasn't all I heard in your song."

She didn't want to know. Each of his comments picked away at the scar surrounding her heart. After mom left and Grannie died, Isi decided things went better when you relied only on yourself. Trusting others only resulted in disappointment. If you didn't let someone in, they couldn't hurt you. Words to live by, and she held them close.

"It's nothing like that," she said. "You heard nothing. The song is from a cartoon movie completely unrelated to me."

He tapped her chest. "Your song came from in here."

She shrugged away from him. She couldn't look at him, couldn't let him see that vulnerable side of her she kept hidden. "It's not true."

He nodded slowly. "I imagine when you say this, others believe, but I see something else. You sang about being a person who had nothing but longing for what could be. Hope surged in your song. You carry this feeling because you pray one daela, you will feel complete."

"This isn't true," she said through a throat choked off with pain. "I'm complete. I don't need anyone else to make me feel real."

"You are correct. You only need yourself."

"That's right," she huffed, her arms snaking across her chest. "I only need me."

"Relying on oneself is the first step."

She didn't like where this was going, but she also had a feeling nothing she said would stop him from naming it. Another thing she kept hidden inside. She started counting to ten—

"Once you love yourself, your heart will open to others."

"I love myself." It came out defensively, but she heard his words. Had she pinned Mom's leaving on herself? For so long, she tried to figure out what she'd done to drive Mom away. Grr. "I don't have time for this."

She didn't want to make time for this.

"Are you sure?" He turned toward her. "Isi, I know what it is like to feel this way, to hold yourself back to keep from being hurt when, deep inside, you are still that child who wants to give and receive love. Your song spoke to me. One day, I hope you will trust me enough to share all of yourself."

"You're wrong. Your mom left but she still loved you. Mine took off to spend a weekend with a boyfriend but never returned. Sure, we got a nice, legally written letter in the mail, saying Grannie could have custody, but Mom bailed on me when I needed her. I was a kid who loved her, not trash to be thrown away. She left me with my grand-mother, who did her best to give me a home, but she had Mom late in life. She was old. And she died, leaving me alone like Mom did."

He tugged her into his arms and held her. Bucko

offered his version of sympathy, cooing in her ear and stroking his beak on her face.

She didn't cry. She cried herself out when she was ten.

"I am sorry," Lyel said. "I did not wish to upset you."

Tipping her head back, she looked up at him, trying to read his face. It was cloaked in shadows, but pain came through in his voice, a feeling echoed in her heart. "You said something about obedience."

"He… I defended him for so long. No, I defended him until the bitter end. When all that time, he did not defend me. Not against the world and mostly, not against himself."

"It was wrong of him to hit you." Her chest spasmed at the thought.

"If a youngling is not disciplined, he will grow up wild."

"Do you think that or are you repeating what you were told? He hurt you, and that's so wrong." Her eyes stung. No denying she felt pain for the child Lyel had been, for the man his upbringing molded him into.

"It is done."

"Is it ever over, though? I'm here to tell you I don't think it ever is." She stepped out of his embrace but kept a grip on his forearms, needing the connection. "You were right about me. What you see is the glued together bits of a life that was shattered. Even now, there are times I can barely keep from falling apart."

"Isi." A world of emotion came through in his voice, and while it was too much, too soon, she couldn't pull away. Stepping back from him now would undo the progress she made and it could hurt Lyel. Something she realized she never wanted to do.

"I think, in some ways, you're also pieces of yourself glued back together," she said softly.

His chest rose and fell. "Perhaps."

"Only perhaps?"

"It is hard to open myself up."

"Boy, do I get it." She laughed ruefully. "But if you don't let it out, if you trap it inside, it festers, and that does you no good." She well understood how holding back feelings could make things worse. Perhaps it was time for her to let it out, too.

"I will think about this."

"It's a start. Let me know if you come to any conclusions."

They started walking again, and Isi's steps felt lighter, as if sharing had released a fifty-pound weight she carried on her shoulders. She hoped Lyel felt the same. Life was too short to cling to past pain.

He approached a scraggly tree silhouetted in the moonlight, its shadow stretching across the arid ground in ghostly fingers. Stooping down, he dug at the base of the tree.

She joined him, placing her hand on his shoulder. Again, she needed this connection. "What are you doing?"

He pointed to where he dug. "See?"

She dropped to her knees beside him, and Bucko hopped from her shoulder to her knee then to the ground. The bird limped to the edge of the depression and peered inside like Isi did.

Lyel carefully shifted the bird to the side and reached into the hole with both hands. He pulled his cupped palms out and held them toward her. "Drink."

"You found water?"

"This tree has deep roots that pull liquid from deep beneath the ground. Wherever you find a juliter tree, you will find something to drink."

She held his hands and sipped the brackish liquid. It might not taste the best, but it granted life. After she quenched her thirst, she did the same for Lyel, reaching into the hole and cupping water for him to sip from her palms.

His fangs flashed in the moonlight, and he traced his finger down her cheek before drinking.

There was something wildly intimate about sharing this way. Did she like it? She sucked in a breath. Yes.

While danger lurked in this direction, it was also free-ing, like she faced a tall wave roaring in from the ocean. If it broke over her, she would drown. But if she jumped up, she could crest the peak and glide down the other side.

They drank their fill and got to their feet while Bucko leaped into the tiny depression. He floated across the thin surface, dipping his beak into the water.

"Finished, Bucko?" she asked, and she swore he nodded. She scooped him up out of the hole and dropped him onto her shoulder. He settled on his fluffy butt, damp-ening her shirt, but she didn't care. She was grateful to have his friendship.

"Come on, matey," she said. "It's time to weigh the anchor and hoist the mizzen."

"Mizzen?" Lyel asked as they started across the desert again.

"It's another pirate saying, but I'm not sure what it means." Her laughter snorted out. "I'm warning you. I won't be able to stop coming up with them. I'm stuck in a pirate rut, which is kind of funny considering there's next to no water around and we're not on a ship."

"Teach me as you teach Bucko, then. We will be pirates together."

"Sure, thing, Jack."

"Jack?"

"He was a famous pirate. He had hair," she tapped the end of a naanan, "a bit like yours." And he was equally sexy, though Jack had been sexy in a flirty way while Lyel was pure, unending, masculine heat.

"I do not know if I prefer the name Lyel or Jack. How about you?"

Lyel. She preferred Lyel.

"I think…" She tripped over one of the black rocks and scowled as she kept moving. Damn thing. Rocks couldn't jump, could they?

"You think…"

She stared straight ahead; her emotions too raw to share yet. But she was nothing if not honest. "I prefer Lyel."

"Isi." He said her name like something precious.

Too much. Too soon.

Maybe.

She pulled ahead of him, jumping over yet another black rock, and he caught up.

"You mentioned your song came from a cartoon, but I do not know what this is," Lyel said lightly. She appreciated that he wasn't pushing this. Despite resting together and his kisses…well, and all the rest, they were only starting to get to know each other.

"A cartoon is animated like a drawing come to life, played out in a movie form."

"Like a vid?"

"Yes. Crakairian males matched with Earth women send video introductions to their prospective, right?"

"They do."

"Have you sent one to an Earthling woman?" Why had she asked that? She truly didn't want to know.

"I have not applied for the Selection."

"Did you plan to?"

"No…" He paused and looked around; his head cocked.

"Ahoy, matey," Bucko said softly by her ear. He ruffled his wings and settled onto her shoulder again.

Lyel shook his head, his naanans flaring out before settling around his shoulders. He started walking, and Isi stayed with him, weaving around an open area peppered with black rocks.

When she started to speak, he lifted his hand.

A mass of black rocks skittered across the desert, rushing toward them.

NINE

Lyel

G rowling, Lyel rushed forward, his kalina lifted. He met the wall of dark creatures scampering toward them and swiped out with his blade. Vardeks. He'd heard of beasts like this. They emerged from the ground at night to feed.

They would not eat Lyel or Isi.

"Ahoy! Ahoy!" Bucko squawked, flapping his wings. Isi, her knife in hand, backed toward the hill they'd descended.

When his kalina hit the lead vardeks, they snapped and cackled. His blade deflected off their hard shells. They marched toward him with their retractable pincers extended.

Sheathing his kalina, he ran to Isi. He scooped her up and raced toward the wall of vardeks, leaping up and over them, landing with a jolt on the soft ground beyond.

Bucko yelped but clung to Isi's shoulder.

"What are those things?" Isi shouted. "They don't seem friendly."

"Vardeks, and they will eat us."

"Let's avoid this, secret agent Lyel."

"I am doing my best." The vardeks spun and charged them. Bolting across the wasteland, Lyel leaped over more clusters and darted to the sides to avoid others.

The vardeks jumped, attempting to latch onto him, their claws scraping his hide, but his scales protected him from penetration. This would not last, however. They'd pinch and slice until they broke through. His blood would draw more, as they hunted by scent.

"You didn't tell me you were a superhero, able to leap tall buildings in a single bound."

"I am super, but I am no hero." His feet churned through the sand as he put distance between them and the vardeks. Fortunately, they hunted in groups and did not coat the entire desert.

"What you're doing is heroic to me."

His steps faltered, and he slowed. A glance over his shoulder showed the creatures were not following. "How is taking you away from the vardeks heroic?"

"Oh, I don't know." Her arms linked around his neck, and he liked how she leaned into him. "Maybe it was the way you ran forward, taking on the…vardeks all by yourself with only a spear."

"What else would you have me do?"

She shrugged. "I have a feeling hitting them wouldn't have done much, and my knife is too short to make much difference. I could've kicked them like balls, I suppose."

"They would have latched onto your feet, and your blows would not have penetrated their exoskeleton."

"Latched on, huh? Let's avoid that." She shuddered, and he tightened his grip on her. "Blow is being generous. I studied martial arts, but I'm no ninja. But that's not all you did. You picked me up and leaped like Aquaman over the creatures." She patted the charlong perched on her shoulder. "Even Bucko wasn't dislodged."

"Who is this man of aqua? He is someone you admire?" He was not jealous.

"Just sayin', Jason Mamoa is something else, and he has many admirable features, but he's an actor. In Aquaman, he plays a superhero. It's a cartoonish movie."

Like the other, where she found her songs? "Did he sing in this vid?"

Cresting a hill, Lyel continued down the other side at a jog. They'd left the vardeks behind for now, but he liked holding Isi. Would she mind if he carried her longer?

She snorted. "He did not sing, and I'm not sure I'd want him to, either." Her fingers traced through his naanans, and he ached to close his eyes and savor her touch. It made his cock twitch. "He had lots of muscles, scales, and he had hair a bit like yours."

"My naanans and scales are better than this man of aqua's."

"They are." She said it in a solemn tone, but her lips curled upward. "They move independently, which is better than hair."

He liked her hair, lying like the softest down on his arm.

"I like them," she added.

And they liked her, if their weaving into her hair and across the back of her neck was any indication. One teased her collarbone, and he swore it ached to dip lower, but naanans did not have emotions. He controlled them, not the other way around. The naanan stroking her cheek suggested otherwise.

Heille, they did what he wished he could do.

"Another Aquaman move?" she said. "You're carrying me as you run across a desert, and I'm no lightweight."

"You are tiny."

"Everyone's tiny compared to you."

"I am of average build."

"The Crakairian average, perhaps, but where I come from, men are not as tall or broad as you."

Lyel puffed out his chest. "I feel bad for the remaining Earth men." A thought occurred to him, and his chest deflated. "Are you saying I am too big?"

The lines above her eyes rose. "That's an interesting question."

"In what way?" She should tell him. Put him out of his misery.

"You're big in ways I shouldn't mention, but no worries, I'm not scared. Not that we're going there yet."

"Where are we not going yet?"

"Into that realm."

He was confused.

"As for the rest of you, I wouldn't be the only woman to call you big, but you're impressive not intimidating."

Rest of him. Rest of him. Oh. "You refer to my cock. I will show it to you when we stop to rest."

She grinned. "Are all Crakairian males eager to flash women?"

"Flash of what?"

"You know." She wiggled her face. Tipping her head to the side, she peered behind them. "We seem to have left the vardeks behind. You can put me down now, and I'll move under my own speed."

He slowed, stopped, and lowered her to her feet.

"Hey, this will work." She darted a few feet away and hefted a stick, swinging it through the air as she pivoted. "I appreciate your heroic efforts on my behalf, but next time, I'm going to play baseball with the vardeks."

"Their bite can be deadly."

"I'll kick them, too."

"Jump over them. That is best."

"As long as you're aware my jump is puny compared to yours. I'm short in case you didn't notice."

"I will carry you again if more vardeks attack."

"That's the thing. I don't want you to carry me. I get wherever I go under my own steam."

"You are independent. I appreciate this in you." If he couldn't help her with this, how could he convince her he was a worthy mate?

Remember the courtship rituals.

He had not prepared a meal while dressed in his fake garlong, as she refused to allow him to kill Bucko. He found water and from her behavior, he could tell she was softening but not sufficient to win her agreement to marriage.

"Thanks." Jumping forward, Isi slashed the stick. She poked at the ground and smacked a rock. "This will work nicely. I took karate for a while, though it was ages ago, but I still know some moves."

"Karate?"

"It's a type of martial arts, a system of unarmed combat where those fighting use their feet and hands to deliver and block blows. Some do it for exercise and to hone their fighting ability. I did it because…"

"What?"

"I needed to protect myself. I also took self-defense classes, so watch out."

He bowed. "I respect your defensive abilities."

"Hello!" Bucko called. "Ahoy, matey."

"Cute," Isi said with a grin. She stroked the charlong's back. "Aren't you a clever bird. How about thar she blows? Remember that one? Thar she blows."

"Blows," the charlong repeated.

Isi snickered. "Close enough."

"On Crakair, we have khatalm warriors. They are

deadly." His father used them for protection. "You have khatalm warrior skills?" This would be helpful.

"Don't get too excited. I only got to blue belt, which means I learned just enough to be dangerous." She rushed forward and stabbed the sand with her stick. "Bucko, try this one. Shiver me timbers."

"Shiver she blows," Bucko twirped.

Isi slashed out at a clump of wispy grasses, severing the seedpods from the main shaft. She stopped, staring forward, and the stick trembled in her hand. "Oh, shit. What's that?"

He followed her gaze to a small herd of jiera. The spindly legged creatures with dusty gray fur, extended their necks and peered their way. Their musky scent tainted the air. Shifting their feet, the lead one stomped to give warning.

"Will they attack?" Isi whispered, backing toward Lyel.

"They will not but—

The ground rumbled around them, and the jiera bolted, racing in the opposite direction.

Anxiety clawed up Lyel's spine when the ground shook again.

Isi turned as she walked toward him, and fear spiked her voice. "Is that an earthquake?"

The ground erupted underneath her.

As a xarton shot up through the ground, its enormous mouth opened. Isi was sucked downward, into the gaping maw.

"Lyel!" She stretched her arms toward him, but she tumbled away from him too fast.

He leaped forward, landing on his belly and snapping his arm out toward her. He latched onto her fingers, and her panicked gaze met his.

"Don't let go!" Isi cried.

"I will not." Easing forward, he tried to get a better grip on her arm.

The xarton's tongue wrapped around Isi's body and yanked, pulling her from Lyel's grasp.

As he bellowed with rage, the xarton's mouth snapped closed.

It sunk back into the sand with Isi inside it.

TEN

Isi

"Wailing never did a soul any good," Grannie always said, and Isi believed it with all her heart. When in trouble, fight instead.

"Thar she blows," Bucko shrieked, clinging to Isi's shoulder as she tumbled down into a mouth the size of a school bus. She kept a death grip on her stick. *Death* being a word too close to comfort. Dank, musty slime coated the surfaces around her and teeth about three feet long glistened with spit.

She'd never forget the look of devastation on Lyel's face as his grip loosened and she fell away from him, into this monster.

After the jaws closed, darkness enveloped her in an odorous pall. What she wouldn't give for a flashlight. The creature's tongue worked, shoving her down its throat. Not tonight, Satan.

Like a freight train, the body moved. Isi wavered, trying to remain on her feet on a squishy surface that felt like a tongue.

Thinking was all well and good, but actions bring results—another Grannie phrase.

It was now or never, and Isi wasn't a girl who believed in never.

"Hold on, Bucko!" Spinning, she delivered a roundhouse kick to one of the front fangs and followed it up with a gouge of her stick on the tongue.

The creature came to a grounding stop, making Isi pitch against the side of the mouth. She pried herself off the gooey wall and stabbed the stick into the beast's upper palate.

It shuddered, a groan worked its way up from the belly.

"Shiver me timbers," Bucko cried, clinging to her shoulder. Extending his neck, he pecked the beast's mouth.

"Hold on, matey," Isi cried. She punched forward, thrusting her fist against the wall, then used the kin geri move she perfected in karate against a fang. The tip snapped off, and the beast swayed, trying to knock Isi off her feet.

Using a pirate's wide stance, she bucked along with the ride, using the opportunity to spear the sidewall with her stick.

Another kick, and the creature blasted upward, a rocket aiming for Crakair.

Thrashing, the beast's tongue worked, thrusting Isi up instead of down.

She flailed at the wall with her stick and kicked a lower fang, breaking another tip. Yeah, that'll teach it!

Smack, smack. She thrust the stick up, impaling the upper part of the mouth, its cry bursting up from below.

The mouth opened, and like Isi was a giant hairball, she was hurtled forward, passing the teeth close enough they scraped her arm.

She landed in the sand on her butt, her body coated

with slime, and her arm stinging. Miraculously, Bucko held on, his claws creating a death grip on her shirt that would leave holes in the fabric. Leaping to her feet, she watched as Lyel flung himself off the ground and onto the back of the creature. It flailed like a giant worm, trying to toss him off, but he held true.

He lifted his spear and brought it down, impaling the creature in the neck.

It shuddered and whipped back and forth.

Lyel went flying. He tumbled through the air and landed on his feet, making sticky, sand-coated Isi envious. Racing forward, he slashed the creature beneath the chin. It bellowed and dropped back into the sand like a subway leaving the station at high speed.

A sandy whirlpool swirled before the ground went still.

Lyel nodded curtly at the bare ground. His gaze sought Isi's and in one leap, he stood in front of her. "Are you injured?"

"I don't...know?" Her arm hurt but at least it was still attached to her body. "Its teeth..." She pointed to the scrape. Blood beaded on the surface and trickled across her skin. The world went into sharp focus then blurry. Focus. Blurry. "Something's not right, Lyel."

"Isi," he groaned.

He caught her before she hit the sand.

I si woke with her arm on fire and elephants stomping through her brain. She wiggled, and Lyel's arms tightened around her.

"I'm alive," she croaked. When she opened her eyes, sunlight stabbed deeply.

"It will take more than a xarton to defeat you."

"Ahoy, matey," Bucko cried from Lyel's shoulder. If he wore an eye patch, his pirate appearance would be complete. Seeing her awake, the bird hopped along Lyel's upper back and jumped, his wings flapping. He landed on her chest and clambered up onto her shoulder. "Hello! Hello!"

"Hello to you, matey." She shifted her arm, grateful Lyel didn't need to cut it off, and ran her fingers across the bulky dressing. "Xarton. Is that what that thing was called? What was it?"

Lyel walked, his footsteps eating up the desert.

"How long was I unconscious?" she asked.

"A day. The xarton's poison invaded your body. I made the antidote and gave it to you, but it took time to work. I carried you while you recovered."

"Have you been traveling long?"

"All daela."

She lost an entire day, and nothing around them had changed.

Lyel's feet churned through the sand, taking them up a small hill and down the other side. He made it seem effortless, but it couldn't be.

"Put me down, and I'll walk," she said.

"If I carry you the entire way, I can protect you." The stark pain in his voice hit her in the chest like a blade.

"I appreciate it." She stroked his face. "You already have protected me. You found an antidote and gave it to me. You didn't abandon me to die."

"Never," he vowed.

"Let me walk. Please. I feel useless. And we should stop so you can rest."

"At nightfall."

Which hovered nearby. Gold and pink beams streaked across the sky as the sun approached the horizon.

"Please." She squirmed, and he sighed. Coming to a stop, he eased her feet to the ground and steadied her when she would've fallen.

"See?" she said. "I'm stronger than a…xarton."

"Blow me down," Bucko said.

"Don't rub it in," she said. "I know my legs are shaky, but a girl has to start somewhere."

"How did you escape?" he asked, taking her hand. His arm went around her back, and though it stung where she was hit, she needed his support. He was right; the poison had done a number on her body and it would take time for her to fully recover.

"Wait. My stick." She couldn't shake her need to keep it close by. It had served her well. "Did I lose it?"

He pulled it from the sheath on his back containing his spear and brandished it, holding it toward her like a king bestowing knighthood. "I kept it safe for you."

"Thank you." She dug into her pocket but found nothing. Silly that she hadn't thought to use her blade against the xarton. "I lost my knife."

"I also collected it for you." He stopped and untied a slender pouch strapped to his calf. "A warrior braver than a man of aqua deserves a noble sheath to hold her blade." He dropped to his knees and secured it to her leg. Looking up, he bared his fangs. "You are a mighty fighter. Stronger than a battalion of khatalm warriors."

She snorted. "I doubt that, but I'm proud of how I handled it. I'm not sure what would've happened if I hadn't fought back."

"I would have come for you."

"How?"

"Dug my way into the xarton's warren and killed it. Sliced it open to find you."

She held onto his shoulders, outlining his larger

shoulder scales with her fingertips. "Lyel. How can you suggest you have no honor after that?"

He straightened. "I had honor, but my father threw it away."

"He threw away his own honor, not yours." She tilted her head. "You came to Mara to destroy the compound, feeling that would restore your feeling of worth, but don't you know? It was there all along. Your father could hurt you. He could demean you. But he could never take away that core person inside you who makes you who you are."

He cupped her face. "Isi. Please."

"Please, what? Don't point out something you need to hear? You can't stop me. You're a good person. Your father was not. But you're not tied together. His actions have no impact on who you are." She pressed her palm against his chest. "Not inside here."

"You do not understand."

"Like I don't understand about my mother? I wish you believed in yourself as much as I believe in you."

"Isi." Bracing her shoulders, he captured her lips with his own.

She moaned and pressed into him, her arms going around his waist. Why was she fighting this when it was something she wanted almost from the moment she met him?

His naanans glided along her shoulders and cupped her neck, while others teased the sides of her breasts. She wanted to tug off her clothing and drag him down onto the ground on top of her.

He had a hard-on, and she savored the feel of his full length pressed against her. Other than a few hours hiding in the tiny rock cave, they hadn't had a moment together where they weren't on the run or injured. What would it be like to relax and savor time getting to know each other?

Lifting her off her feet, he spun her around. He bared his fangs then nuzzled her neck, his laughter tickling her skin.

A fluttering sound tugged at her attention, but she ignored it. This moment was for her and Lyel.

He lowered her to her feet but kept his arms around her. "I like you, Isi. It is not just the symbol on my hand saying this."

"I don't have a symbol, but I like you, too."

He grinned. "What shall we do with this liking?"

"I think we should—"

Something slammed into Lyel's back, thrusting him forward. He pulled her with him, shielding her body with his. They tumbled to the ground and Lyel rolled across the rough surface, taking her with him. He jumped to his feet and thrust her behind him, but he staggered.

Six flying Al'kieern hovered nearby with stun sticks and laser guns lifted.

"Take them," the leader shouted. "Fedeema would like to speak to them."

They rushed toward her and Lyel.

ELEVEN

Lyel

Lyel's back stung from the stunner, but he shrugged off the pain. He had to protect Isi.

She liked him! But he might die before he had the chance to show her how much she was starting to mean to him.

Snarling, he pulled his kalina. Isi moved around to stand beside him, brandishing her stick and knife, one in each hand.

"Let's kill them," she said.

"My thought exactly." But how?

"Split up," she said, bolting to the right. Two Al'kieern took off after her, their jeers filling the air. They might find Isi a greater challenge than they assumed.

This left four for Lyel, an easy number to defeat. As two rushed toward him, he flicked darts from his shoulder sekairs. A direct hit took two of the Al'kieern out as the poison darts killed them immediately. They tumbled to the ground and the others paused, frowning.

A quick glance at Isi told him he'd been right. She stood, swinging her stick, while the Al'kieern flew around her, looking for a way to grab her. One came too close, and she thrust forward. Her stick connected with the Al'kieern's face, and he reeled away, bellowing.

Lyel's two remaining challengers flew wide and came in from each side. His sekairs flicked, but his darts missed. One of the fliers hit him on the right, and he flung himself forward. Rolling, he came to his feet and slashed out with his kalina. The Al'kieern zipped backward. They lifted their laser pistols and fired.

Lyel dove to the side, the blasts hitting where he'd been standing.

The ground rumbled. Heille. His gaze met Isi's, and it was clear she felt the movement as well. Flying, the Al'kieern probably hadn't.

He waved for her to come closer.

When the second flier dove toward her, she spun, swinging out with her leg. Her foot connected with the Al'kieern's chest. He shrieked and tumbled backward, spinning through the air.

Lyel's jaw dropped.

Joining him, Isi grinned, her feet planted solidly in the sandy ground. "You need help with the last two?" Her smile faded fast. She hefted her stick and swung it at one of the three remaining Al'kieern darting in close. "We need to get out of here before a xarton arrives for a snack."

The ground shifted again, sand swirling to their right.

"I've got an idea," Isi said. She grabbed Lyel's hand and tugged him toward where the xarton was rising from below.

Run toward the xarton? It was suicide, but if Isi said she had a plan, he'd follow. He kept his kalina ready, however.

The Al'kieern gave chase, flying in close and trying to

grab them. They ducked and then bolted again, aiming for the swirling sand.

"When I say go," Isi called out. "Grab me and jump." She stomped her feet, and the sand shifted faster. The xarton was coming, aiming straight for them.

The Al'kieern swept over them, carrying a net, but he and Isi split, darting to the sides.

As the Al'kieern reeled the empty net in and came around for another pass, the xarton erupted from the sand, its mouth agape.

Lyel grabbed Isi and leaped, soaring over the xarton.

The net dropped and snagged on the xarton's fangs. Its jaws snapped closed, and it flopped onto its side, dragging the Al'kieerns down with it. Two let go, but the other was trapped, his hands snagged in the mesh. The creature dove into the sand.

Lyel landed on the opposite side of the xarton as it snaked into the ground. Its tail whipped out, and Isi was snagged by its forked tip. The ends wrapped around her ankle and she was swept off her feet and dragged toward the hole.

Latching onto her arms, Lyel was pulled along with her. They plunged into the sand behind the xarton and were sucked down beneath the surface.

TWELVE

Isi

As she was hauled into the ground, Lyel grabbed her wrists and held on. Bucko leaped off with a squawk and flew toward safety.

Isi and Lyel slid into the hole after the xarton together. The sun winked out as they dropped below the surface, and darkness coated the world, gritty and scratchy. Sand was shoved into Isi's mouth, and she gasped, unable to breathe.

This was it. They'd die and be eaten by the xarton.

She hadn't had a chance yet to… What did she want? Her sole goal had been to escape Earth for Crakair and find a way to eke out an existence.

She hadn't planned on Lyel and now, when it seemed the choice would be taken from her, she wanted more. So much more.

They were pulled deeper into the ground, smacking against what vaguely felt like walls, as well as each other. Through it all, Lyel held onto her, protecting her with his own body. When he could've released her and saved himself, he tightened his grip.

"Hold on," he shouted over the shifting sand and creature's growls.

The xarton emerged into a tunnel deep below the ground. Isi flopped along a hard surface, dragged behind the creature down the passage. Miraculously enough, Lyel hung on. Their gazes met. How was it possible she could see? This wasn't a manmade structure but some sort of tunnel system where the xarton must live.

"It's taking us to its nest," she shouted, her voice filled with panic. "We're gonna be eaten alive." She kicked, trying to break free of the tail but the grip tightened, choking off the blood to her foot.

Lyel released one of her hands, and her eyes widened. He wasn't letting go. She'd stake her life on it. But what was he doing?

Using her for leverage, he pulled himself toward her.

When their faces were close, he bared his fangs. "No worries."

She found herself grinning, which was silly. She was about to die; how could she find even a speck of happiness in this moment?

The xarton flicked its tail, and they were tossed against the wall. Isi's teeth clanked together, and her bones shuddered.

Lyel grimaced and latched onto her shoulders, then her waist, moving down her body. Reaching over his head, he hefted his kalina.

"No worries," she said through chattering teeth. "Love your attitude, Lyel!"

A slice of his spear, and Isi was cut free.

As they tumbled away from the xarton, the creature screamed. Its tails smacked out, aiming for them, but Lyel scooped Isi up and bolted in the opposite direction. The xarton shrieked and scrambled around to give chase.

A glance showed Isi where the light was coming from. The blob-like creatures pinned inside globes in the compound, the ones who tried to attack her, peppered the ceiling. They shifted as she and Lyel ran beneath them.

"Watch out for the blobs on the ceiling," she hissed. "They're not friendly." What if they dropped down onto them?

"Arins. They taste good."

She shuddered, remembering the beastie from the dungeon below the compound. The creatures of light flung themselves against the glass. Their long teeth and claws stood out in her mind, and she tried to shrink closer to Lyel. "You eat them?"

"Roasted, they have a nutty, sweet flavor."

Somehow, she couldn't equate nutty and sweet with the gleaming blobs. Maybe with barbeque sauce…

"When we pause for a break, I will roast one for you and serve it to you while naked."

She must be mishearing him. "You didn't say naked." Panting, she continued to race beside him.

"I do not have a true garlong. Naked is almost as good."

How could Lyel wearing a garlong be better than him striding around without clothing? She shook her head, dismissing the thought. Right now, it was run or be eaten. No time to think about Lyel naked.

But her mind kept leaping in that direction. Curiosity supposedly killed the cat. Would it burn Isi?

While the xarton roared and slithered behind them, they ran faster, down one tunnel and into another. At an intersection, they took a right, then another.

"Do you know where we're going?"

"To the surface."

"How can you tell which way will take us there?"

"I have an excellent sense of direction."

"If you're like most guys, you think you have an excellent sense of direction when, in reality, it sucks."

"What do you wish me to suck?"

Her mouth dropped.

"Suck as in stinks."

"I do not stink." He sounded affronted, but he was right. How was it possible for him to still smell good? He'd run for hours through the desert yet here he was, tossing around a woodsy sandalwood smell while she probably looked and smelled like overcooked broccoli.

"Never fear, I will suck," he added. "Soon."

Her mind, naturally, went to all the areas she'd like Lyel to place his mouth. What kind of person thought of sex at a time like this? The xarton could catch up—though they were running awfully fast—and gobble them down in one bite. She could almost feel its teeth sinking into her skin. Rocking in a corner and wailing was the normal response in a situation like this, but it was hard to be scared when she had a big, mossy-green alien protector willing to do almost anything to keep her safe. He was armed and rather savvy with his spear, if she did say so herself.

"What would you have me suck first?" he asked, and she swore she heard humor in his voice. Could he tell she wanted to rip off the tiny scrap of material he wore around his waist?

"I think you should suck whatever you please," she said. There. Let's see what he did with that!

"All of you," he said. "I will suck all of you."

"Our timing is off."

"We will hold this thought for later."

The idea of what he would do later sent tingles shooting through her bones. "Do you think we'll get a later?" she panted out.

"We will have many laters." He scooped her up in his arms, which was good because she was flagging. Though neutralized, the xarton's toxin still chugged through her veins.

While being dragged into the ground by a predatory beast, Isi had an epiphany. She wasn't intimidated by the idea of being with Lyel any longer. Sure, she was scared. It was hard to trust someone not to hurt you. But if she didn't take this chance… If she didn't give *Lyel* a chance, she'd regret it for the rest of her life.

"Do you think Bucko is all right?" she asked. "He jumped off me when the xarton grabbed my leg."

"He survived without us before we found him."

"Not very well. He was hobbling though the desert, hurt. That big, mean predator was after him. I bet he's scared and wonders where we are. I hope he hides."

"We will find him." The certainty in his voice eased her concern a tiny bit, but she wouldn't feel good until they escaped the tunnels and tracked down her friend.

"We're a family," she said. "We stick together."

His steps slowed, but he bared his fangs. With a shout of joy, he picked up his pace, running faster. "Yes, *we* are a family."

"How are we going to return to the surface?" she asked. The tunnel appeared to widen ahead, and the number of gleaming blobs on the ceiling had lessened.

"There will be an exit somewhere soon."

"You'll run until you find it." It wasn't a question. She was beginning to know Lyel well. He never gave up. Kinda like how he continued to pursue her affection. She had to admit she liked that about him.

"I will."

"We've been running a long time."

"You?" His naanans flared out and his brow ridges

scrunched together. She was tempted to kick him, because damn, he was cocky.

"Yeah, me. I've been running, too. Put me down and I'll run some more."

His brow ridges lifted. "How long and how fast can you run?"

"Long and fast enough. Didn't you see me kicking Al'kieern ass a short time ago? I'm good for it."

"I did not see kicking of the ass, but…"

When she wiggled, he released her. She slid down his body, trying not to get turned on by the friction. So much for that idea. Heat flushed through her, centering below her belly. What was it with this guy? Did he strew Isi catnip around wherever he went? Good thing she decided to stop resisting.

Yes, yes. Give in, a little voice inside her said. *You know you want him.*

"Shut up," she said.

Lyel shot a confused look her way.

"Nothing," she said. "Absolutely nothing." Waving her arm, she indicated they should keep going.

She jogged beside him and they continued down the tunnel that gradually widened. They stopped at the end where it emptied into a cavern rising multiple stories. Vines draped down the stone walls, and way up high, much higher than even the Jolly Green Giant—who was not Lyel—could reach, a tiny pinprick hole in the ceiling let in light. A few light blobs oozed along the walls, generating enough to see, and big bugs or birds flitted around near the hole. She hoped they were birds.

"This doesn't look good," she whispered, gaping at the recliner-sized eggs evenly spaced around the football field sized room. "Xartons in waiting, I assume."

"Yes."

"And the momma xarton is going to catch up to us, and she's going to be fuckin' pissed off that we're here."

"We will not be here long." He gestured to the opposite side of the room where another tunnel waited.

"How are we going to get across the room?"

"Any way we can."

"You're an awesome jumper, like Olympic quality, but I think the distance is too far even for you."

"We could…climb."

She tipped her head back. "The hole looks too small to fit through."

"For me, but not for you."

"If you think I'm going to leave you here as xarton bait, you've got another thing coming. You promised me a meal cooked while naked, followed by sucking, and I'm holding you to it."

"Isi." He tugged her into his arms and his mouth landed on hers, stealing her breath and any thought she had about the eggs, the xarton, and escape. He lifted his head too soon.

They hadn't been matched like the Earth brides going to Crakair, but did that matter? When you find someone who could mean the world to you, you grab onto them and don't let go.

Determination drove her to the lip of the big depression where the eggs had been laid. She was going to get out of here and see what came next with Lyel. "Why don't you climb the vines and work your way over to the other tunnel? Meanwhile, I'll book it across the egg patch. I didn't do well in gym class when they made us climb a rope. I got about halfway up then slid down. I was picking rope splinters out of my palms for days."

"The urdranes would sting me."

Great. They weren't birds. Giant hornets? "Avoid the urdranes." She peered up at him.

"Normally, they eat carrion, but they will also hunt and kill moving prey."

"Here we are, moving."

One of the hornets spied them and with wings whirling, dove toward them. Others joined in, creating a discordant sound that grated on Isi's nerves.

She tipped her head back and belted out a middle C worthy of an opera singer. Holding the note, she lifted her voice and added a lilting cadenza.

The hornets slowed then started flying into each other and smacking against the walls. Stunned bodies dropped around them. Some twitched, others lay silent.

Lyel gaped at Isi.

"I had no idea if that would do anything but stir them up, but hell, that was fun."

"How... I heard you sing before, but nothing like this."

"I've had a little training. A lot actually, courtesy of Grannie. I'll never be asked to perform at the Metropolitan Opera, but I sure did wow Grannie's neighbors."

"You are amazing. Someday, would you sing for me?"

That touched her, deep inside. "I'd be happy to sing for you, Lyel."

"Then let us escape this trap and get off Mara. We have so many things left to do together." He took her hand and they jumped off the edge, landing with a thump on the soft ground near an egg.

"We're going to just stroll across the room?" she whispered. "Seems anticlimactic."

"Sometimes, the best solution is the easiest."

"Lead on. We've got some courtship to do."

Marriage? That was a bit too much to contemplate

right now. And for the third component of Crakairian relationships, the fucking? Was it wrong to be excited about that component?

She went from being afraid to being eager to drag Lyel off to the bedroom. Or the ground. That would do, though not *this* ground.

They moved around the eggs, rushing for the other tunnel.

"How long until they hatch?" she asked softly. Silly to think talking in a regular tone would make them spontaneously burst from their shells, but with her luck, they might.

"I do not know, but we will not remain here long enough to find out."

Crack.

"You jinxed it."

The sound came from behind her and was echoed by a high-pitched shriek coming from the other tunnel.

Isi spun. A fissure etched down the side of an egg. And momma xarton was going to whip their butts for being around for the blessed event. After that, she'd feed them to her soon-to-be hatched young.

"Time's up," Isi hissed. "How about more of that running?"

With a nod, Lyel bolted, and Isi stayed right behind him as he wove around eggs forming cracks. Chunks of shell rained down, but she didn't pause long enough to see what the babies looked like. People said all babies were cute, but she had a feeling she wouldn't be cooing about mini xartons.

They were only halfway across the room when a roar from behind told them Momma was home and she was about to kick some alien ass.

"Faster," Isi cried. She hadn't much speed left in her.

Worn out from the running and poison, she couldn't keep up.

Beside her, the top of an eggshell popped off. It crashed to the ground in front of her and rocked.

A series of clicks was followed by a grunting shriek.

Isi's legs pumped. Sweat trickled down her spine, and her heart had to be galloping a thousand beats per minute. She wasn't stopping to count.

More shell fragments bombed them, dropping like jagged rocks. They jumped over some and darted around others but were not making progress fast enough.

The mother xarton plunged through the room, somehow avoiding hitting her babies. She saw them and was determined to pin them down for her babies' first meal.

A large hunk of shell smacked on the ground in front of them, blocking the path between two hatching eggs. Without pausing, Lyel swept Isi up in his arms and leaped, carrying them to the other side. He dropped her to her feet and, holding her hand, kept going.

Only thirty feet or so left. They were going to make it!

The adult xarton shrieked and oozed toward them, her segmented body squishing into itself before snapping forward. She was gaining and there wasn't anything they could do about it.

A shell ahead of them split wide open and a xarton—mini compared to Mamma—plopped out. It rose onto its lower body and wavered in the air.

Fangs snapping, it plunged toward Isi.

THIRTEEN

Lyel

It was clear Isi wanted to defend herself, and she'd proven she had the skills to do so. But against a xarton youngling? Only together did they stand a chance of escaping this heille-hole.

While she gritted her teeth and brandished her knife, proving yet again how fierce she was, the xarton youngling's head wove in the air. If they didn't avoid eye contact, it would hypnotize them with its gaze.

Isi mumbled something. Her fingers twitched, and her arm started to lower.

Lyel placed his hand over her eyes and spoke close to her ear. "Do not meet its gaze. It will hold onto you, and you will not wake up."

When Isi nodded, he released her. Kalina in hand, he plunged forward, and she bellowed, following with her knife raised.

A few lethal slices with his spear, and the youngling plopped on the ground in pieces.

Behind them, the mother xarton screamed. With fire in her eyes, she rushed toward them.

Sheathing his blade, Lyel grabbed Isi's hand and pulled her to the right, around an unhatched egg. A crack sliced down the center, and another youngling stuck its head out. Its attention locked on them, and it oozed out of the shell, falling onto the ground with a wet smack.

They reached the end of the room and, wrapping his arm around her waist, Lyel jumped up onto the raised area. They didn't stop, but ran for the tunnel, ducking into the darkness. If they were lucky, the mother would be too preoccupied with her surviving younglings to follow. If they were unlucky, the mother and younglings would rush into the tunnel, seeking revenge.

Overhead, arins oozed along the jagged rock ceiling. One dropped down, smacking into Lyel's shoulder. Before he could respond, Isi jumped and knocked it off. It hit the wall and slid down the side, leaving a wet streak on the surface.

"They're attacking?" she asked, her voice shaking.

"It fell." So he said. He wasn't sure. He'd never seen one behave in this manner before.

As they jogged through the tunnel, other arins released their hold on the roof and plunged downward, hitting the ground around them and smacking against their heads and shoulders. Ducked down, they continued to run, leaping over clusters of arins and beating others aside before they made impact.

"Where's my stick when I need it," Isi panted. "These things are falling like bowling ball sized hail."

"We will find a way out of here soon."

"What were you saying about eating arins?" Isi groaned as she ripped one off her head and flung it toward the wall. "I'm going to take a hard pass on that, if you don't mind."

"I will serve you something else."

"While naked," she puffed as they raced around a corner and started down another passage. "Don't forget the best part of your upcoming meal preparation."

"You wish to see me naked?" he asked, unable to keep the amazement from his voice. She responded favorably earlier when he mentioned serving her without a garlong, but he wasn't sure if she was teasing. In a few daela's span, she went from telling him there would be no benefits to their friendship, to suggesting he strip off his clothing. And to think he had yet to formally court her. He did not understand, but he would not complain. He was beginning to believe he would never understand this Earthling female, though he would be happy to spend his lifetime trying to figure her out.

"Oh, shit." Ahead of him, Isi came to a stop and her arms whirled in circles in the air. A vast pit stretched ahead of them, filling this section of the tunnel. "We've got to turn around and find another way."

Hissing groans followed by slopping smacks told Lyel the xarton younglings had caught their scent and had entered the tunnel to hunt.

"There is no going back," he said. "Only forward."

Isi gulped. "The jump is too far."

"We have to try." Taking her hand, he backed up while assessing the gap ahead. It was farther than he's ever jumped before. But what choice did they have? Staying here meant being killed and consumed. Better to fall to their deaths than wait for the xartons. He stooped down. "Climb onto my back and wrap your arms around my shoulders. Hold on."

"I'm nervous but…I trust you."

She offered what so few others had. How could he show her how much this meant to him?

With a nod and a shimmer in her eyes, Isi darted

around behind him. She scrambled up onto his back and her hands linked together beneath his chin. "Ready!"

He straightened and stepped back a few paces. After taking in a gust of air, he ran forward, his feet smacking the ground and his heart on fire. He would make it. He had to make it. He failed his mission to kill Fedeema, but in this, he could prove he had honor.

At the edge of the pit, he jumped, soaring over the dark, inky blackness. Straining forward, he hoped he—

His right foot hit the lip, but the ground gave way.

They plunged down into the darkness.

Isi yelped but hung on to him while they tumbled down the side of a steep, black cliff. Too far. They were going to fall all the way to the bottom. His heart thundered, and his matebond blood roared with rage. He had to save them —save *her*.

His hand snapped out and latched on to something jutting from the side of the cliff. They dangled while his furious breathing echoed around them.

With fear and disappointment in himself clouding his mind, Lyel looked around for handholds and places for his feet, but found nothing but a smooth, almost glossy surface and the root he snagged while falling. No, on closer inspection, it was a fang from a long-dead xarton. How it got here was a mystery.

"That was scary," Isi said in a shaky voice.

It was still scary. How was he going to get them out of this? The side of the cavern he was aiming for was too high up from where they dangled. Down could be an option, but he had a suspicion about what might wait for them if they were able to make it there.

How was he going to save his mate? He was foolish to take on this challenge. He should've grabbed her when he heard her singing and run. They could've hidden some-where until he got them off the moon.

Stupid Lyel for hoping to restore his family's honor by completing this mission single-handedly. He should've let Vork and the military handle it instead of—

"I have an idea," Isi said softly, her words breaking through his downward spiral. He swallowed back the lump of pain in his throat, but it would not move. "Can you reach that branch sticking out to our right? It looks like it's higher than this one. If we can find another, we might be able to climb. At least we're on the right side of the hole."

"Yes, that branch will do. I am going to ease you off my back."

"Tell me what I need to do." Her legs wrapped around his waist dropped down and she hung against his body.

"While we do this, I will not let you go until I am sure you will make it there," he vowed. "If you start to slip, I will catch you and keep you secure."

"I know you will, Lyel." The quiet confidence in her voice amazed him. Did she truly trust him or was she pretending?

"I will grab your hand and throw you over to the branch. Actually, I believe it is a fang, not a branch."

"I wondered. I recognized it from when I was inside the xarton's mouth. How did it end up here, sticking out of the cliff?"

He assessed the distance between him and the fang. Once he released Isi, she'd be airborne. One misstep could mean her death. "I have heard of this but never imagined seeing it. When a xarton is close to death, it throws itself into a pit such as this. Other creatures wait at the bottom to consume the carcass. I assume, over time, a few are snagged on the sides and do not reach the bottom. They fuse with the cliff face."

"So, we're literally hanging out in a burial pit."

"Yes."

"Let's get out of here A.S.A.P., then. Once you throw me to the branch, what should I do next?"

She *did* trust him, and that humbled him. They dangled inside a pit that plunged what appeared to be half a klek deep, and she didn't fear he'd make a lethal mistake.

"Once you reach the fang, I want you to try to climb up onto it. It is closer to the top than this one. From there, you will be able to reach the edge. Once you reach the top, keep going down the tunnel and you'll find an exit from the warren."

Her pause went on a few ticks. "Not me, *us*. *We'll* find an exit from the warren."

And here was where he had to be honest. "I will get you to the branch, but I do not believe I can reach for myself."

"You're an Olympic material jumper. You can do it."

Not unless he could brace himself, and there was nothing around for him to stand on. "Are you ready?"

"Hell, no. I'm not leaving you here. Don't even suggest it, Lyel." Her voice came out tight with what he assumed was anger, but a glance at her face revealed gleaming eyes. Tears. He'd read about them in the booklet about Earth women. Their eyes seeped when they were happy or sad. Lyel doubted this was from happiness.

The notion made his heart expand in his chest, making it a challenge to breathe.

She cared, and it was shredding him because finally, he found someone who might be willing to share her life with him, only to lose this chance. Just like he lost his chance at a lasting friendship with Vork. Only now, when he faced his likely death, did he fully realize his regret. If only he had reached out to Vork sooner...

"Instead of flinging me to the fang on our right," Isi said, interrupting his doom-filled musings. "Why don't we go down? I see a few more fangs and branches projecting from the surface, and they seem to continue for some distance."

"I told you, creatures wait at the bottom to consume the xarton."

"So you've heard."

"Many say this. It is not a myth."

"I'm willing to chance it. It beats me trying to get out of the warren without you while you fall to your death. Let's go down there and kick some beastie butts then find a way out from that direction."

"And if we cannot kick the…beastie butts or there is no way out?"

"Then we'll climb back up and find a different route, one that keeps you with me." Her voice broke. "Because Lyel, I want you with me, now and for as long as we have left."

"Isi. It breaks me when you say things like this."

"And it breaks me when you suggest I go on without you. We're a team, Lyel. Maybe at first, we were pseudo adversaries, but we're together, right? If you, um, still want me. I might've put you off already because I'm not exciting enough, pretty enough, or kickass enough to be worthy."

"Isi, you are so much more than worthy."

"And so are you."

He sighed, and with the exhalation, some of his self-loathing eased. "We will try to go down."

"Yay." She pressed her face against the back of his neck. "I want to kiss you, but with our positions, a hug will have to do." Her legs linked around his waist again. "Can you make it to the fang on our left? It's a few feet away and lower."

With her faith in him, he could climb the tallest, most jagged cliff in the Ikeline Mountains.

Swinging his leg out, he used the motion to propel them down and lower, catching the spike sticking out with ease. The second fang was closer, and he barely stopped before reaching out and taking them in that direction.

"This is working well," she said. She kissed the back of his neck, making his scales tingle. "Thank you for trying, for giving us a chance."

Each time he tried to sacrifice himself for her, she refused to take his offer. Some might feel this diminished him but, for whatever reason, it made him proud. Of himself and of her. She was right. They were a team. It was time for him to start acting that way. This gorgeous Earthling female was offering him a future. He would be a fool—a *dishonorable* fool—not to take the hand she held out to him.

Reaching out, he snagged another fang, then moved to the next, slowly weaving his way down the steep gleaming surface. A few of the stretches were almost more than he could handle, but with Isi's confidence in him, he was her agent of secrets. He would not betray the trust she put in him.

He swung his leg out, using the motion to carry them down and to his right. If he gauged the distance correctly, they were nearly halfway down. What waited on the bottom? He would make sure his kalina was ready before dropping the final distance.

"Almost there," Isi said, echoing his thought. "You're amazing, by the way. I'm in awe."

"You would do this yourself if I was not here with you."

"I told you about my school rope incident. There's no way I could do this by myself."

"With strength of will, one finds the way."

"We have a similar phrase on Earth, where there's a will, there's a way."

"Two cultures, two vastly different species, yet so similar. We are entwined."

"Entwined," she breathed. "I like that."

Once his honor was restored, he would claim his mate. A glorious future waited them on Crakair. But first, escape this trap then the Orcal. Once they reached the city, he could contact Vork.

He swung a leg out and reached for the next fang, but it shifted when he grasped it.

The projection loosened, coming free.

Isi gasped. Her hands tightened on his shoulders, and she buried her face in his neck as they shot down the smooth surface.

FOURTEEN

Isi

As they slid down the cliff, Isi reached out and snagged a root sticking out of the wall. She was ripped from Lyel's back but held onto the root to break their fall. He tumbled farther but grabbed onto her ankle before plunging to the bottom.

Close! She'd come very close to losing him.

"You okay?" she asked, her breathing jerky. The strain on her body was immense. He was no puny, five-footer, but a big, tall alien. She wouldn't be able to hold him for long.

"Yes. Are you o…key. Is that a word, okey?"

She released a rough laugh. "Only if you use it with dokey."

"I do not know what a dokey is. Or an okey. But I am all right. I see a fang projecting from the cliff face directly below me and will let go and drop down to it. Dokey okey?"

"Dokey okey." She swiped the tears of relief from her eyes and sniffed. What if he kept falling? Losing him would've—

He let go of her ankle, and she watched as he slid

down the wall, easily latching onto the fang. Pulling himself up onto it—something she could never do in gym class or anywhere else—he balanced on the projection, lifting his arms toward her. "Let go and join me, mate."

"Mate, huh?" Her smile made it clear she teased.

"Mate." Pure satisfaction rang in his voice. "We are going to be friends with many benefits."

Her skin shouldn't tingle. Not here in this dangerous place. But there it was. Love came at you no matter where you might be. It didn't wait for the perfect opportunity. And that's what this was, love. She'd never been a fan of insta-anything except her instapot, but how could she not fall for Lyel? When she fled Earth, she hadn't expected to meet someone special, but Lyel was everything she could ever hope for in a guy. A mate. LOL. Who would've thought she'd end up falling for an alien?

"Let's renegotiate our deal when we reach the bottom and have finished kicking unknown creature butts, dokey okey?" she said.

"Dokey okey."

"I'm letting go now." She closed her eyes and released the branch. Her body glided down the surface, into Lyel's waiting arms.

"I have you," he said gruffly against her throat. He nipped her skin, and her tingles went haywire, zipping around inside her like tiny lightning bolts.

"You do have me." Man, did he ever. Now wasn't the time for sharing her feelings, but she could take a second for a quick kiss, right?

Wrapping her arms around his shoulders and her legs around his waist, she placed her lips on his. He groaned and pulled her against him, secure, safe, and set aflame. His tongue teased across the seam of her lips, and she opened, letting him in. She clung, taking all he had to give.

When she lifted her head, he bared his fangs. "Isi." The satisfaction in his voice made her want to cling to him forever. And she would, sorta. She'd hold on as long as he wanted her. But they had to get to the bottom of the cliff, out of the sub-tunnels, and off this moon before anything else could happen.

"We need to get off this cliff, dude, because I have plans for you," she said.

One brow ridge cocked up, and his eyes sparkled. "Plans?"

She grinned. Damn, it felt good to let go, to let a moment take her wherever it pleased, even in this tenuous situation. "You'll see."

"See I will. Dude." He rolled the word across his tongue, his glorious forked tongue she also had plans for. "You used this before and I like it." He nodded. "You may call me dude whenever it pleases you."

"Glad you like it…Dude." She chuckled. "How about getting us to the ground, *Dude*?"

"Watch me."

With renewed superpower energy, Lyel dropped down to another fang, swinging forward without stopping and leaping to a root. He used branches, fangs, roots, and jutting rocks to quickly carry them downward, but stopped before dropping the last ten feet or so.

She expected to see bones littering the ground, but maybe the giant worms didn't have bones. They oozed, like the arin lights, and could be made up of…she was no biologist, but cartilage, skin, and…gook. That was scientific. Gook. Sue her. She was an accountant and avoided gook.

About the size of a small pond and circular, the room was made up of black stone. Knee high lumps of purplish things she didn't want to examine closely lay strewn about on the flat surface. The cliff rose up on all sides around them, smooth except for the handholds she and Lyel used to descend. Worst case, they could climb back up, but she hated thinking of that option, as the xartons would be waiting. The room had two exits, like a gladiator arena, which wasn't a good thought right there. Why had that idea popped into her mind?

She leaned in close to his ear. "Where are the beasties?"

"Hiding?"

"Do we dare sneak down there and find a way out? If they can leave, so can we, right? Maybe we can scoot out a convenient exit and avoid them altogether."

He nudged his head toward the thick root he clung to. "Take hold of this. I would like to go down and look around by myself, if you do not mind."

"I do mind. We're together, dude. Get used to it. Well…" She gulped, realizing how demanding her words had come out. She and Lyel weren't exactly committed yet, though he was calling her mate and insisting she was "his". "What I mean is, I want to cover your back. Remember, I'm a wannabe ninja. A khatalm fighter. Sort of. Maybe. Someday. I'll need more training but I'm badass already."

"Your ass *is* bad. We will remain together. You have proven you are capable of protecting yourself."

Heat filled her face, and she wanted to hug him to show how much him saying that meant to her. "Thank you for believing in me."

"Always."

And that warmed her up even more.

"You are perfect the way you are, but I will train you further if you wish," he said.

"You're a khatalm fighter?"

"I studied with them for many yaros."

"How many…yaros are we talking about?" And what was a yaro?

"Since I was five-yaros-old."

Oh, yaro meant year. But talk about being impressed. "You really *are* an agent of secrets."

Nodding, he showed her his fangs, but his gaze darted away. Jeez, was he shy? As far as she could tell, Crakairians —and the Al'kieern—didn't blush, which could be because they had scales instead of skin. She liked seeing a hint of shyness in him. It made him more…human wasn't the right word as he was alien, but it was the only one she had in her vocabulary. It made him relatable.

"Since you wish to come with me, get ready," he said. He released the rock and dropped the final ten feet to the ground below. Made up of what looked like big slabs of ledge, his boots made barely a sound.

She slipped off him, savoring the feel of his rock-hard body on hers. Other things were stirring, but they didn't have time for that. Damn creatures kept getting in the way of the important things in life.

Turning, she put her back to him and looked around. Her trusty stick was gone, but she had her knife, secure in its sheath. Time to pull it out.

On closer examination, the mounds appeared to be dried out lumps of…intestines? She wasn't sure and it might be best to leave it at that. Alien flies the size of her palm buzzed around the clumps, their low hum filling the air.

Above the hum, a scraping sound drifted into the room from one of the exits, echoing around them.

"I'm not feeling good about this," she mumbled, squinting toward the arched opening. It was too dark to see beyond a foot or two, but she sensed something lurked there. "Let's run in the other direction?"

He jerked his head to the archway on their right, and they raced that way. But as they got close, scraping sounds came from this opening, too. Coming to a stop, they backed away.

"Should we wait in the middle of the room where we can see what's coming before it bites us?" she whispered.

"Yes." Lyel took her hand and they hurried to the center then stood back-to-back. He lifted his sword while she tightened her grip on her knife.

Spying a fang lying on the ground, she snatched it up. "Two weapons. Look at me, closer to ninja status."

Lyel tossed a grin over his shoulder, and his eyes sparkled despite the lines of desperation on his face. "You are amazing."

"So are you, agent of secrets. We're going to fight off whatever's coming and escape. Any ideas what we'll face?"

"I have heard—"

A pack of five-foot-tall, gray and pink, alien kangaroos hopped into the "arena" from both archways.

"Aw," she said, unsure if she wanted to fight them or skip over to them and dole out pats. "They're cute. Well, except for their fangs. What is it with everything around here having fangs? And my, look at those claws. I imagine they're good at eviscerating prey."

"Why would you think of things like that now?" he asked, keeping his sword handy.

"Because they are. They're sweet and fuzzy and I bet they're cuddly."

He looked at her like she had two heads, but that would be the alien kangaroos.

One hopped closer, its gaze intent on them. The others followed, spreading out to surround them.

"Do you know anything about them?" she asked through clenched teeth.

"I have never seen or heard of them before. I only believed something waited at the bottom."

"Do you think they have weaknesses?"

"All do, do they not?"

"Not you, honey. You're my agent of secrets. You have no weaknesses."

"That…is not true, but you are kind to say so."

She and Lyel eased backward, aiming for one of the archways. The kangaroos, followed, cooing and tilting their heads.

"Maybe they haven't seen anything live before. You said those dying throw themselves off the edge. The fall must kill them."

"Does it matter? If they see us as food, they will attack."

"Unless they're waiting for us to flop on the ground."

"We will not do this."

"Good plan. How about this one?" She darted a glance his way. "Run."

They bolted for the closest exit. As they approached the archway, Isi had a dilemma. Should she encourage Lyel to enter the unknown first or take the lead in case something horrible waited inside? Silly to think she was best to face the horror, but as eager as he was to protect her, she felt the same.

"You go first," she said, stopping beside the opening. She hefted her knife and growled at the kangaroos galloping toward them, their heads lolling around like demented bobbleheads. How in the hell did they function with rubber necks? They shouldn't prove a challenge, but her skin prickled with fear. Sometimes, the unknown was worse than what was before your eyes. In this case, both ruled.

"No, you go first," Lyel said, leaping in front of her

and hefting his sword. He swung it at a kangaroo who came to close, and the creature whistled and reeled backward.

"They seem more curious than eager to bite," she said. "I wonder…"

"We are not going to try to tame one. Our family is growing, but this," he waved his sword toward the lead kangaroo, "is too big to ride on your shoulder."

"Might be fun to teach it pirate phrases, though, amirite?"

"No."

Chuckling, she stepped closer to the exit. "Maybe we should enter at the same time; it's wide enough for that. Then we can protect each other."

"I like this plan."

They plunged into the darkness.

Lyel groaned and reached for his back as if something hit him. His body hitched, stumbling forward.

Her heart on fire, she reached out to break his fall and tumbled to the ground with him.

FIFTEEN

Lyel

Lyel woke with his head lying on something soft. Where was he and why…?

Isi!

With a groan, he started to rise.

"Hold on there, dude." Isi stroked his forehead. "Lay back down and rest. You were," her voice choked, "I swore the kangaroo killed you when it rushed forward and kicked you."

"In the back." A dull ache was working its way down his spine but when he shifted, he could tell he had no lasting injury.

"You were pushed forward, and you hit your head on the wall." Her voice choked off. "You fell like a chopped tree and didn't move."

He shook his head, and his naanans fluttered. His right temple pounded, and a dull throb in his mind made him wince, but again, no lasting injury.

"Where are we?" He peered around, taking in a small, stone-walled room with a ceiling so low, he would not be able to stand upright. A dirt floor beneath him. Isi sat, leaning against the wall, with his head on her lap and her fingers woven into his naanans. They coiled around her wrist, holding tight.

"I couldn't wake you up, so I dragged you in here." She sniffed. "Other than your head injury, which bled a bit but seems to have stopped, I don't think you were badly hurt. I… I hope it's okay that I checked you out."

"You…?" What did it mean to check out?

"I ran my hands over your body to make sure you weren't wounded or hurt." She stroked his forehead, taking care not to touch the stinging place on his temple. Tears shimmered in her eyes.

He hated seeing her sad. He was going to be dokey okey. How could he reassure her?

"I have one regret," he said gravely. Perhaps he could tease a smile out of her.

"What?" Her face fell.

"My regret is that I was not awake while you…checked me out."

Her laughter snorted out, followed by more tears welling in her eyes. They trickled down her face. "I was scared, Lyel."

"I am sorry I was not here to protect you."

"That's not it. Don't you see? I was worried you wouldn't wake up and not because I needed you to protect me. You know me. I love—mostly—to kick ass. I'm able to defend myself. But I can't bear the idea of losing you." Stark fear filled her face, it was his undoing.

He sat up and tugged her into his arms, holding her while she sniffed and snuffled against his chest. "I am sorry for teasing."

"It's okay. I'm sorry I'm soaking the front of your chest."

"I will dry."

Leaning back in his embrace, she ran her fingertips over his naanans. Unruly things, they entwined around her wrist and stroked her. Continuing her assessment, she ran her fingers across his shoulders. "Is your back all right after moving?"

"I am dokey okey."

"I'm glad to hear it but you still need to rest." She helped ease him over to sit beside her, leaning his back against the wall. "We can stay here for a while. The giant kangaroos tried to get inside but I stabbed them, and they backed off. They howl every now and then, but they've been respectful."

"You amaze me."

Her hand dropped onto his thigh, and she squeezed. "You would've done the same."

"You say one of the creatures hit me?"

"It leaped up and smacked its feet against your back. You tumbled forward and were knocked unconscious."

"I am sorry."

"Not your fault! I'll be honest, I was furious, which made me act stupid."

"What did you do?"

"I grabbed your spear and charged them. They took off like, well like a xarton mama was after them, and bolted through the exit on the opposite end of the arena. I looked around and found this small alcove and dragged you down the halls to it and pulled you inside."

He peered at the stone walls surrounding. A small room, he couldn't imagine what its use might be.

"The stupid kangaroos were scared at first, but they're curious things, which is why I think one poked its head inside the small opening. I haven't heard a peep from them since I poked the first one in the snout. It roared and yanked its head out of the opening."

"You…I wish I could have seen this." He could picture her standing over him like she had when he was bound, his kalina in her hand, thrusting the steel blade at the creature.

"I've never fought with a weapon like it before, but I'm a quick study. I'll freely admit, I'm a marginal fighter. We're lucky we weren't both killed. I'm going to need training to take on bigger challenges."

"I will teach you."

"You're going to be teaching me for a long time."

"We have this time, do we not?"

"Do we?" She leaned her head against the wall and tipped it backward, staring toward the ceiling. "I'm beginning to think we'll never escape this moon. We'll be stuck in these tunnels until I'm sixty years—yaros—old and then we'll spend my next twenty yaros crossing the desert. I'll be gray haired, hobbling along beside you by then."

"I will be hobbling beside you. Always."

Her breath caught and her eyes swam with tears again. "Lyel, you say things that wreck me sometimes."

Had he offended her? He spoke from his heart. "Is this…dokey okey?"

"It is." She leaned her head against his shoulder, and he put his arm around her waist. "If I'm going to be wrecked, I want it to be with you."

"Isi. You say things that wreck *me*." So simple yet profound. Lyel had rarely felt love. His father's affection came with conditions Lyel could never meet. His mother loved him enough to speak up for him once, but she left. His sister…heille it hurt to think of her. She had truly loved him for who he was, and he missed having that in his life.

Isi was not saying she loved him, but her emotions spoke to him. She cared—*they* cared—and it was a huge step for them both.

"Rest," he said. "You watched over me and now I will do so for you."

"You hit your head and were knocked out. You could have a concussion. I think you should rest. I'll keep *you* safe."

He dropped his chin onto the top of her head. "We will keep each other safe."

"We will," she sighed.

He was proud of his mate. She defended him from the creatures she called kan-gar-oots. She found a good place to hide. How she had dragged him through halls and the tiny opening, he did not know. As much as he would like to remain here until they regained their strength, without food or water, they would be driven from this place soon.

The gnawing pain in his head crowded out all other thoughts, and he allowed himself to doze. She was right. He needed rest to regain his strength.

Isi slept and while he let himself relax, he watched over her as she had him. This was honorable behavior, correct? It counted for something.

Mumbling but not waking, she climbed up onto his lap and faced him, wrapping her arms and legs around him. As she leaned into him, he held her, praying he could protect her, not only in this small room but until he could take her to his estate on Crakair. She would not be sixty-yaros-old before they left these caverns. He would get them back to the surface and then through the wasteland. Soon, they would reach the city. A port many species visited, they could blend in, though an Earthling would stand out among the others. It was unlikely humans had visited Mara other than when Crown Prince Axil and his mate, Julia, crash landed here months ago.

Once he secured their location in the city, Lyel would

contact Vork and his former friend would send a ship for them. Except…

Lyel must finish his mission before departing Mara. The queen still lived. If he was unable to take care of this soon, he would need to remain on the planet until his assignment was finished.

Then, he could leave Mara and proudly claim Isi as his mate.

S he woke all at once and stretched. Gazing up at him, she smiled, soft and sweeter than jinjin fruit. His emotions in a tangle, all he could do was smile.

"Hey," she said in a low voice. "How's your head feeling?" Her concerned gaze scanned his temple. "No bleeding."

"I am well." The throbbing had eased off to a dull ache. He could live with it.

"And your back? How does that feel?"

"Also well." He was more focused on how wonderful it felt to hold her. That feeling surpassed all others. If he buried his face in her neck, grazed his fangs along her jawline, and captured her lips, what would she do?

She cupped her hands at the back of his neck and urged his head down to meet hers.

They kissed, and fire burst through him, centering in his groin. He wanted her. He'd want her forever.

Taking things at a slow pace was not easy, not while his matebond blood surged through him demanding he make her his, but his patience would be rewarded when she came to him willingly.

She stroked her tongue across his fang, and he groaned.

His naanans glided along her back, while others stroked her breasts. He couldn't get enough of her. He needed more. Pulling her into him, he deepened their kiss, teasing her tongue with his own.

They burst apart, and she arched her spine, inviting his naanan's touch.

"I want…" She shook her head. "I need you, Lyel."

Claiming her fully would have to wait. Their first time would not be here, in a hole beneath the Maran desert. But there was no reason he could not give her pleasure. In fact, satisfying a mate was part of ancient Crakairian courtship rituals.

He eased her back on the ground and followed, bracing himself over her, memorizing the breathless expression on her face.

"Lyel," she moaned, tugging him closer. "Kiss me. Touch me."

"Are you sure?"

"Yes."

He kissed her jaw and nibbled her earlobe. While his naanans stroked her breasts, focusing on her nipples, she writhed beneath him, moaning. He cupped his hand between the legs, and she bucked against him.

Tugging on the waistband of her odd pants, he eased them down over her hips. She kicked them off her feet and removed the odd scrap of fabric she wore beneath.

He started at her mouth, kissing her again as passion grew inside them to a fever pitch. Moving down her body, he paused and helped her remove her tunic. He could not get enough of her beautiful breasts, so different from a Crakairian female yet infinitely exciting.

He stroked them, and his naanans could not stay away. One latched onto her nipple and vibrated.

"I love it when you touch me," she gasped, her head thrashing. "You did say something about sucking…"

Sucking sounded wonderful. He took one of her nipples into his mouth and stroked his tongue across it. His reward was her moans. While a naanan tugged on her other nipple, he nibbled her sensitive flesh, drawing it out deeper, bringing more furious cries from his mate. If only he could love her body forever.

"Lyel," she sighed, stroking his naanans. His cock throbbed, and he ached to bury himself deeply inside her. Waiting would only make the moment they came together sweeter.

He kissed across her belly, teasing the small indent in the middle, then moved between her legs. A feast lay before him, and he planned to indulge. Bringing her joy would satisfy him more than anything else.

Lifting her legs onto his shoulders, he exhaled on her exposed flesh, making her shiver. She rocked her hips up to meet his fingers.

He stroked her folds then bent closer and licked up her slit.

"Ah," she cried out.

"Tell me what you like, my mate," he said, his voice hoarse. She tasted exquisite. He had to have more. He nibbled the nub at the top of her slit while she thrashed on the floor.

"Don't stop. Don't! I like it all." Her fingers sunk into his naanans, and they twined around her arms. "Whatever you want to do. Just do not stop."

"I will not. Not until you come for me, mate. And then I believe I need to ensure you come again."

"Lyel," she croaked. Sliding a finger inside her, he stroked her inner walls while wrapping the forked tip of his tongue around the bud at the top of her slit. "This is…" Her words dissolved into a moan.

While his naanans teased her nipples, he pumped his fingers inside her, gliding in and out. She bucked, rising to meet his touch. He pulled his fingers out and licked them. "You taste amazing. And you like this."

She snorted. "What gave you that idea?"

"Do you like this?" He pressed his tongue inside her, sucking and stroking her inner walls while she groaned and urged him on.

"You're killing me!"

He yanked his head back, dragging his tongue from inside her. "This is not true."

She fisted his naanans and snarled. "If you stop now, I'm going to scream."

Chuckling, he returned to her body. "Oh, mate, I do wish you to scream. Let me see what I can do to make that happen."

"It's gonna happen. Hell, this is torture."

"Sweet torture, correct, mate?" He felt her heat rising beneath his palm resting on her belly. Her body quivered, and her moans became frantic. He captured the bud at the tip of her slit with a naanan and the inner vibration motion engaged while he licked deep inside her again.

She gasped; her body wracked with quivers as he carried her over the edge. Her keen lit up the room as she shuddered around him, as she lifted her body to him. He kept sucking and licking her while she eased back down. Still, that was not enough.

"Lyel," she said in a lazy voice, her fingers stroking his quivering naanans. His cock was a solid bar beneath his scrap of clothing, and he ached to drive inside her, but he would wait.

"I wish to do this again," he said. Bringing her pleasure was all that mattered.

"I don't think I can so soon."

"Are you sure?" He teased the nub at the top of her slit, and her body jolted.

"Oh fuck. You're right. I can."

Nothing made a male happier than to satisfy his mate. Multiple times.

Rising over her, he flashed his fangs. He nibbled her breasts and worked his way up to her jawline. Her earlobe got extra attention and a bite before he claimed her lips.

Soon, he would claim all of her. He could not wait.

"That was…" She smiled. "You're awesome. I don't know how you were able to make me come so many times."

Grinning, he leaned forward to kiss her. "I *am* an agent of secrets, am I not?"

SIXTEEN

Isi

Isi lay curled up in Lyel's arms, her body tingling with satisfaction.

He still had a substantial hard-on.

Easing back onto the ground, she smiled up at him. "I think my favorite alien is uncomfortable." Actually, he looked quite pleased with himself. His Cheshire cat smile told her he enjoyed making her fall apart multiple times. She was eager for him to do it again, but it wasn't fair she had all the fun.

She'd seen her share of Al'kieern alien dicks when Fedeema's nightly boyfriends strode around the room, but she had not seen a Crakairian male until Lyel. Was his cock similar to the Al'kieern's or was it more like a human? The Al'kieerns had long, skinny cocks with big bulbs on the end.

Lyel had one and that was about all she knew.

Reaching for his pants, she undid a fastener she had never seen before but was simple to use.

"Isi," he groaned, strain filling his face. "I cannot take—"

"No, let *me* take. It's my turn to please my mate."

"Mate." His fingers wove into her hair, the soft look he gave told her all she needed to know. He felt the same way about her as she did about him. "Isi. I do not know what to say."

"Maybe sit back, or lean back in this case, and just feel? No talking needed."

His tight nod spurred her on.

She tugged the scrap of material out from around his hips like she unwrapped a package on Christmas morning —the one she looked forward to the most.

With his clothing gone, she sat back on her heels and looked him over. Long and thick, his cock fit his seven-foot-plus size. It had a bulbous tip like a golf ball, and ridges encircled the shaft. It grew thicker as it reached his large balls beneath. As she watched, it vibrated, but that couldn't be true. She leaned in closer, watching it. Hell yeah, it did vibrate. Did it do that while it was inside?

His lips twitched as he watched her watching him. "Should I be worried?"

"Only if you don't know how to use it." Bold of her, but accountants were into more than numbers.

"I do, mate. I promise you this."

"All talk. You didn't use it yet."

"I wish to wait."

She placed a hand on her hip. "That's a new one, coming from a guy."

He stroked her face, and she leaned into his touch. "I wish for," his gaze took in the tiny room, "more. I wish for our first time to be perfect."

"I'm not sure the location makes a difference. Some people do it the first time in the back of a car."

"I do not know of this car, but when we will *do it*, it will be special."

"So we wait? For how long?"

"Until the time is right."

"I'm not pushing this." Her hand flapped toward his rigid cock. "I'm not pushing you. But if you don't want me to touch, lick, and suck on your cock, tell me now."

He groaned. "Lick… Suck… I have not experienced this."

"For a guy who just drove me out of my mind at least three times with his mouth, I'm a bit surprised."

He shrugged. "I have not wished to do this with anyone else."

"Wait." Her jaw dropped. "Are you saying you're a virgin?"

"What is this virgin?"

"It's a name for someone who hasn't had sex."

"Then yes, I am this virgin. A virgin of secrets to go with my other name. Perhaps I need to work in dude, as I like that as well."

"You…" He undid her, and she loved it. "Should I tell you I'll be gentle?"

He flashed his fangs. "Please do not."

"For you, I'm more than willing to accommodate." She leaned in close and nipped his neck. While she might not have fangs, she could bite every now and then, too. "You tell me if something doesn't work for you, K? It's been a while since I was a virgin."

"You can touch or…lick all you want."

His voice, low and deep, shot zings through her body. He'd given her three orgasms already. How could she want more?

"Oh, I want," she said, her voice so low, she barely recognized it. "I want more."

Leaving his scaled, delectable neck, she worked her way downward. "You have the most amazing chest, and this case you're wearing on your abs drives me out of my mind."

His deep chuckle rang out. "What would you do with my case of abs?"

"Later. For now, I have a single focus."

"What might that be, mate?"

"This." She stroked her finger down his cock, and it twitched. It released a steady vibration that almost made her come, and a slippery liquid coated the tip. This dude was lethal if he could turn her on with only visual stimuli. But she had a taste of what he could give her. It was only natural to want the full package.

"Isi," he growled in warning. "Do not tease."

She cocked her head. "Is it a tease when I fully intend to deliver?"

His naanans flared out before settling on her shoulders. "How…?"

"Watch me." Scooting down, she took his glorious cock in both hands and stroked it.

"Isi…"

No warning there. Pure lust filled his voice, and it drove her on.

She bent forward and licked the underside. He groaned and shifted his hips, impatient. She wanted to make this—his first time! —as perfect as possible. He was right, though. They should wait to have full sex until they weren't scared about being eaten or dying. Her snort vibrated through his cock. He huffed, but the sound she made wasn't intended as a turn-on. Her rueful laugh had slipped through.

Time to focus on giving him as much pleasure as possi-ble. Who knows what tomorrow or even the next twenty minutes could bring? He deserved the best and while she wasn't sure she was it; she'd show him what he meant to her and hope it was enough.

She took the head of his cock into her mouth and sucked. Damn, he tasted good. Like everything perfect and male. A bit salty with a hint of sweetness. Cinnamon? Maybe. Or some other spice. It hardly mattered. Taking as much of him inside her mouth was her goal, not evaluating his flavor.

He groaned and tipped his head back against the wall, pumped up, mimicking the movements she ached to feel between her legs.

She couldn't get enough of him, but he was big and wide. Swirling her tongue along him, she held him at the base and pressed her lips and tongue along his length.

His wonderful, huge cock vibrated, showing her his pleasure.

Sucking the end into her mouth again, she moved fast, tugging and pulling.

He pitched his hips up, and his eyes rolled back in his head. "Isi…" he hissed. "I…"

"Just feel," she said, coming up for a breath. She dove back in, taking as much of him as she could, determined to show him how awesome he was.

He pumped in a frenzy. His cock lengthened, vibrated faster, and then he stilled. His gaze met hers, and he cupped her head with his big palms while his body shuddered.

Groaning, he moved faster, driving himself into her mouth. She took him in, her tongue sweeping his length.

When he fell apart, she caught him.

SEVENTEEN

Lyel

L yel had died and drifted up into the clouds.

"Isi."

"Was that okay? You liked it?" She smiled and licked her lips.

His cock, satisfied, twitched again eager for more. "It was amazing." He had never imagined anything like this.

If only he could lay her on a soft bed and love her for daelas.

But they had to leave.

Rising to his knees, he wrapped the material around his hips and secured it. He helped Isi up and kissed her long and deep, trying to show her how special this moment was for him.

They burst apart, grinning at each other.

"There's more where that came from," she said.

"Soon, mate."

"I think the term mate is growing on me."

He did not know what a word growing on her meant, but the happiness shining in her eyes made his heart surge. "Do you prefer mate over dude?"

She leaned against him, looking up at him. "Either works but mate… It feels special."

His arms tightened around her. "You are special."

"So are you." Her gaze darted to the opening. "Let me make sure the coast is clear."

More unusual Earth words but he vaguely understood.

Crawling to the opening, she carefully poked her head out. "Nothing out here. I think we should make a run for it."

They left the tiny sanctuary and he glanced around. More tunnels, but he swore the one on his left sloped upward.

He held out his hand, and she took it. They moved quickly through the tunnels. There had to be a way out. The creatures would not survive solely on the inconsistent rate of dying xartons.

Shuffles and thumps behind them told him the pack followed. Would they attack? He kept his kalina ready. Isi held her knife and kept shooting concerned looks over her shoulder.

"How much farther, do you think?" she panted.

He hated that she's been on the run almost exclusively since the compound exploded. If only he could find a secure place where she could rest and feel safe. Maybe once they reached the surface, though he was not holding out hope for that. They still had a considerable distance to cross before they reached the fence on the opposite side of the wasteland.

Coming to an intersection of tunnels, they paused.

"Which way?" Isi asked. She raked her unruly hair back and swiped her flushed face. "Left, right, or forward?"

"It continues to slope upward if we go forward."

"For now. We don't know where any of them go." She

frowned. "I have an idea." Using his kalina, she sliced a strip of material off the bottom of her tunic. She entered the chamber he suggested and jumped up, snagging the tiny piece of shirt on a root jutting from the surface. "There," she said, returning to his side. "This way, we'll know we took this channel already."

"Very wise."

She tapped her temple and grinned, though her smile showed strain. "Accountant brain right here. It's not just about the numbers." Looking past him, her eyes widened. "Oh, shit. Time to run."

He didn't need to turn to know the creatures had caught up. Grabbing Isi's hand, he bolted. They rushed up the tunnel, and he swore he smelled fresh air. But it soon sloped downward, and Isi's fear was proven true.

They rounded a corner and found themselves at the intersection again. Without a word, Isi pulled another scrap of fabric from her pocket and tagged a second passage. They ran downhill, and he worried this would be a wrong turn as well.

Grunts and huffs reached him from behind. Too close.

Isi kept going, her face pink, and her breathing uneven. "We're gonna make it. You can do it!"

"As can you."

They rounded a corner and a steep, rising hill waited for them.

"Love hills," she panted out. "But I hope this one leads to the surface." She started up, her pace slowing. By the time they reached the top, she'd straggled to a fast walk. "I can do it but damn, let's avoid hills from now on, okay?"

Ahead lay a section of the tunnel with no light. Had the arins been eaten? Lyel's assumption was the glowing plant made up the majority of the kan-gar-oot's diet.

"Creepy," Isi huffed, jogging forward.

The kan-gar-oots crested the top of the hill behind them, their numbers grown. At least thirty gave chase. If they didn't find a way out of here soon, they'd be fodder.

He let Isi pull ahead and hefted his kalina. If she slowed or the kan-gar-oots caught up, he would stop and do battle. He should be able to kill five or more before he was overrun. That would buy Isi time to keep going.

"No," Isi cried from ahead.

He spun back to face her and stifled his groan. Rushing forward, he stopped and gazed up the smooth wall surface.

"Dead end," she said. "We've got to turn around and go back to the third option." Pivoting, she released a soft cry. "Too late. We're trapped. But…" Staring upward, she scowled. "How energized do you feel, agent of secrets?"

"Very energized." What she had done for him back in the small room… The wonder of her mouth and the satisfaction she gave him. He would never forget. He wanted to be with her again, which meant he needed to tap his agent of secrets power. "Climb onto my back."

She grinned. "You're gonna do it, aren't you? Damn, you're amazing." She pointed. "There's light up there, at the end of the passage." Scrambling around behind him, she jumped and latched onto his shoulders. "Ready. Do it, dude."

Dude. The nickname lit him on fire. He could do this, for them both.

He crouched and sprang upward, soaring into the narrow tunnel. Almost there. It was going to happen!

His fingers scrambled on the stone edge, but he lost his grip.

They started falling.

"Roots!" Isi cried. "Grab on."

He caught one as they slid down the cliff and brought their descent to a halt.

"Yes," she hissed. "You are awesome, and I'm crazy about you."

He hoped that was a positive thing but would wait to ask later.

"Here we are again," she said, breathless. "Just you and me, hanging out together, taking a moment to chat. Trying not to be eaten by ginormous kangaroos gathering beneath us. If we drop, well, we'll hit them like a bomb or a bowling ball impacting pins. Strike!" A thread of anxiety wove into her high-pitched giggle. "I'm okay. Really. Or dokey okey. I love the way you twisted that, by the way. Thought I should say it before… Not going there."

"We are getting out of here, Isi," he said. If he had a free hand, he would place his fist to his chest, but he would not let go of her or the root.

"I don't see how we're getting out of this one, Lyel. There are no roots or fangs or rocks above us we—well, you—can grab onto."

"Watch me." He released the root and dropped down onto a fang he spied while they rose toward the top. Crouching, he sprang upward again, landing securely on a flat surface above the shoot.

"Whoa," Isi said, sliding down his body to the ground. "You…" Barreling around to his front, she leaped into his arms and clung. "You did it. You did it," she said into his neck, over and over. "You're so much better than Aquaman."

"You are amazing." One of his arms went around her, holding her tight. "You have been braver than anyone I know."

"You've guided us and kept us safe." Leaning back in his embrace, she gave him a watery grin. "And you give great orgasms."

"I need to give you more."

"You do."

She turned and backed into his arms. "Do I see light ahead?"

"Could be arins."

"Or a way out. I think we should look into it, don't you?"

He took the hand she offered, and they strode through the tunnel. Reaching the end, they could go left or right, but light beckoned on the right.

Isi squeezed his hand. "We're going to get out of here soon. I feel it in my bones."

"I do, too."

"We'll be in the desert again."

"We will."

She lifted her chin. "And we'll be closer to the end of the Orcal."

"I hope so." Underground, it was hard to tell.

They reached the end of the passage and found another stretching above them, narrow but with protrusions they could hold onto.

"Jump or climb?" he asked. "I think I can reach the top." Where the light shone brightly. Were they finally at the end of this?

"Climbing is a bigger challenge, I assume."

"On my back, mate, and I will take us there."

She clambered onto him and pressed her face into his neck. "Why do you still smell good? I know I reek. Yet, here you are, smelling like fresh-cut grass and cinnamon, and everything naughty."

"This is natural for me." He bared his fangs, overwhelmed with happiness. Their situation was dire, but somehow, they'd found each other while taking on each part of the challenge. Nothing could tear them apart.

"Go-go! I hear kangaroos scrambling up the wall."

Would they follow all the way to the surface, or did they know something he and Isi had yet to discover? Perhaps this was another end of the dead, as Isi called the tunnel below.

With a jump, he sprang upward, driving them up through the chute. He propelled them forward once they cleared the tunnel and landed easily on a sand-strewn platform.

"No more going up," Isi said, tipping her head to the side to look around his shoulder. "Straight ahead it is. At least there's natural light in that direction."

He strode forward with her still on his back, his strides eating up the sandy distance to the end of a wider tunnel opening into a large room filled with xarton eggs.

"Mama's gone shopping," Isi whispered. "Why don't we creep around the slumbering babies and escape out the other side before she's standing in the doorway, her claws filled with groceries?" She pointed to a wide archway on the opposite side of the room. "I'll climb off you."

"Stay." After making sure she held on, he leaped forward, landing partway through the room. Not stopping, he continued with another jump, taking them deeper. Around them, eggs rocked, but none hatched, and no mother xarton appeared to issue a challenge.

He raced around a row of eggs, aiming for the archway only to see a smaller opening on the right. It was too late to stop and take another route. As he passed the opening, the enraged cry of a xarton echoed in the big room.

"Forget grocery shopping. Mama's awake and she hasn't had her coffee," Isi said.

He did not know what coffee was, but he got the gist of what she said: Run!

He bolted for the archway and leaped up onto the flat surface in front of it. Not stopping to see if the mother xarton gave chase—she most likely did—he raced through the opening, finding yet another tunnel. Would this ever end?

"She's behind us. Go!" Isi pumped her hips against him as if she rode a wildarn across the plains of dunare.

Picking up speed, Lyel took them up an incline and down the other side. Another hill was followed by a third, but with each, they climbed higher.

Meanwhile, the mother xarton chased them, her body rolling through the passage.

"She's gaining on us," Isi said. "Any rooms nearby where we can hide?"

Lyel had one goal, to get them out of the tunnels and back to the surface. He pushed for speed, his legs pumping, his blood roaring through him like flames licking across dry tinder.

At the end of the channel, they came to an opening. Sunlight poured in.

"You're gonna do it, agent of secrets?" Isi kissed the back of his neck. "Have I told you how amazing you are yet?"

"You have. Recently."

"But not within the last second. You're freakin' amazing. You got us through it. You—"

He stepped out into the light and came to a shuddering halt.

Fedeema floated above the desert floor with a full battalion of Al'kieern soldiers flanking her.

Each pointed laser pistols at Lyel and Isi.

Isi

Isi slid off Lyel's back. "Damn, the wicked witch is back in business. Any ideas for getting out of this alive?"

"Step to the side of the opening," he said softly, inching her over to the rock wall to their right. "We will wait here. Do not move."

"I don't think I can," she said, her teeth chattering despite the oppressive heat rolling off the wasteland. "I swear, I can feel a collar tightening around my throat already. Although this time, I'll probably avoid the collar since I'll be dead."

"Not happening," he said.

Fedeema drifted closer. "Come forward into the light, Songbird. I wish to see you before I kill you."

Isi said nothing, but what could she say? Let us go wasn't an option, and she doubted pleading to finish the challenge would result in Fedeema agreeing and waving for them to continue.

The ground rumbled, softly at first but with growing volume.

Awesome. Were more xartons arriving for the feast?

"The hills are alive," Isi sang, her voice shaky but loud enough to overwhelm the jeers of the Al'kieen troops.

Fedeema paused, staring at Isi. "I do not wish to hear you sing, not even a song you have not gifted us with before."

Isi had been saving the Sound of Music for a special occasion. Why not now?

She lifted her voice. "With the sound of…"

As Fedeema and her entourage floated closer, compelled by Isi's voice as they were whenever she sang, the mother xarton burst through the archway. She leaped toward the queen but Fedeema reeled back, her wings flapping. The xarton's fangs snapped closed and she dropped back to the wasteland. Her shriek of frustration blasted through the air.

A pack of giant kangaroos galloped from the opening, grunting and squealing, delighted by the feast on display.

Isi and Lyel inched farther to the side and found a small, recessed area on the hill's surface. In the shadows, they could hide.

Lasers blasted from the Al'kieern, taking down the front line of kangaroos, but others surged from the tunnel. A never ending stream of hopping furry bunnies with long tails, fangs, and beady eyes. They leaped and snatched Al'kieern from the air. Tumbling to the ground, they stomped on the blue-skinned aliens and proceeded to rip them apart, swallowing great gulps of flesh, not caring if their victims were dead or alive.

Fedeema rose above them, shrieking in fury. She glared toward where Isi and Lyel hid and with a few straggling Al'kieern beside her, fled, leaving the rest of her crew to be eaten by the kangaroos and mama xarton.

"I assume we'll remain here until they're…done eating," she whispered, having no interest in drawing attention.

"Yes." Lyel sank to the ground and stretched out his legs. He patted his lap, and she dropped down onto it, facing him.

"We leave at sunset, I assume?" she said with a shudder. She swallowed deeply more than once. "Too hot to travel during the day?"

"You may not have noticed while we were below ground, but we are closer to the fence. I anticipate most of a nights' walking to reach the end, but I could be wrong."

If they could avoid xartons and whatever Fedeema planned next, they might stand a chance. "She'll be after us once she rallies."

"We can handle her."

Isi snorted. "So you say."

"So we will do."

"And then what?" she asked. "You said the fence is tall. Can we climb over it or will you jump?"

"The top is electrified."

"We can't risk jumping then."

"From what I hear, it is too high for even me. We will find another way."

"You say that so casually."

His arms tightened around her. "Do not fear. All is not lost yet."

"I love how you remain confident, no matter what happens."

"I have a mate to protect. Someone I am growing to care for very much."

Her heart pinched, and she strained toward him. "Lyel. You're killing me here."

"That is not my wish, but it is a sweet death, is it not?"

She buried her face in his neck. "Very."

In a surprisingly short time, the kangaroos and xarton finished the Al'kieern. The xarton melted into the sand, and the kangaroos hopped back into the cave.

Silence ruled, punctuated only with a rare bird cry as carrion eaters moved in to pick over the bones.

She and Lyel got off the ground and looked for a way down off the ledge.

Lyel plunged down onto the sand, and held out his arms. "I have you. Jump."

She did without thought. Trust had grown between them. She had his back and he had hers.

Holding hands, they started walking.

While she didn't want to draw the attention of a xarton, she did want to find Bucko. "Hey buddy?" she whispered, hoping he'd hear. "Ahoy, matey?" She turned to Lyel. "I'm worried about him. Maybe we should go back and find him? I hate to think he's somewhere injured, hoping I'll—"

Twirp!

She spun around to find Bucko half-flying, half-scurrying across the sand toward them.

"Buddy!" she cried, racing toward him. Tears stung behind her eyes, and she let them fall. They'd been through one hardship after another. It was wonderful to find something to smile about if only for a few moments.

Scooping him up, she danced around in the sand while he stroked his face against hers.

"Watch the fangs, little guy," she said with a snort as they scraped her sensitive skin. She lifted him up onto her shoulder, and he settled down on his fluffy bird butt.

Tipping his head back, he twirped. "Ahoy! Batten down the hatches!"

She frowned. "I didn't teach you that." Tipping her head to the side, she studied his birdy face, but he only bared his fangs and twirped again. With a shake of her head, she caught up to Lyel, who waited with a grin on his face. "Did you teach him to say that?"

His ridge brows lifted. "Me? How would I learn Earth pirate phrases on my own?"

This was weird.

They started walking. She knew they'd soon locate a place to settle until the sun set. Hopefully in the shade, though very little existed.

"Pirates are everywhere," she said.

"They are. The Al'kieern are our quadrant's pirates. Mara is a pirate planet, and we will need to take care once we reach the city."

"If we reach the city." She peered over her shoulder, but the sky remained clear. Chills tracked down her spine. "I'm surprised the queen isn't after us already."

"She will be."

"Again, I hate how confident you are about some things, but only because this means we'll have to face her again."

"I plan to kill her," he grated out.

"Take a number. Can I call dibs?"

"You wish to kill her yourself?"

"Don't sound too amazed." Her steps slowed. "She… hurt me. You know that." While her back only ached with vigorous activity, the sting inside would take a long time to go away.

His arm went around her waist, below where she'd been hit. "I do understand the need to show someone you are not powerless."

"Your father."

He nodded.

"I think we're both carrying our past around with us on our shoulders. It weighs us down."

"It does."

"How can we be free?"

"I came to believe that I must prove I was not my father's actions."

"And now?"

"Hmm…" He squinted forward to where the desert shimmered. If she believed her eyes, something moved ahead of them, but that was mirage for you. They were deceptive beasts. "I do not know how I feel now. After my father forced the vengeance and I fought on his behalf, as was the correct thing to do for my family, I thought my honor was gone forever. I volunteered for this mission."

This explained why he was so determined to carry it through.

"I believed I would die but completing my quest would restore my family honor."

She leaned into his side as they walked. "I can see where it would be easy to think that. But you know honor lies with the person. You're not responsible for your father's actions. He was a big boy; he knew what he was doing."

"He did, I agree. But family…"

"They can be complicated. I get it. Remember my mom?"

"Who made it difficult for you to trust."

"Yeah." Her voice hollowed out. "I'm working on that."

"As am I."

"Back to killing Fedeema. She left. Maybe she doesn't intend to come after us. We trounced her—with our creature friends' help—enough times to teach her a lesson."

"Hello!" Bucko cried. "Jack! Jack! Hoist the mizzen."

She soothed the bird, wishing he'd be quiet. They didn't need to draw the attention of anything lurking nearby.

"Completely destroying the operation is a worthy goal," she said. "They kidnapped me. I want it shut down. But perhaps the best way to do it is by taking the battle to her instead of waiting for her to give chase. That puts us on the defensive."

He cocked his head. "You are right. Do you have ideas?"

She was grateful he didn't go all alpha and suggest he would handle this while she, the little woman, hid in the background. From the moment she met him, she could see he respected her and her abilities. It made her like him even more.

"We could put me out as bait," she said.

He growled. "We will not."

"She wants me."

"She wants to kill you. There is no guarantee she would not simply fire her lasers at you."

"You're right."

Lyel led her over to a juliter tree, where he dug for water. Once sated, they walked again. She swore she could almost see the fence stretching across the desert far ahead of them, but she must be imagining it.

"We don't have much to work with," Isi said.

"I believe she will wait at the fence and challenge us there."

"Then let's fool her and go back the way we came."

He glanced over his shoulder. "Your idea has merit."

"We need to do something unexpected. We're walking toward the fence that's supposed to be our only way out. We need to turn this around and do something else."

"Going back is not a likely option."

"Maybe some of their ships survived the blast. We could steal one and escape the moon."

"You are suggesting we not kill Fedeema."

"We keep coming back here, but does revenge serve either of us? Yes, we want to eliminate the kidnapping operation, but maybe we should get to Crakair and talk to someone who can help us do that. Many minds thinking up solutions instead of one."

"It was my mission."

"And you've done a wonderful job. You killed most of them and blew up their compound."

"Fedeema was the true target."

She sighed as they stomped to the top of a hill and paused to survey the desert around them. Nothing but sand, sand, and more sand. If there was a fence waiting, she couldn't see it now.

"So you're saying we have to kill her, no matter what. Why can't we let this go until we reach Crakair, regroup, and discuss options?"

"She is sending a fleet to Earth." The dread in his voice made her mouth go dry.

That didn't sound good. "I assume not on a *we come in peace* mission."

"For the Al'kieern, it has always been about profit."

"They don't want to negotiate for brides." Why hadn't she seen this? "They're going to invade and take people, aren't they?"

"There will be no negotiations."

"This is horrible."

"Which is why I must stop her."

"Blimey, throw them in the brig," Bucko cried.

Good thought, but... "Are you sure you didn't teach Bucko new phrases when I wasn't looking?" she asked Lyel.

"When have you not been looking?"

Never. She watched him all the time.

Isi started down the hill and then across a flat, open area, with Lyel beside her. The sun hovered on the horizon, and she assumed they'd keep walking into the night, as they hadn't located a place to escape the rays. "You're right. I do look."

He grinned. "As do I but it is the nature of the mating."

"Mating. What convinces you we're destined to be mates?"

"This." He showed her his palm.

"I saw that back at the compound." She flipped her hand over, showing its blank surface. "Only guys get the mate symbol thing?"

"Usually, it is both."

"Maybe I'm not your mate. He or she could be someone else."

He huffed. "It is not Fedeema."

"Maybe you're bi and it's one of the guys."

"Guys… This could be true, but I do not believe it in my heart." His fist pressed against his chest. "In here, I know you are my destined mate."

"Does anyone have a destined mate? I mean, you meet someone, and you like them. Or you don't but he slowly grows on you."

"Like a plant."

She chuckled. "Sorta." Staring forward, she tried to see the end, but it didn't appear as if they'd made any progress despite hours of walking. "On Earth, we don't have mates and we don't show a sign that someone is the one we're meant to love."

"How do you know when you have found that person?"

He sounded astonished. What would it be like to *know*?

"Maybe we decide inside here." She tapped her chest. "But lots of couples don't make it. They break up, sometimes for valid reasons but other times because they just…I don't know. Fall out of love, I guess."

"This does happen on Crakair."

"Where someone with one of those symbols breaks up with their mate?"

"Never that. Somehow, fate knows. But when one carries the symbol and the other doesn't, it can mean they are not fated mates."

She didn't like where this was headed. Now that she was committed, she worried she wasn't his "true" mate, that they'd choose to part. It hurt to think that. "It sounds like you have something like divorce too. That's what we call it on Earth when a couple breaks up permanently. Their marriage legally ends."

"This will not happen with us."

She showed him her hand again. "No symbol." Why did that sting? It shouldn't. They weren't fated. She was silly to believe in something like that. It was time to decide in her heart if Lyel was the one. If he wasn't, she needed to end this before they took things too far.

"I trust in the bond, Isi. You must as well. Life would not share you with me only to snatch you away."

She grimaced. "It happens."

Pausing, he turned to face her, taking her hands and squeezing. On her shoulder, Bucko snored. Lucky him, being able to sleep while they walked. "You do not trust easy, but can you give this to me?"

Could she? She wanted to. Since she was little, she wanted to believe a forever home waited for her. Could it be with Lyel?

Now or never, Isi.

No, he was not asking her to choose; he was asking her to give him her trust.

For the first time in forever, that was easy.

She nodded, a shy smile blooming on her face. "I trust you, Lyel."

NINETEEN

Lyel

H is heart soared at her words. He would not abuse her trust, as he knew how difficult it was for her to give it.

Leaning forward, he kissed her. A promise that he would not betray that trust.

Perhaps he did have honor after all.

They walked through the night and when dawn crested the horizon, they approached a hill and climbed to the top. Ahead stood the fence. Isi was right, though. They could not do what Fedeema expected.

"We will surprise her," he said.

"How?"

He stared toward the long metal structure spanning the end of the desert. Beyond, rolling hills speckled with deep blue grass led to the city. There, they could find sanctuary and a shuttle off the planet. Freedom was close, but it could be snatched away from them any minar.

She cleared her throat to clear the dust. "Two options as far as I can tell. We could say she'll expect us to try a different route, rather than straight across. Thus, she'll have traps waiting everywhere else. Or she'll decide we assume that, and we'll instead run straight forward, so she'll lay traps there."

"Or there are traps in all the possible routes."

"Which is likely the reality." She huffed, sending hair shooting up off her face. "Then let's bull in a china closet our way forward. We'll take on whatever might be waiting for us and reach the fence. Then what? You said the top is electrified. How will we get through? Is there a gate or weak area in the fence? Can we break or cut it?"

"I do not know," he said. "We will find out when we get there."

"Our odds are not looking good."

His sigh showed he agreed. While frustration poured through him, he studied the terrain between here and the fence, looking for indications someone had created traps, but the wind smoothed the surface. If something lurked, waiting to spring on them, he couldn't see it.

"Hello!" Bucko cried.

Isi jumped and gave Lyel a sheepish grin. "I've created a monster." She stroked the bird's feathers. "But he's cute. He can do whatever he pleases," she said in a sing-song voice.

"Hello!" echoed behind them.

Lyel spun, lifting his kalina, but he saw no movement and no one coming at them. With a huff, he lowered his weapon, but he was slower to turn back to the fence. Something had echoed Bucko. He would remain on high alert, as he'd been for much of this journey.

"I'll keep my knife handy," Isi said.

They started down the hill, their feet sliding on the sand, dragging them down quicker than they might wish to traverse the distance. When they reached the bottom, they walked cautiously toward the fence, taking care where they placed their feet.

Bucko peered around but didn't seem concerned. A good sign. Animals often sensed danger and sounded the alarm.

"Oh, shit," Isi hissed, coming to an abrupt stop.

"What?" Lyel also paused, his weapon ready, but he didn't see anything of concern. His sekairs lifted, prepared to shoot poison at the threat.

"Something shifted under my foot." She peered down, unmoving.

"The sand?"

"It felt different. Harder, but not stone."

Lyel's heart thumped once then raced like a wildarn being chased by a javeess.

"Climb onto my back," he said softly. There was still no one around as far as he could see, but that meant nothing. "I will run."

"I don't dare move my feet." Her voice shook, but her posture remained stoic.

He reached out and grabbed her, hefting her up onto his back in one motion.

A bang, and metal bars thrust up from the ground, creating a fence around them. Another clang, and a top snapped into place, securing them in a cage. The ground shifted, lifting from the sand, showing a base attached to the rest.

"I'm sorry," Isi said, her voice breaking. "I caused this to happen."

"One of us would have. I am sure this area is filled with hidden cages."

She slid off his back and strode to the edge. Gripping the bars, she tried to shake them, but they didn't move.

With gritted teeth, she strained, trying to pull them apart. He joined her and added his strength, but they didn't shift.

Dropping to his knees, he ran his hands around on the bottom, looking for a way out. There had to be one, and he'd find it. Sweat coiled down his spine, and he ached to scoop up Isi and run as far and fast as he could, but they were trapped.

Isi kicked the bars, over and over, until he stilled her by tugging her into his arms.

She wept silently into his chest while he rubbed her low back.

"It is dokey okey," he said, hoping his twist of her phrase would bring on a hint of a smile, but how could it? She had every right to be upset.

He needed to get them out of this before—

A fluttering sound sent him spinning. Three winged Al'kieern approached. As they drew near, they cackled.

"Caught like a moosa in a trap. How do you like your new room, *Songbird?*" a male cried.

"Sing for us, Songbird," another shouted.

Isi stiffened and remained silent.

"Ahoy," Bucko cried. "Ahoy! Matey, ahoy!"

"Ahoy!" someone cried, and Lyel swore it was not one of the Al'kieern.

Odd, but nothing he could investigate now.

"The queen suggests we leave you here to bake in the sun," an Al'kieern said. "I think poking you sounds better." He flew in fast and threw a rock at the cage. It deflected off a bar but the next he chucked passed between.

Bucko cheeped shrilly.

Lyel and Isi ducked, and the rock sailed over them, hitting a bar behind them with a bang. Another flew into the cage, and Lyel knocked it to the side with his kalina.

"This is stupid," Isi said. She stormed to the edge of

the cage. "You really intend to fly around and throw rocks at us?" When a rock flew into the cage, she snatched it out of the air. Quicker than he could blink, she hurled it back at the Al'kieern. It hit him square in the chest and he reeled backward, spinning end over end before correcting.

Growling and rubbing his chest, he flew in close. "I will kill you for that."

"Old news, buddy," she said dryly as she handed Bucko to Lyel. "Try something else." Tumbling forward, she rolled and swept up another rock and hurled it. This one hit the Al'kieern in the head.

He dropped to the sand like the rock and lay unmoving.

"One down, two to go," she said to Lyel, who watched her with his mouth ajar. She casually took Bucko back and placed him on her shoulder.

"Walk the plank!" Bucko chirped. "Walk the plank!"

"I didn't teach him that either, but I'm runnin' with it," Isi said.

"After what I saw, *you* need to train me in fighting skills, not the other way around."

She blew pretend smoke of her finger pistol. "Watch me. I've got a few more tricks up my sleeve."

The two remaining Al'kieern flew up high and conferred. Snapping and snarling, they shot down to their unconscious friend, grabbed him by the arms, and darted toward the fence.

"Don't leave so soon," Isi called after them. "The party was just getting started!"

The Al'kieern continued up and over the fence and flew toward the city.

Isi's arms dropped to her sides. "This feels anticlimactic. Like, something more should be happening, shouldn't it?"

"You must not—"
The floor gave way beneath them.

TWENTY

Isi

When the metal floor shifted underfoot, Isi latched onto a bar and Lyel at the same time.

Instead of being swept downward with the rocks and sand collected on the metal, they dangled with only Isi holding on.

"Been here, done this already," she said. "We're not going down again."

Bucko flew off Isi's shoulder and clung to a bar. He peered down at them as if to say, *why are you foolin' around?*

Lyel grabbed a bar, and she released her knuckle-white grip in his arm. That had been close. While she showed bravado on the outside, inside, she quaked. Her hands wouldn't stop shaking and spent adrenaline made her knees ache.

He pulled himself up beside her and hung as if he stood leaning against the bar at the local club, grinning while he flirted with a girl he just met.

Oh, true. They hadn't known each other long. But in the time they'd been together, they saved each other's lives, had hot not-quite-sex, and learned to trust each other. Who needed a lifetime for that?

"So, since I kept us from being sucked into the ground," she said. "It's your turn to come up with a way out of this trap."

"Challenge accepted." Baring his fangs, he tightened his grip on the bars and used them to ratchet himself higher, until his full body hung against the wall of the cage. He swung out and when his body flew toward the bars, he lifted his feet and hit them solidly against the side of the cage. Over and over.

The cage rocked, tipped, and toppled over. Isi found herself lying on the bars with the floor of the wasteland beneath her. Letting go of her death grip, she stood. Bucko flew from the cage to her shoulder and settled, chirping as if to scold her for misbehaving.

"Not my fault, buddy," she said, gulping at the big hole. If she fell in, she'd be swallowed.

"Aye, aye, Captain," he cried.

She really had no idea where he was learning these phrases, but he was cute. It was funny. And it wasn't as if she could ask him.

"I have an idea," she said.

He grinned. "It *is* your turn to act."

"Walk with me." She strode the edge and looked downward. "Good thing we avoided that." The hole went on forever and this time, there didn't appear to be roots, fangs, or rocks to grab onto to break their fall.

They'd be dead, which was Fedeema's goal.

The thought of dying, of losing Lyel… It filled her with sorrow and rage.

Lyel joined her, and she jumped onto his back. "You'll have to perform again, sweet cheeks, but maybe you can take us across that opening?" She waved to the gap beneath where the cage's floor had been.

"I will take you anywhere but please, I prefer dude to sweet cheeks." With a simple leap, he landed on the other side of the pit. Free. Sort of.

"Dude it is," Isi said. "Although…" Damn, it felt good to smile. "Are you sure I can't call you sweet cheeks?"

He swept her up and spun in a circle. When he lowered her to her feet, he kissed her.

She clung to him, having no problem admitting she loved this. She wanted his kisses, his touch to last forever.

His kiss ended too soon, and she growled, feeling greedy.

He stroked her face. "I guess I could live with sweet cheeks."

Her laugh snorted out of her. "You…"

"Me…"

She shook her finger at him. "One of these days…"

"I am going to hold you to that promise."

"Oh, no worries," she said. "I intend to keep it." Turning, she leaned into him and looked around. "What are the odds there are more cages between us and the fence?"

"There must be. I think…" He turned her around and honestly, she wanted more kisses, but he waved to his back. "Hop on."

"You have a plan?" she asked.

"It is my turn, is it not?"

"One of these days, it's going to be *our* turn."

"That it is, mate. That it is."

"Heave ho!" Bucko cried. "All hands-on deck!"

Isi rolled her eyes. "I'm being outdone by a bird, but he's right. Time to heave ho and get out of here." She jumped onto Lyel's back and gripped his shoulders, wrapping her legs around his waist.

They must look like the fable where the dog stood on the donkey, the cat stood on the dog, and the rooster hopped on top of the pile. Except she was on Lyel, and Bucko perched on her. As if to cement the impression, Bucko fluttered up onto her head.

"Dude," she said.

"Yes?" When she said nothing, just grunted, Lyel tipped his head to look back over his shoulder. "Are you holding on?"

"I am. Where are we—"

He leaped forward and the second his foot hit the ground, he projected them again, running the distance between the cage and the fence in huge bounds.

Bucko squawked and his claws wrapped around her hair. Ugh. She hoped she had some left by the time they stopped.

Behind them, cages jutted out of the ground, giant steely jaws, but they snapped shut empty because she and Lyel had already left the area.

He stopped when they were inches from the fence. Bucko released his death grip on her hair to hop onto her shoulder. She rubbed her head to take the sting away and make sure she still had hair. So far, so good.

She gazed upward. "This sucks, huh?" The damn thing had to be fifty feet high, as if they knew Crakairians might try to hop over it. "Can we dig underneath?"

"I have heard the fence extends some ways beneath the surface."

"So, no." She slid off his back.

"Ahoy? Ahoy?" Bucko cried.

She swore his voice echoed in the low hills behind them. "Do you think it's safe to walk alongside the fence or is that booby-trapped, too?"

He shrugged. "Do not go far."

She held out her hand. "Let's face whatever waits together."

He bared his fangs, but his smile fell fast.

Their situation was tenuous. They couldn't stay here long as Fedeema would arrive with new backup. Xartons would sense their presence and attack. Other creatures must be lurking about, eager for a snack.

The fence stretched for miles in either direction, which meant there would be no walking around it. Not in this lifetime, that is. No going over. No going under.

She growled, squinting at the metal mesh fence. "You don't happen to have wire cutters with you, do you? Or claws you can use to snip the metal?"

"I do not. Sadly, Crakairians have evolved beyond our Driegon heritage and lost our claws."

"Driegon. I haven't heard of them before."

"We believe they have died out. Ages ago, everyone lived in an enormous cave system below the surface of Crakair. Something happened. An argument, perhaps? No one remembers. But many left the caves and migrated to the surface, where they evolved into the Crakairians you see today. Occasionally, someone is born with Driegon features, but most appear as I do."

"I see." She gripped the fence and tried to shake it, but it remained solid. "What features are we talking about?"

"The claws you referred to, though the Driegons were said to only have claws where we have a thumbnail. Tails, horns, wings, spikes down their backs, scales like mine, though rumor has it they were bigger."

"Naanans?" She loved how Lyel's stroked her, how they functioned as independent limbs.

"I do not believe so, though I am not sure why."

"Your Driegons sound like Earth's mythical dragons. Do they have any human-like features?"

"Two arms and two legs. Faces like Crakairians, I believe. I do not know otherwise. We have no pictures."

She wiggled her eyebrows. "They sound sexy."

He growled. "You wish I had a tail or wings?"

"Only now." She tipped her head back and took in the fence looming over them. "If you had wings, you could fly us up and over the top."

"Now I wish I *was* Driegon."

Stopping, she squeezed his hand. "It's okay. I think you're perfect just the way you are." He was cute, kind, and he wanted to please her.

Twirp.

"Not now, Bucko," she said with a wave of her hand. There had to be a way past this fence; they just needed to find it. In frustration, she kicked the fence but got nothing for her effort other than sore toes.

Twirp!

Sighing, she tipped her head, crossing her eyes to look at Bucko, but he wasn't gazing at her. She turned to where the bird's attention was fixated.

"Holy shit," she said.

"Heille," Lyel echoed.

At least a thousand birds like Bucko littered the ground a short distance from them.

"Ahoy!" they chirped in unison.

Lyel

For the second time in a span of minars, Lyel's jaw dropped.

"Aren't they cute?" Isi cooed, starting toward them. He held her back.

They were … not cute, but he would wait to see how this played out before making final judgment.

"Ahoy!" they called again, tiptoeing across the sand toward them.

Isi dropped to her heels and held out her arms as if she would hug them all. "They're gorgeous." She tipped her head back to smile at Lyel. "Look at their beautiful grayish blue feathers. Yeah, they resemble skinny chickens with fangs, but chickens are sweet creatures. Aren't they amazing? Bucko, are these your friends?"

Bucko twirped. He flew off her shoulder and joined the other birds clustering around Isi.

Lyel wasn't sure if he should keep his kalina ready or drop to the ground and join Isi in welcoming Bucko's family. Family? Wait a minar. How was he going to provide for all these birds, let alone get them to Crakair. This could be a problem.

This was demented. Unnatural.

Entertaining.

Isi was the cause, somehow. And if nothing else, she would bring humor to his life as long as she remained a part of it.

He hadn't had much chance to court her, yet she showed she cared. Was it possible to woo a mate without the formal courtship rituals?

"I can't believe how many of you there are," Isi exclaimed, patting one bird after another. "You're all so awesome." She tumbled backward, onto the sand, and a few jumped up onto her chest for pats.

"Take care, mate." Their claws… Yet they treated her with utmost gentleness, walking cautiously across her body. Soon, they surrounded her.

She sat up, grinning, and the tension that had creased her face since he met her was gone. "I'm not sure what to do with them all."

Bucko flew up onto her shoulder and others joined him, crowding together. Their claws sunk into her shirt, but she didn't flinch, so they must not be digging into skin.

A few flew up onto Lyel's shoulders, and he peered at them, unsure of their intentions.

Isi stood. "It was nice seeing all your friends, Bucko, but they should probably leave before Fedeema gets here." Her worried gaze met his and the creases reappeared on her face. "We should leave, too."

"Walk the plank," Bucko chirped. "Walk the plank! Ahoy!"

More birds flew to Isi's back and latched onto her shirt. Others did the same with Lyel, clinging to his scales. They pulled, but not unpleasantly. Yet.

"Should I fight them off?" he asked, seeking a cue. She bonded with Bucko, and he trusted her instincts in this. His hand tightened on his kalina, but there was no way he could fight them all off if they chose to attack.

"Hold on," she said. "I think…"

Their wings flapped, and they lifted her up off the ground.

"Holy…" she squealed. "This… I don't know what's happening, Lyel, but I'm going to find out!"

He was lifted as well, higher and higher. If they dropped him, he'd suffer grave injuries, but they didn't appear to be hostile. Their wings flapped, creating a stiff breeze that swirled around him.

The birds flew him and Isi over the fence. They continued to fly half a klek or more, taking them away from the fence and closer to the city.

Slowing, they drifted down to the ground and carefully set them in the scraggly blue grass. Releasing them, the birds settled on the ground around him and Isi, watching them.

"I wish we had something we could give them as a reward," Isi said. "That was unbelievable. I never imagined anything like that could happen."

"Perhaps this is *our* reward for helping Bucko. If you had not protected him, he would be dead."

"Maybe." She dropped to her knees and held out her arms. The birds fluttered in close, seeking their share of affection.

Movement in the desert drew Lyel's eye. In the distance, dark specks appeared, coming this way.

His heart flipped. Fedeema.

"We need to leave," he said.

Isi followed his gaze and groaned. Rising to her feet,

she flicked her hands toward the birds. "You guys better hide. Trouble's coming."

As if they understood her—maybe they did—the birds shot off the ground en masse, Bucko included. They circled around overhead before splitting, each flying away in a different direction.

"I guess we're not taking a bunch of birds to Crakair," she said forlornly.

"This is a very sad thing," he said, not actually meaning it but wanting to reassure Isi.

Her shoulders slumped. "Even Bucko left."

He gathered her into his arms. "He is with his friends."

She sniffed. "True, but I'm going to miss him."

"There are many creatures on Crakair you can befriend. My home is in the country. You will see." This was the first time he'd suggested she come with him, not only to Crakair, but to his estate. How would she respond?

Tipping her head back, she gave him a watery smile. "I can't wait to see your home."

"Our home, if you would have me."

She took in a deep breath, and he girded himself for her refusal, but her smile grew. "I like that Lyel. Our home." She held out her hand. "I know we need to get away, but my heart is happy for the first time in a long time. Let's get out of here and find a way to Crakair."

He nodded as he took her hand. As they raced toward the city, he shot a glance over his shoulder, but they'd moved far enough away, he could no longer see the fence.

A cry of rage rang out, echoing across the hills.

Fedeema had reached the fence and found them missing.

As Isi would say, the so-called queen was fuckin' pissed.

TWENTY-TWO

Isi

As they ran toward the city, low sandy hills with scraggly vegetation gave way to lusher blue grass and trees.

"We're going to get away, aren't we?" Isi puffed as she raced beside Lyel. "Thanks to Bucko and his friends."

"We might."

"You don't sound sure of that."

"Fedeema will not be stopped by a fence."

"You're right. She's got wings, and this is her turf. Can we hide in the city?"

"For a short time," he said.

"Once we're inside the city streets, we can blend in with everyone, except… I don't blend well." She scrunched her face. "But we'll find a way to avoid notice and escape Mara. Is there a regular shuttle going to Crakair?" Wouldn't that be nice? To think, they could be close to leaving this wasteland behind.

"There is no shuttle, but we will find a way once we have finished here."

"You still want to kill Fedeema."

He dipped his head. "The mission must be completed."

"To restore your honor."

"It is more than that. I do this for us. For Crakair. And for Earth."

"We do need to keep her from enacting her plan, but will killing her accomplish that? Won't someone else take her place?"

"I assume the explosion killed most."

"You'd think her own government wouldn't want her drawing attention to this planet." They raced through an area peppered with spiky trees with dark blue trunks. Overhead, broad, golden leaves reminiscent of banana trees, blocked the sun and hopefully kept Fedeema from finding them.

"She is doing this outside the jurisdiction of the Maran government."

"Then let's go to them and let them handle it."

"The former government approved of her actions."

Ah. She nodded. "And no one knows the new leader's thoughts. Fedeema seemed frightened of the new leader. She mentioned providing a distraction when the leader visited the compound."

"Which I destroyed."

"The evidence is gone. Do you think the leader will be suspicious about the explosion?"

"Perhaps." His naanans flared out before settling on his shoulders. "We cannot take a chance until we know this person's thoughts."

When they reached the outskirts of town, they passed rundown, abandoned buildings with overgrown lawns. Their pace slowed to a walk.

She had to admit, she was worn out. Days of hiding on the Crakairian starship, followed by pleasing Fedeema to avoid her strap, had been topped off with a run through the desert with creatures trying to eat them. Isi needed a rest or even ten minutes where she wasn't frightened. Would that time ever come?

"Why not notify the Crakairian government about the new leader and let them handle it?" She asked, staring at the broken-down equipment sitting in a fallow field.

"I plan to." Lyel's brow ridges lifted. "Though I do not expect much will come of it. There are few laws on Mara and those in existence are lax, permitting most to do as they please."

"And we're walking into this town."

"There is no other way to escape."

They stopped on top of a small hill.

"The city awaits," she said, staring toward the cluster of buildings, none higher than three or four stories. It wasn't big; maybe a mile across, though she couldn't see how far it stretched from here. "How many people live in the city?"

"There are about a hundred thousand residents in Qe'ket, though the number changes substantially depending on the seasons and what is happening in this quadrant of the galaxy. Qe'ket is a pirate port where those skirting the law come for ship repairs, to sell merchandise, and for refueling."

"And here I am, without my pirate sidekick." She missed Bucko already, though she knew he would be happier with his friends and family.

"You are welcome to teach me your pirate phrases and I shall…I love to twist your words, but I cannot say I will kick your side."

"I like that in you, Lyel." She squinted up at him as they stepped onto a gravel road winding through the wooded area, heading for the city. "Yer the finest pirate's booty I've ever laid me eyes on."

Lips twitching, his brow ridges quivered. "You have not seen many pirate booties, then."

"Lyel, you're gorgeous. You know that, right? You're the hottest guy I know."

"I am the only…guy around."

"Still the hottest." She tapped her chin. "How about this one? Show me yer buried treasure." Before he could speak, she held up her finger. "Would ye like to shiver me timbers?"

He chuckled. "Whenever you wish, mate."

"I believe I want to be shivered soon."

His steps slowed. "You do?"

She squeezed his hand. "You didn't know that already?"

"How could I?"

"Lyel," she said. "One of these days, we're going to be safe enough to explore this."

"Not now, but you are right. Soon, mate."

She hoped their time would come. She wanted to share whatever the future gave them.

Ahead, a road wound from the right, cutting through a forest that continued in that direction as far as her eyes could see. Small caravans of creatures vaguely resembling horses except with six legs and spiked tails pulled carts with blue-skinned aliens driving.

"You are an Earthling," Lyel said. "We need to find you a disguise before we travel farther."

"Short of getting wet and rolling in the sand, we're out of disguises." She peered backward. "Unless we want to go back and see if there's something I can wear in one of those abandoned houses."

"Anything of value would have been stolen by now."

Turning to face her, he took her hands. "I will need to leave you. Once I have acquired something we can use to hide your appearance, I will return."

She nodded. "Will a Crakairian stand out in Qe'ket?"

"Not as much as an Earthling female."

"I'd be seen as breeder material. Something to be stolen and sold to the highest bidder." That's what she was initially threatened with. If Fedeema hadn't heard her sing and used her for entertainment, who knew where she'd be now? She wasn't grateful to Fedeema, but she was grateful she had not been sold as a breeder.

Glancing around, she didn't see any good hiding spots. "Where can I wait?"

Leaving the path, he wove through the woods, taking her deeper into the thickets. Birds called overhead, and the low hum of insects rippled through the air.

Lyel approached a small, falling down house, the word "house" being generous. Hovel would work better. Boards had been secured together to form an A-frame structure. Most of the roofing had peeled off, and if there had been a door, it had fled the scene. He ducked inside, but he wouldn't be able to stand upright, as he was taller than the building. Poking his head out, he waved for her to join him.

"Cozy," she said when she entered and looked around. About six by eight feet in length, holes peppered the rotting floor, and straggly bluish grass grew up through where some boards were missing. A tiny fireplace covered the back wall, and a cabinet with a cracked door leaned forward, ready to topple forward. Other than a chair with two legs and the remnants of a straw-stuffed mattress, the solitary room was empty. Light peeked in from all sides. No cobwebs but Lyel may have gotten rid of them. "Do I dare sit?"

"I would trust that." He waved to a flat rock propped up beside the fireplace.

She wiggled it flat and dropped down onto it.

He knelt in front of her, cupping her face in his big, warm hands. "I will not be gone long, but try to…"

"Keep quiet. I get it. The last thing I want to do is draw anyone's attention." She gave him a quick kiss that turned into a lot more. It felt like a promise.

With a curt nod, he rose and crept from the tiny house. His footsteps faded, quick and filled with purpose.

She stretched out her legs and hugged her waist. It was easy to come across as confident when Lyel was here, but this place was a bit too creepy for Isi. She was glad daylight streamed in through the cracks in the roof and she wouldn't be alone in the hovel long. To think someone once lived here. Maybe when the door and roof were secure and the fireplace was lit, it was cozy.

A thud outside made her freeze. Her skin rippled with goosebumps, and she swallowed the lump of fear in her throat. It could be Lyel but… He hadn't been gone long.

She carefully rose to her feet and gripped her knife tightly. Glancing around, she spied the fire poker lying near the opposite wall. It was a question of did she dare cross the rickety floor to reach it. That poker would add to her reach. It would make a difference.

She started toward it, keeping her footsteps light to avoid making a sound.

The building shuddered, and the roof collapsed on top of her.

Knocked forward, she hit the boards hard. The world wavered and went out of focus.

TWENTY-THREE

Lyel

The moment Lyel entered the part of the woods where he left Isi, he knew something horrible had happened.

He wanted to rush forward with his kalina raised, but a move like that could see them both killed.

Moving stealthily and using the trees as cover, he worked his way to the small building. He bit back his groan when he found the structure collapsed and no one around.

He listened and when he determined no one waited to attack, he leaped forward. Landing near the building, he ripped off the roof, praying Isi was beneath while also praying she was not. Crushed, she could be… He shook his head, and his naanans were a riotous mess around his head. He did not wish to think about what it would mean if she was lying beneath the rubble.

He would find her.

"Isi," he whispered as he searched the remains of the structure.

Gone.

Frantic, he searched the ground around the building in widening circles, finding tracks leading deeper into the woods.

He hefted his kalina and with fear and anger licking through his veins, he picked up his speed to a run, following the tracks made by at least three beings.

Utter silence surrounded him, and his furious breathing cut through the air.

Ahead, the tracks led to an open area with tall grass and sunshine beating down from above. He burst into the clearing to find wagon dents in the grass leading from the open area to a road.

Unless someone had flown Isi from the destroyed building, whoever made these tracks had taken her. Since the marks in the grass were fresh, he bet on the latter. Few bothered to capture another unless they hoped to make dinars in the market.

He bolted toward the city, his footsteps eating up the distance.

Unfortunately, while he overtook wagons heading to the market, none held trussed-up Isi in the back. He garnered much anger and raised brow ridges with each kalina-induced inspection of their wagons.

Darting around the last vehicle he inspected, he rushed toward the market, taking the narrow back streets at a dead run, his heart aflame, and his hands shaking. What if he did not find her?

Isi!

Al'kieern and Trugeons, plus others of races he hadn't seen before, plastered themselves against buildings as he roared, shoving his way through the crowd.

As he drew closer to the marketplace, jeers and boisterous voices reached Lyel's ears. Would he get there on time? Rarer than cut corlire stone mined deep in the Ikeline Mountains, an Earth woman would fetch a high price. She would be the featured auction in the marketplace.

He hit the open area where they put items on display at a run and wove through the crowd gathered around the stage.

Isi stood in the center. With her hands tied in the front, she stared forward dully. A red mark on her face told him she'd fought, and they subdued her. They drugged her to ensure she behaved.

His blood roared, and he ached to lay waste to everyone around him.

How was he going to rescue her? He had no credits to bid, and his kalina and his strength of will alone would not be enough to defeat the crowd surrounding him.

Fuck this. There was no way out, but that never stopped Lyel before.

This wasn't about honor or proving something to those who scorned his family. This was about rescuing the woman he loved.

Crouching, he leaped, bursting above the crowd. He soared over them and landed hard on the wooden platform. Tumbling forward to break his landing, he rose to his feet in front of the auctioneer whose single eye widened.

The auctioneer bared his jagged teeth. "Capture heem! Take the Crakairian and throw him into the dungeon!"

Winged Al'kieen flew at Lyel, and he spun, his kalina whistling through the air. It sliced through the Al'kieern, and they reeled back, squealing.

A solid punch in the plexus sent the stubby zennier male backward against the rail. But he rallied and pulled a laser pistol from his belt.

As he lifted it, Lyel rushed forward and used one of Isi's moves. His leg swung out and knocked the pistol from the male's hand. Lowering his head, the auctioneer ran toward Lyel, determined to impale him with his horns.

Lyel leaped up and flipped mid-air, landing in a crouch behind the auctioneer.

Guards rushed up the stairs to the auction platform.

Lyel ran to Isi.

"Lyel," she gasped, and her pained gaze met his. "They…" She shook her head. "My brain… Help."

"I will get you out of here, love," he said, lifting her into his arms. When a guard came near, Lyel kicked out, sending the guard back into the others rushing up the stairs. They tumbled down and jumped to their feet, growling.

"Love." Her lips quirked upward before falling again. "I…" She sagged against him.

As more winged Al'kieern flew toward the stage and the crowd roared, he flung himself from the platform. He landed solidly on the cobbled street behind the crowd and raced away from the marketplace.

Al'kieern flew after him, the lasers hitting the buildings around him. He zigzagged down a narrow street and when he hit an intersection, he turned right, weaving into another busy market area. The smell of roast wildarn filled the air. Vendors selling various wares shouted as he passed, telling him to slow down, to stop and check out their "special price for the female".

When a laser blast hit the ground near Lyel, the vendors faded back against the stone buildings behind them, hissing.

Lyel ran through the crowd, shoving aside anyone who got in his way. He turned into an alley and raced to the end, finding a solid wall. A crouch, and he flew upward onto the roof of a low building. He raced across the top while Isi clung to him, her face buried in his neck. She kept repeating his name, over and over, and it ripped his insides apart to hear the sadness in her voice.

He jumped, spanning the distance to another building and plunged to the ground on the other side, landing in the seedy bar district of the city.

Blending in with the boisterous patrons, he remained beneath the awnings stretching across the main thorough-fare, hoping to lose the Al'kieern. When no lasers hit his spine, his hope grew.

He darted into a narrow alley beside one of the "nicer" inns in the city, remembering a stay here when his father visited the city in an official capacity for the Council.

A jump took him up to a deck on the second floor, and another to the platform of the third. He peered into the window and seeing no one inside, carefully lifted the glass panel.

He climbed through the opening and after ensuring the room was unrented, laid Isi on the bed.

She clung to him but when she gave him a sleepy smile and whispered his name, he took heart. He reached her in time.

He smoothed his fingers along the mark on her face, wishing he could erase it with his touch and cut her bindings.

"I will be back," he whispered.

She smiled again. "Matey…" Her unfocused gaze drifted across him, and she swallowed. "Wanna swab your deck." Her arms lifted toward him.

"I want you to swab my deck, but only when you are in full control of your mind, love."

She yawned. "Tired…"

"Rest." He crept to the door and turned to look at her, reassuring himself she was okay.

Then he went downstairs to procure this room for the night.

TWENTY-FOUR

Isi

Isi woke and stretched, savoring the squishy mattress beneath her and the scratchy yet warm blanket on top of her.

Until memory set in.

A lizard alien hauling her out from beneath the rubble of the tiny A-frame. Trying to run but him tackling her to the ground. The alien hauling her off the ground. He yanked her arms in front and tying her wrists, binding them tight enough they bled.

She kicked and punched with both fists, but the gray-skinned, lizard-like alien snapped his five-inch fangs and snarled. He socked her in the face with his tail and hauled her to her feet when she fell, dragging her through the woods to a wagon, where he tossed her inside.

The long, bumpy ride into the city while the alien shouted something over and over resulted in other aliens cheering and following like the lizard was the pied piper.

When the wagon stopped, aliens crowded around, pointing and jeering. A round, one-eyed alien grabbed her ankle and dragged her out of the wagon. Propping her up in front of him, he exhaled into her face and the world swam.

He'd drugged her with his breath. Somehow.

She vaguely remembered…an auction.

And Lyel? But he couldn't be here, or he wouldn't have left her alone in a room.

Shit, she must've dreamed him rescuing her and calling her love.

Had she been sold? A quick scan of her body told her she hadn't been violated, but whoever bought her might plan to wait until she woke up.

No way in hell would she lie here waiting to be raped.

At least her hands were untied. Leaping from the bed, she staggered but righted herself, grateful whatever the one-eyed alien breathed into her face had cleared. She turned back to the bed and using pillows, made it look like she still slept underneath the covers.

A quick look around told her she not only lost her knife but there were no weapon up for grabs. That didn't stop Isi. Striding to the desk sitting along the side wall, she poked through the drawers and found something vaguely resembling a pen long forgotten in the back. It was better than nothing.

Gripping it tightly, she crept over to stand beside the door. When it opened, she'd be ready. After she stabbed her alien captor, she'd flee.

Then she needed to find Lyel, if it was possible in an Al'kieern city.

The doorknob rattled, and a key turned in the lock.

Fear made her skin flush, and she tightened her sweaty hand on the pen. When the door opened, she leaped, landing on the person's back.

"You're not raping me," she shrieked, lifting the pen.

"I would never rape you, mate."

"Lyel?" Her terror fled, replaced with remorse. She'd almost stabbed him!

Sliding off his back, the pen clattered on the floor. When he turned, she leaped into his arms, trembling. Her legs went around his waist.

"Hey," he said, patting her low back. "It is dokey okey." Leaning back, he bared his fangs. "I tease when I say dokey, you know."

"I did know," she said against his neck. "I like it. It's ours." She inhaled his scent, drinking it in through her pores. She wanted to melt into him and never break free. "I didn't know it was you."

"I understand." He cupped her bottom and turning, nudged the door closed. He backed until his legs hit the bed. Sitting, he pulled her close, murmuring in her hair. "I am sorry I left you alone. I told you I would be back and thought you understood."

"I don't remember. My mind was mush after the one-eyed alien breathed in my face."

"This species secretes a drug through their fangs, something that relaxes the victim and makes them compliant. I thought it was wearing off when I left you here. I went downstairs and secured this room for the night, plus transport to Crakair."

Her heart leaped in excitement. "We're leaving?"

"Tomorrow."

"This is wonderful."

He nodded against her hair. "We will remain here until it is time to leave. You are safe."

A weight dropped from her body, leaving her light and carefree. "It's truly safe?" She trusted him, but after what happened, she would need time to feel secure again. Actually she might not feel secure until they reached Crakair.

"The innkeeper will send up a meal soon, but we will

remain here until morning. I will not leave you again, and when we go out on the street, you will be well disguised."

Was it truly over?

When she left Earth, she was determined to find her way alone. She didn't plan on Lyel, but she wouldn't have this any other way.

"What about Fedeema?"

"I…" He sucked in a breath and released it. "I spoke with my friend, Vork, and the Crakairian government will handle it."

"How do you feel about that?" Leaning back, she watched a myriad of emotions flick across his face, ending with resolve.

"This is how it should be."

"Should."

"I will not risk your life again."

"What aren't you telling me?" she asked.

"I will work with the Crakairian government. If they need my help, I will give it."

"You'll endanger yourself." She held up her hand but frowned at it. "This isn't me saying I want a kiss, though I do. I want you to hear me out." At his nod, she continued. "I understand wanting to do something, and I know how much your honor means to you, which is why I will state right now that I support you in whatever you choose to do."

"Even if that means I need to leave to go after Fedeema once you are safe on Crakair?"

It hurt to swallow, but she forced the lump down. "Yes. You do what you must. If it's important to you, it's important to me."

"Isi." He drew her into his arms. "Thank you."

She didn't have to like it, but she did feel she had to be here for him no matter what he chose to do. Who was she to say how he lived his life? If she held him back, it wasn't true love, was it? As everyone always said, someone was only yours if you set them free and they came back on their own. It wouldn't be easy, but it was something she had to do. Keeping her face buried in his chest, she blinked back tears. Being supportive was tearing her apart.

"I will be careful, no matter what I do," he said. "And if I leave, I will come back to you."

She nodded and sniffed. "And I will be waiting."

He held her in the silence that followed, until her heart lightened.

Leaning back in his embrace, she looked up at him. "We'll stay here tonight, then."

"Our meal should be here soon."

How could she be hungry when her emotions had hitched onto the back of a rollercoaster?

A scratch on the door made her jump. "Our food?" she whispered. When Lyel nodded, she slid off his lap and slunk around the bed. "I'll hide." Dropping to the floor, she hunkered underneath the frame.

The mattress creaked when Lyel rose, and she tracked his footsteps to the door, which he opened.

"On the desk, please," he said.

The clang of dishes, on what sounded like a cart bumping across the floorboards, was followed by the smell of meat and something sweet.

"Thank you. I will not need further services tonight," Lyel said.

Whoever delivered the food spoke in a language Isi did not understand, then left, shutting the door behind them.

Isi waited to the count of ten to make sure they didn't come back, then crept out from beneath the bed. She took in the cart loaded with food. "How are we paying for this? When we arrived, you were almost naked."

"Once I communicated with him, Vork arranged for dinars. In the morning, I will go out and buy disguises we will wear to reach the spaceport."

"Sounds good." Her belly rumbled.

"Are you hungry?" he asked.

For whatever reason, her mind shot to hunger for something other than food. Though she denied it, she's wanted this guy almost from the moment she met him.

Her mouth went dry. "I am…hungry."

He curled his finger her way. "Come closer, love, and I will serve you."

"What are you going to…serve me?" she stuttered out. Was serving meals a Crakairian custom? If so, she was all in. She hated cooking.

"I believe I made a promise, did I not?"

"Which one?" she stuttered out, gulping.

"I said I would court you naked, my mate."

TWENTY-FIVE

Lyel

"Court me?" Isi said, her eyes widening. Her voice dropped to a bare whisper. "I was hoping you were going to give me a strip tease. If only I had a dollar…"

He did not know what a dollar was. As for strip tease, he could cipher that out. She wished to see him strip off clothing. It would be a tease. He liked this idea and would add it to his courtship repertoire once he had clothing.

"Please be aware, I do not have a garlong," Lyel said, his voice deep and gravelly. Strips and teasing would have to wait. He must approach this in a serious manner. Now that this minar was at hand, his hands shook, and his heart fluttered behind his ribs. Isi made it clear she wished to be with him, but a Crakairian courted his mate, he did not drag her across a desert then rescue her from slavers. None of that would win a female's affection.

A matebond had to be handled in a formal, Crakairian manner. This was not about his family's honor, but about his own.

Isi was the most special female he had ever met. She deserved to be wooed.

"I'm not sure it matters if you have a garlong, though I don't know what a garlong is." Her gaze remained fixed on his groin, and his cock twitched, eager. It would need to wait. "You're enough for me already, Lyel. You don't need to do anything else to win me."

But he did. This was important. How could he help her understand? "I wish to court you, as all Crakairian mates are courted. I honor you by doing so."

"That's sweet, and I want that if it makes you happy. The last thing I want to do is interfere in something you feel is important, but know I'm all in, Lyel. You don't need to jump through hoops to convince me you're the one."

Hoops? He was not sure how him jumping through a circular object would convince her he was worthy of mating, but he would do so once he obtained a hoop.

Wait. She said she was "all in," stating again she wanted to be with him.

"I am all in, as well, Isi, which is why I will use this evening, here in this lowly inn, to court you."

She strolled toward him, her hips swaying. He could not drag his eyes away from the languid movement of her body. His throat choked off with longing. Soon. Very soon.

Stopping in front of him, she traced her finger down his chest to his abdomen before lingering. "How long does courtship take?"

"For some, a yaro."

She blinked fast as if processing his statement. "Do you plan to court me for a full yaro?"

"If you wish. It will be torture to wait that long, but I will do so."

"I'm not saying I want a yaro of courtship."

"If you could set the time limit, how long would you suggest?"

"You said we have tonight? That works for me."

He bowed. "I will do my best to show you I am your fated mate."

"I want you, Lyel. If it takes a night or even a year for us to be together, I'll be patient, but as far as I'm concerned, you already courted me."

He tilted his head, and his naanans strained toward her. Pesky things: they revealed his heart. "How do you mean?"

"Don't you see? You don't need to do things to win a person's love. It's about showing you care. For example… Tell me what a Crakairian courtship entails."

"First, a Crakairian feeds an intended mate a ceremonial meal while dressed in a garlong."

"Kind of like first dates on Earth. Dressing up to impress and going out to dinner."

"Interesting. Earthlings and Crakairians are not that different."

"Our appearances may vary, but we all want the same thing, to impress someone we like," she said. "What else?"

"Next, a Crakairian male would emulse their intended's feet with a boodler."

"I assume we have no boodler."

"This bothers me deeply."

Her lips twitched, but she nodded solemnly. "I can see it does. If we have no boodler, how else could you…emulse my feet?"

"The emulsion is a form of massage."

"If you massage my feet, I'll be in heaven." Her eyes sparkled, and he appreciated how seriously she took his suit.

"After that, I would bathe you in a zinter bath."

She cocked her head toward the corner. "That's a tub, right?"

"It is not a zinter bath."

"Can we pretend it is?"

"Without zinters?" he grumbled. "That would be difficult."

"Are there zinters on the menu?"

His gaze shot to their covered meal. "We do not eat zinters. They eat us."

"Why am I suddenly concerned about this form of bathing? But since others have taken a zinter bath before, and they're still alive and kicking, I'm going to assume "eat us" is a general comment and not reality."

"They do not eat us, you are correct. They…nibble around us while we lounge in the tub."

"Maybe, um…" her fingertip teased his abs. Completely distracting. His cock throbbed, and he suppressed the urge to take her to the bed and climb on top of her. He must do this in an honorable way. "Perhaps…" Her finger poked his chest. "You could substitute for the zinters?"

His flesh went hot. "I would…" He gulped. "I could do this if you feel it would be an adequate substitute." Why had he not thought of this?

"I'll try not to be disappointed. I mean, we're talking about zinters." She tipped her hands back and forth as if weighing something. "You nibbling or zinters. Hmm. It's a tough choice."

He could not tell if she was teasing or completely serious. But courtship was serious business, so he would treat her comment in this manner.

She stepped in closer. "Here's what you need to understand, because I think you're coming at this from the wrong angle. Your courtship was in the way you listened to my song and heard so much more than the words I spoke. You heard my soul. It was in the way you protected me in the tunnels beneath the wasteland. And in the way you leaped to my defense in the auction market, which I thought was a dream but was really you. I can't believe the risk you took. Am I mistaken or did you jump over the crowd, land on the stage, punch the one-eyed alien, sweep me off my feet, and then run through the city with multiple aliens chasing you?"

"I did all that."

"And you don't think that impresses me?"

"Did it?"

Her heartfelt sigh fell between them. "More than anything else you could do."

"Isi, you break me."

She cupped his face. "I don't want to hurt you."

He gathered her close. "You do not. You humble me. When I am with you, I wish to be your hero and a hero always acts with honor."

"I've been holding out for a hero, and he is you."

"We can…" His naanans, nervous, lifted and settled on her shoulders. She tipped her head and rubbed her face on one, and he swore it hummed. Or his body hummed. It was hard to tell because his soul was singing. "I do not remember what I meant to say."

She stepped back and sat on the bed. "Why don't you show me your version of the Crakairian courtship rituals. Like you said, we have tonight, and this gives me a chance to learn more about you. We can wait for…other things until you've completed your rituals."

"We will." She was open to his formal courtship! He would not disappoint her in these simple tasks. Stepping back, he bowed deeply. A feeling of rightness filled him. "Dreafillar."

The smile she gave him chased away his shaking limbs. This was going to work out as it should. He would court her tonight and tomorrow morning, he would worship her body. "You said that before when we first met."

"It is the formal courtship greeting."

A smile flitted across her lips. "Is there a formal courtship greeting women say in response?"

"Dreafillay."

She dipped her head forward, and the movement did not hide her sweet smile. "Dreafillay."

TWENTY-SIX

Isi

____

I si woke the next morning, nestled in Lyel's arms. She traced her finger across his chest scales, though softly with no intent to wake him. Savoring being close to him was all that mattered. They hadn't had sex—yet, but he'd taken time to court her. Who could complain about that?

His scales felt smooth and supple, which he'd need for quick movement, but also firm enough to withstand an attack by something resembling a dragon, if his talk about the Driegon race was to be believed. Crakairians had evolved, but they held onto some of their dragon features.

She rose onto her elbow and watched him sleep. There was something both sweet and fearsome about Lyel at rest. When challenged by a foe, this male was lethal. Yet he could be gentle, as he was last night when he emulsed her feet. She did her best not to giggle, but jeez, it tickled. They both ended up tumbling onto the bed together with her trying to find even one ticklish spot on Lyel without success. They ended up making out, but when she wanted to give him everything, he told her to rest, that he still needed to bathe her. He said she was tired, and he wouldn't take advantage of that. Again, he showed her how caring he was. They laid together in the dark, talking about their former lives. Night stole through the room, and she drifted to sleep.

She wanted to show him how much she cared, to give instead of take. There was no denying her heart. Fire licked through her, and she had no wish to put the flames out this time.

Rising over him, she stared at his mouth, eager to taste him again. Fangs. Scales. Nannans. This person was truly alien. But somehow, like two pieces of a puzzle, they fit together.

Would he know if she kissed him?

Leaning forward, she put her mouth on his, drinking in the feel of him beneath her. His arms rose to wrap around her, and he tumbled to the side, taking her with him and then rising over her.

"You dare to wake the beast," he growled, showing her that he was a quick study and *she* had ticklish spots.

Her lust turned into laughter, but when he spoke again, she stilled.

"Are you ready for nibbling, mate?" he asked.

"Oh, please," she moaned. "Feel welcome to nibble at will."

He rose off her and strode to the tub. Dragging it out into the center of the room, he stared down at it. "It is not a zinter pool."

"I can see this bothers you, but I'm interested in your nibbles, not a fishes." She sat up on the side of the bed. "We need water, though."

He returned to the wall and fiddled with a long dark tube, stretching it out until it reached the side of the tub. He stroked its length with his fingers, and water spurted from the end.

"Is there a faucet in the wall?"

"Hmm?" He looked up from the hose. "This is a yarl-ish. The creature lives in the walls. If we are kind to it, it pulls water up from beneath the ground, heats it within its body, and gives it to us." Stroking the "hose," he hummed.

"Does singing help?" she asked.

"Your singing always helps."

"I'll keep it low. I don't know how thin the walls are. No need to draw attention."

"Wise."

She sang softly. "You'll be in my heart… From this day on! Now, and forever more." Her song rose and fell, and she put everything inside her into the words.

"Isi," Lyel's guttural voice cut through the silence once she finished. "My mate." Swallowing deeply, he directed his gaze to the water, blinking rapidly. "I would bathe you. I wish to show you even a fraction of my feelings for you with my courtship."

She slid off the bed and approached him. "You have more integrity than anyone I know. I just wanted to say that. This," she waved to the room, "and everything you've done for me show me what an honorable person you are."

He wrapped his arms around her and dropped his chin on top of her head. "You continue to break me, love."

"If I break you…" She tipped her head back, hoping her feelings showed on her face. "Then let me put you back together."

He bared his fangs. "This makes me happy, but I am eager to nibble."

"Far be it for me to stop you from nibbling if that's your goal." She stepped out of his embrace and tugged off her shirt. After shimmying out of her jeans, she faced him in her undies.

He gulped, his heated gaze falling down her body like a heavy caress.

Her underwear joined her jeans on the floor, and she stepped into the tub.

He crossed the room to the desk and returned with a bristly plant the size of a quarter, handing it to her.

She stared down at it; grateful it wasn't alive. As far as she could see. "What does this have to do with nibbling?"

He placed a second one in his mouth and chewed.

"Food?" she asked.

"This…cleans one's teeth? Freshens one's breath."

"Oh, like a mint, only bushy." Without reservations, she popped it into her mouth. It tasted vaguely like spearmint and as she chewed, it shifted across her teeth. Back at the compound, she'd done the best she could with water and her finger, but she hated not being able to floss and brush. "Do we swallow it?"

He nodded.

Her mouth feeling better than it had in too long, she sank deeper into the water.

Lyel dropped down beside the tub and lifted a small piece of cloth.

"That's not going to nibble me either, is it?"

"Once I bathe you, *I* will nibble."

Her grin couldn't be denied. There wasn't anything sexier than a guy you loved eager to please you. He was going to rub a cloth all over her body before using his mouth on her flesh.

He started with her back, covering it with broad, gentles strokes, dipping lower. Eyes sliding closed, she sighed as he washed her hair with something vaguely floral, then washed her feet and legs.

The cloth climbed higher and higher. She scooted down and propped a heel up on his shoulder, and he moved the cloth closer. A few more inches, and she was going to scream, but he teased, rubbing almost to where she wanted him before gliding away.

He moved to her breasts, where he was bolder, running the cloth over them until her nipples peaked.

When she moaned, he dropped the cloth. Lifting her from the tub, he dried her quickly then carried her to the bed. But when she tried to pull him down on top of her, he slipped backward.

"Let me…"

He ripped off the scrap of cloth he wore to bed and jumped into the tub, giving her a decent view of his ass. He cleansed himself quickly then rose from the water, standing and watching her while liquid sluiced down his god-like body.

Stepping over the edge of the tub, he ran a dry cloth over his body but tossed it aside before finishing. He strode to the bed and climbed up over her.

"Isi," he sighed. His mouth caught hers and when his tongue glided over the seam of her lips, she opened to him. She ran her heels down his calves, delighting in the scratchy-smooth feel of his scales. Lifting her legs up around his waist, she welcomed the heat and firmness of his body on hers.

His rigid cock probed her opening, but he lifted his head before claiming her. "Time to nibble."

"Don't tease. I want you now." Her body aflame, she ached to feel everything.

"Soon." His mouth trailed along her jawline, and he did nibble, biting down with his fangs on her neck, across her clavicle and down to her breasts. Sucking and nibbling, he gave equal attention to each breast before moving down her body. He spread her legs wide. "Lovely." Playing with her folds, he rubbed her clit, driving her to a fever pitch.

She thrashed on the bed while he replaced his fingers with his mouth. His fangs grazed her clit, and her hips bucked. She panted, moaned, and begged him to give her everything, but he kept teasing, nibbling on her clit while pressing a finger only a tiny bit inside her.

When she thought she'd scream, he backed away, his mouth curling up with satisfaction.

"Come, love," he said, tugging her upward, onto his lap.

"I need you, Lyel," she whispered into his neck.

"And you shall have me. Take me as you wish, mate."

"Lay on your back," she said, feeling bolder than ever before.

"Tell me what you want, love." When he complied, she climbed up over him, centering his big, vibrating cock at her entrance.

"I want this," she said, stroking his enormous cock. "All of you." Only now, when she was about to feel everything, did she wonder if it would fit. "I, um, I've never been one to compare cocks to vegetables or fruit before, but…"

"Fruit? Vegetables?" His chest shook with his laugh. "Which am I, mate? I do hope you name a decent-sized vegetable."

No matter where you went, guys still worried about cock size?

"More than a banana," she said with a grin. "Though not as wide as an eggplant."

"Is it acceptable that I am not as wide as the plant with an egg?"

"If you want to be inside me, yes."

"I do wish to be inside." His voice came out deep and husky.

"Maybe we could call you an overgrown cucumber."

His thumbs glided across her clit.

Her eyes closed, and she shifted forward, welcoming his touch. "I am wetter than I've been in my life."

"I want you wet, mate. Very wet."

"I'm gonna do it. I am going to take all of you."

"My cucumber."

Her laughter snorted out. "Other Earth women have been with Crakairians. I can make it fit, too, right?"

"We will. Together." The need on his face and in his voice pushed aside her lingering doubts.

"I want you and I'm going to have you." Pressing down, she felt her entrance expand to accommodate his girth. "Oh, wow."

"Too much cucumber?" he panted.

Do. Not. Laugh. But it felt awesome chuckling through sex.

His naanans stroked her breasts while others teased her spine.

"I think your cucumber is just the right size."

Sweat beaded on his scales and trickled down his temples. His body shook with anticipation. "Take as much cucumber as you wish."

"I wish for it all." How awesome would it be when he was buried inside her? She pushed down harder, and he slipped deeper. It ached and burned but felt fantastic. She had to have it.

Rising, she spread herself and dropped down hard.

He pressed upward, ramming himself into her, and they both gasped.

"Yes," she hissed.

"Isi."

She lifted and plunged down again. Damn, he was big, but she could take him all.

Holding her steady, he sat up and they rocked together.

Her moans were echoed by his groans. Their pace got furious as they ground into each other.

"I… I need you," she cried.

He lifted her up and onto her hands and knees then braced her hips to drive himself deeply inside with one stroke.

"Yes." Her guttural cry rang out, and she quivered around him.

He went faster, nearly driving her into the headboard, but she held on, taking him, while her orgasm crashed over her.

He groaned and his cock tightened as he released himself inside her. Muscles straining and his body rigid, he gasped and shuddered.

She dropped to the bed and he lowered himself onto her, keeping them connected.

"You are amazing, mate," he said, kissing the back of her neck.

She shifted slightly, and his body stirred. Oh, my. Stamina in addition to size? She wasn't sure she was ready for…

He pumped slowly, and his cock vibrated, the sensation sinking through her bones. Her spine tingled. Everything tingled.

He nibbled her shoulder, biting down with his fangs. Heat shot to her clit. Okay, maybe she *was* ready for more.

TWENTY-SEVEN

Lyel

H e left the room only long enough to fetch breakfast and obtain disguises.

After eating, they left the room with Isi covered from head to foot in draping cloth and Lyel wearing a headdress that made him resemble a verdisque warrior. It wasn't much, but it was the best he could do without giving away his identity to the world around them.

"Am I going to stand out dressed like this?" she asked as they took the back door exiting out into the alley. He did not wish to bring her through the open sitting area spanning the front of the building. Too many patrons would be eager to collect the bounty.

He saw the posting while he purchased their breakfast in the bakery next door, announcing a reward for a Crakairian and an Earth woman.

"No more than me," Lyel said, adjusting the headdress. It kept slipping forward, covering his eyes.

"How far do we have to travel?"

"The spaceport is half a klek away. We will travel

through the back streets, where there are fewer prying eyes."

She took his hand and squeezed. "We'll get there. Soon, we'll leave this planet."

He kept his gaze trained on everything around them and Isi. Always Isi. He wanted to think about the wonder of them coming together not long ago but did not dare. A simple distraction could prove lethal.

Reaching the end of the alley outside the inn, he poked his head out into the intersection then retreated to lean against the wall of a stone building.

"Anything?" Isi whispered.

"Locals setting up stands. It is market day."

"At least I'm not the hot ticket item."

He tucked his arm around her waist and drew her closer. "You will always be my hot ticket item."

"And you'll be my…"

"Your cucumber?"

They both snickered, but he sobered soon. "We will need to travel down this road to reach the one that will take us to the spaceport."

"I was afraid you'd say that."

"Stay close." He couldn't take her hand as he needed both his hands free for defense. "While I was purchasing our breakfast, I…found this." Pulling a second kalina from under his cloak—an item he also found hanging on a peg in the inn's front room—he offered the blade to Isi. "I realize you still wish training."

She took it and delivered a few careful swipes. "I love it. Let's hope I don't need to use it."

He studied her face, finding only confidence reflected there. No fear. This woman would make any male a worthy mate.

They hurried down the street, passing warnoks and truleeds hawking their wares.

"Fruit for the verdisque warrior? A new shawl for the…female?"

When he and Isi didn't stop, the aliens moved on to other possible customers.

Shouts rang out behind them and while Lyel was tempted to grab Isi and run, he instead paused by a stand full of glittering jewelry. The vendor, believing he might make a purchase, descended.

"As you can see, we have a lovely selection of…"

Lyel nodded while carefully peering over his shoulder, toward the commotion. A fleet of Al'kieern soldiers interrogated a warnok. They dragged him from behind his stall and flew up, lifting him with them. The warnok shrieked, her six arms flailing.

Wailing, she pointed toward where Lyel stood with Isi.

"Oh, oh," Isi said softly. "Time to run, right, dude?"

He clipped a nod and they hurried away from the jeweler.

They were halfway down the road when the bustling crowd ahead of them stilled. A sharp cry rang out, and everyone parted, revealing…

Fedeema stood at the end of the road with a battalion of Al'kieern behind her.

Isi

"Come, Songbird," Fedeema said, her voice a whip on Isi's spine. She pointed to the ground at her feet. "I have decided to forgive you. This time. A new collar waits for you."

Absolutely not! She would not willingly subject herself to what was forced on her by the queen.

Isi lifted her chin and tightened her grip on the kalina. "No."

Fedeema's chest rose and fell with a heavy sigh. "That was your last chance."

"I'm staying with Lyel."

"Then you will die with…Lyel." Fedeema lifted one hand and when it fell, the Al'kieern behind her flew up and over her, roaring toward Isi and Lyel.

Yelping, the crowd scattered, leaving Isi and Lyel standing in the middle of the empty street.

"Run," Isi cried, grabbing Lyel's hand. But when they would've fled, the crowd pressed back on them, shouting taunts and jeers. They crowded around, pushing them toward Fedeema.

While Isi kicked out, taking down the alien in the front, but more shuffled forward, creating an impenetrable alien wall.

"Hold on," Lyel said, lifting Isi off her feet. He jumped, but smacked into a mass of Al'kieern. Rebounding off them with his feet, Lyel flipped and smacked back down on the road.

Angry aliens massed around them, shoving them toward Fedeema.

"I hoped it would not come to this, mate," Lyel said with sorrow.

"It's not over yet," she said, tossing off the cloth drapes that had done little to disguise her and hefted her spear. "We'll fight them."

"Don't. You will be hurt." Lyel snagged the back of her shirt. "I have dishonored myself and you."

"There's no honor in the queen's actions. This is slaughter." Part of her fumed; the rest mourned. They came so close to escaping, to getting a chance to start a life together. "I'm not going down easily."

As her Al'kieen henchmen dropped to the ground and lifted their lasers, Fedeema flew over them.

Isi and Lyel braced themselves, facing her.

Isi snarled, and Lyel's rumbling growl made a few in the crowd take hurried steps backward.

Shouts from the end of the road made the queen turn, but when nothing revealed itself, she turned back to Lyel and Isi. "How did you escape the wasteland?" she snapped. "Who helped you?"

"Birds," Isi said. "Pirate birds."

Fedeema snarled. "Do not lie to me. You know what happens when I am displeased."

"I won't let you hit me again," Isi said, brandishing her weapon.

"You have no say in it."

"I do." Lyel flung his spear forward, impaling the queen in her thigh. She clutched the area with all four hands and staggered backward. Stiffening, she yanked it out, and it fell from her fingers and clattered on the cobble-stone road.

With a roar, Fedeema pulled a knife from her belt and rushed toward them, waving the weapon wildly. Rage burned in her eyes and there would be no more chances.

It was kill or be killed.

Lyel nodded to Isi and stepped behind her, covering her from that side.

Isi rushed forward to meet the queen who was anything but queenly. This horrifying, pitiful alien female had hurt Isi, and it was time to teach her a lesson.

Fedeema slashed out with the knife. Isi blocked the blow with the fleshy part of her arm and twisted Fedeema's wrist, holding tight until Fedeema groaned and dropped the weapon.

Spinning, she delivered a side kick to Fedeema's chest, hurling the woman into her Al'kieern minions. She bounced off them and landed on her ass.

Her Al'kieern contingent rushed to her, their hands fluttering.

"Kill them," Fedeema hissed. "Now!"

As Isi backed away, joining Lyel, the Al'kieern soared toward them.

"Thank you for showing me what it means to love," Isi said, her heart aching.

"Isi." Regret filled Lyel's voice. "When they reach us, run. I will hold them off. Slip into the crowd and hide."

"No way. I'm not leaving you."

"Please."

She shook her head. "I won't. Don't ask me again."

The Al'kieern descended, sneering and waving their laser pistols.

They didn't stand a chance.

He sighed. "I hate that— "

"Halt!" someone shouted.

The Al'kieern kept coming. It would be over soon.

"At least we're together," Isi said. Her voice shook. Facing death would never be easy. She took his hand and squeezed it. "I love you, Lyel. Not sure I told you."

"You showed me, mate, and I love you, too."

"I said halt!" The voice was louder, but really, could anyone control the queen's minions other than Fedeema? And she was fuckin' pissed.

As the Al'kieern engulfed them, Lyel sheltered Isi in his arms.

"Hold tight, love. We will…"

Shots rang out, and the Al'kieern shuddered. They dropped like flies, smacking on the ground where they lay quivering, their eyes staring toward the sky.

"What's going on?" Isi asked, climbing to her feet. Her gaze was drawn to an Al'kieern standing not far from her and Lyel. In the woman's hand, she held a gun Isi had never seen before. She strode toward them, and Isi girded herself for death again. The woman might only be one soldier, but her weapon could level a crowd.

The alien stopped not far from them and dipped forward in a short bow. "You may leave. I will handle…" Her gaze shot toward Fedeema cowering on the ground. "Her."

"Please, my queen," Fedeema whimpered. "I…"

"Silence," the woman shouted, stilling Fedeema. Her gaze fell on Isi and Lyel again. "I should introduce myself. I am Bredera, the newly appointed leader of Mara. Fedeema may think she will usurp me, but it is time for her to learn a lesson. My predecessor suffered an unfortunate…accident, and *I* have assumed command."

Lyel dipped his head. "I am Lyel Tair'im Iradran Sastray."

"I know who you are," Bredera said slyly. "I appreciate your efforts in the wasteland, but I ask you to leave Mara. I will handle eliminating the rest of the operation."

"You will not send ships to Earth?" Lyel asked.

"This is not in our best interest." Bredera studied Isi. "You, I do not know, but I respect a female with your fighting abilities."

"Thank you," Isi said. "What are you going to do with Fedeema?"

"I believe we have the perfect solution for her." Bredera pivoted, and her voice lifted as she spoke to her Al'kieern guard. "Clip Fedeema's wings and throw her into the wasteland. Alone. Allow her one skin of water. No food. And make sure the fence is secure. I do not wish her to escape."

As the Al'kieern guard hauled Fedeema off her feet, Bredera's wings extended and she took flight. The group carried Fedeema up and over the low buildings, in the direction of the desert. Fedeema's scream rang out, but she no longer posed a threat.

Dropping her kalina, Isi turned to Lyel and took his hands. "Lyel?"

"Yes, mate?"

"I want to go to Crakair. I…" She sucked in a deep breath and released it. "I'm ready to go home."

TWENTY-NINE

Lyel

They left Mara in a shuttle for Crakair, and were met at the spaceport by Vork, Lyel's old friend.

After the debriefing, Vork walked them out to the platform where they would book transport to Lyel's estate.

To Lyel's surprise, Vork embraced him. "I am grateful you survived your mission. I worried, my friend."

For too long, Lyel had ached to reach out to his childhood friend. Now, Vork had done it for him. He braced Vork's forearms, the gesture good friends used when they met up after a long parting. "Thank you." His gaze darted to Isi before returning to Lyel. "Perhaps we could get together soon."

"I would like that," Lyel said, his heart lightening. "Com me?" He had to wonder if this was a true overture on Vork's part or if Vork truly would get in touch.

"I will," Vork said.

Isi's gaze flicked back and forth between the two males but she did not speak.

They boarded a craft to take them to Lyel's estate. As their transport left the station, Lyel gave Vork a solemn nod. It contained a promise Lyel would go more than halfway to deliver if his friend felt the same later.

He stared out the window for a minar, unsure what this might mean for his future, until Isi took his hand and squeezed it. He tugged her close and held her as the craft zipped across the city and headed into the country closer to the mountains.

It was late by the time they reached his—their—estate, and they immediately went to bed.

When he woke the next morning, Isi was gone, but she left him a note, saying she was walking in the gardens she saw from the window.

Lyel followed, but a hail on his com stopped him on the front steps.

Vork.

With his fingers trembling, though he had no idea why he was nervous, he tapped to open the conversation.

"Lyel." Vork's voice gave nothing away.

"Is everything all right on Mara?" Was Fedeema stirring up trouble?

"Rest assured. There are no issues on Mara. We are working with the new leader to establish a truce between our nations. All is going well."

In the silence that followed, Lyel ran through a variety of reasons for Vork to hail him.

"I…I wanted to invite you to a party."

This was not one of the reasons. His heart stilled. "A party?"

"Yes. A few males with Earth mates would like to gather together. The females…they enjoy talking."

"I have noticed this."

"Some more than others."

"This, I have also noticed."

"We—*I*—thought you and your new mate would like to join us. It is all right if you cannot—"

"No!" Lyel lowered his voice. "No. I can. We can go to a party. I…I would like this. It would be nice to see you again, Vork. To talk."

"Yes. Bold of me to say, Lyel, but I miss what we had as younglings. I would like to find our way back to that. To friendship."

Lyel rubbed his chest. Funny how it hurt. "I would like that too."

"Time passes too quickly, my friend."

"It does. I am grateful you reached out. We would be happy to come to your party."

"That would be awesome," Vork said. "My mate, Evie, she enjoys to cook Earth dishes." Vork grumbled. "Some are delicious. Others…" He coughed. "We could make… sporgotti. I believe that is what it is called. It is one of the better Earth dishes."

"It sounds…delicious." Truly, just getting the chance to be with his friend…to talk…would make his life complete. He did not care what they ate.

"We were thinking of getting together in two days, if you could join us then."

On what Isi called the weekend, when Lyel did not work. "I—we—will be there." Lyel sagged against the closed door behind him.

"Very good," Vork said. Silence ticked through the com. "Thank you."

"I am glad you called, friend."

Vork's voice deepened with emotion. "I am, too."

They ended the call, and Lyel stared toward the gardens, stunned. Stunned and happy.

His grin soon took over.

This… Such a welcome surprise. He could not wait to

see his old friend again, to bridge their past with the present and move forward together from there.

But for now…Isi.

When he reached the high slester hedges, her lilting voice tugged him along the paths weaving through the maze to the center. His mate called to him, a siren's lure he would be happy to listen to for the rest of his life.

Pausing beside the slester hedge surrounding the small garden where, a yaro ago, he had watched his sister dance, Lyel lifted his com.

This minar. This. He had to record it.

"Waiting here," she sang in a pure, compelling voice that sunk deeply into Lyel's soul. "It's so very clear. This is where I'm meant to be…"

He stepped forward. "Isi." His heart shone in his voice.

"Lyel." She grinned and held out her hand. "You'll never believe what happened." When she flipped her hand over, a matebond symbol gleamed on her palm. "It appeared a few minars ago, when you entered the clearing. Guess you're stuck with me, matey."

He crossed the small grassy area and wrapped her in his arms. A searing kiss followed.

Honor? Restored. Though not in the way he envisioned.

Love? It was his and he would treasure this female for the rest of his daelas.

Happiness?

He bared his fangs as he kissed his mate, and he swore he heard his sister's tinkling laughter.

Isi

"What if they don't like me?" Isi asked as their transport craft zipped toward the city. She smoothed the dress she'd finally chosen, hoping it was the right choice for the party. What if everyone else was wearing ball gowns while she showed up in a sundress? The Crown Prince was going to be there!

Lyel squeezed her hand. "They will love you as I do."

She gnawed on her lower lip. "I'm not one of them." One of the matched brides, that is. "I stole on board the ship. They must think I bumped ahead in the line. And then, when—"

Turning her to face him, he cupped her cheeks in his big hands and kissed her. "Vork said you are welcome."

"Because he's part of the government. He has to say that. I bet I caused a diplomatic crisis. I was a stowaway, and now they're stuck with me."

"Trust me in this?" His words broke through her anxiety. Tugging her up onto his lap, he held her.

She pressed her face into his chest, and his scent and

presence soothed her. Her shoulders drooped. "I'm sorry I'm freaking out."

"No worries."

"I have no reason to be afraid. Here I am acting silly when I should be supporting you."

"I… Strangely enough, I welcome this. I have missed my friend."

She rose up and kissed him. "Tell you what. I'll hold your hand if you hold mine."

He flashed his fangs. "Deal."

The craft landed on a rooftop platform and the hatch slid up. Isi stepped out and waited for Lyel to join her. Night had fallen, and someone strung what looked like twinkle lights around the open rooftop patio but were probably some sort of bug or plant that emitted light. A waist-high wall surrounded the roof, and tables had been set up with cloth coverings topped with flowers in tiny vases. Overhead, the three moons shone down on them. The terror she'd lived through on one of them had started to fade. What happened on Mara was the past. Lyel was her future.

Vork and an Earth woman came down the steps to greet them.

Vork strode forward and braced Lyel's forearms. They performed a sort of bro-hug thing then stepped back, both baring their fangs. "Welcome, friend."

"I…" Lyel's face creased with hope and a hint of joy. "Thank you. It is nice to be here."

"The first of many gatherings," Vork said. It wasn't a question, and he held up his hand. "I am not pushing. Not too hard. But I have missed you and do not want to let more time pass without bringing you back into my life."

"You humble me, Vork. Let tonight be the first of many," Lyel echoed. His gaze met hers, and she read the elation shining there. Tears stung in the back of her eyes, and she sniffed. If they were alone, she'd hold him, kiss him, and tell him how happy she was that he was getting a second chance with his friend. The loss of Vork had left a big hole in Lyel's life. She was glad to see it starting to fill in again. They were taking first steps with many more to follow.

Vork leaned around Lyel, and she marveled anew at how big these guys were. "Welcome, Isi." He stepped back and put his arm around the Earth woman, urging her forward. "This is my mate, Evie. And," he stroked the chin of the baby Evie held, "this is Jacob Lyel Mabir Javaar, our son."

"Vork," Lyel choked out. "You did not."

"I—we—did. I hope it was not too presumptuous. I…I wanted to show faith in our friendship."

"I do not know what to say."

"No need to say anything."

They crowded around Evie to check out the youngling boy.

"Aw, he's beautiful," Isi said, stoking the baby's scaled cheek. His skin was dark green, like his dad's, and tiny fangs poked through his gum line. He stretched his little arms up, and the blanket wrapped around him fell backward. "He has hair!"

"I love it, don't you?" Evie said, stroking the short, silky strands. She grinned at Vork who'd wrapped his arm around her. "Someone around here was hoping desperately for naanans, but now he's decided hair is better. Which it is." The smile she gave Isi included her in the tease.

Isi wasn't sure which she'd prefer in a child. As long as the baby was healthy, it didn't matter. So far, she didn't suspect she was pregnant, but… Wait. When had she last had a period? She couldn't remember, which meant she might be carrying already. Whoa. Her hand went to her belly, but she didn't feel anything yet. The idea made her chuckle. If she was pregnant, she wasn't far enough along for a baby bump.

Lyel winked, but he couldn't know what she was thinking. Once she was sure, she'd share. Hell, she might share anyway, and they could do whatever stood in for a pregnancy test on Crakair together.

Vork's com buzzed, and he frowned down at it.

"A call?" Evie asked, watching Vork's face.

"Hmm. From the Council." Vork tapped into it, and a holoimage of an older Crakairian male dressed in a robe was projected above the device attached to Vork's wrist.

"Commander Vork," the Councilman said. His grayed naanans flared around his head, and his long robe swished forward as he shifted in agitation. "We have a diplomatic crisis, and I need you to come to the Council Chambers immediately to help us handle it."

Isi took Lyel's hand and squeezed. Were the Al'kieern acting up?

"What is the issue?" Vork asked, his voice grim.

"The Driegons."

Vork and Lyel shared a concerned glance, and Vork's posture tightened. "Our extinct ancestors?"

"They are not extinct after all," the older man said. "They have sent an ambassador to the Council."

"This is amazing," Lyel whispered to Isi. "I cannot believe they still live. It has been hundreds of yaros since anyone interacted with them. They are thought to have died out."

"You're talking about the Crakairians with the dragon-like features?" She couldn't imagine meeting someone with horns, a tail, and wings, but she never thought she'd meet aliens. They were an Area 51 myth, not reality. Yet, here she was, mated with a green-skinned, scaled alien, and loving every minar of it.

"What is the crisis?" Vork asked.

"The disease killed most of their females, as it did here on Crakair," the older man said. "They are asking us to facilitate a relationship with Earth. They want—"

"Mates?" Vork's wide-eyed gaze met Lyel's. "How is this possible?"

"That is our challenge," the Councilman said. "We need someone to serve as a liaison for this, and you are the best choice."

"Of course," Vork said. "When do you need me at the Chambers?"

"First thing tomorrow."

Vork's fist pressed against his chest. "I will be there."

"Thank you." The Councilman's image winked out.

Vork sighed. "This is unexpected."

"But welcome, right?" Evie said, leaning into Vork's side. "I have to admit, I'm curious to meet the legendary Driegons. Wings, you said? I can't even imagine." She shook her head. "I wonder how Earth women will feel about matches with a new alien race?"

"I'm curious, too," Isi said, though by the response to the Crakairians, she had a feeling they would be just as interested in getting to know guys who were part dragon.

"It is time, Evelyn," a droid said, whizzing over to Evie. "I will take the child, now."

Tension rippled down Isi's spine. Why would a droid believe it could command such a thing?

"This is Bane," Evie said as if she sensed Isi's worry. "He lives with Lily and Jorg, and he loves kids. Don't you Bane?"

"I have solemnly taken on the task of raising the first

generation of Crakairian-Earthling offspring. I will ensure they are taught proper protocol."

What kind of protocol did a baby need to be taught?

The droid held out its arms. "The child, please."

Evie handed her son over without a care. "Burp him, if you don't mind." She grinned at Isi. "Jacob makes a mess whenever he does it so I tend to foist that task off on Bane, who doesn't mind at all, do you?" She patted the droid's shoulder.

Bane grumbled, something Isi couldn't imagine a droid doing. With the baby in his mechanical arms, he zipped toward the side of the room where someone had set up what vaguely looked like a playpen constructed of living vines. He laid the baby on his shoulder and delivered tender pats to the child's back.

"It seems odd to have a droid babysitter, but this is Crakair, a world completely different from our own," Evie said. "We're a hodgepodge of Earth and Crakairian customs, and Bane somehow fits in with it all. He's actually a sweet guy—droid. Okay, *guy* as he's developing feelings."

Impossible, right? Isi watched Bane carefully settle on the ground, cupping his arms around the baby who seemed quite content to be held by a droid.

"Anyway." Evie latched onto Isi's arm. "Everyone's dying to meet both of you. And food! We've got a bunch of appetizers. But save some room for dinner. I made a big pot of spaghetti, garlic bread, and we have chocolate lava cake for dessert."

"Really, truly lava cake?" Isi asked, salivating already. She loved Crakairian food, but sometimes a girl needed chocolate. "Where did you find the ingredients?"

"Would you believe a few women have come to Crakair—outside the matchmaking program that is—and opened shops in town? The Council freaked out initially but when one of them formed a matebond with the baker, they changed their tune." She led Isi toward the others. "In addition to the bakery, we have a pizza place, and the start of a farmer's market. Jenny brought seeds and is carefully cultivating Earth fruits and vegetables she plans to sell. Right now, she only offers herbs, but everything grows like, well, weeds, here. You know what I mean. Her blueberries are going to be fabulous."

Isi would have to talk Lyel into coming to town every now and then. "Did you really say there was a bakery here?"

"Yup. She makes the best bread. Pastries. Cakes. And despite a few Crakairians sticking their noses up at the idea, many have discovered Earth treats are awesome." Her arm looped around Isi's waist. "While you haven't met everyone yet, I hope once you get to know us better, you'll feel welcome. Vork isn't the only one who needs friends."

"You're sweet to say that."

Evie grinned. "Crakairians are the best, but sometimes it's nice to talk about things we remember from Earth, right?"

Lyel was Isi's best friend, and she was getting to know the Crakairians who worked on the estate, but she missed the camaraderie of Earthlings, too. It thrilled her to think she'd make new friends tonight.

"Axil," Evie said. She raised her voice and waved to a male Crakairian whose back faced them. As he was hunched forward, Isi couldn't see what he was doing. "I'd like to introduce you to Isi."

This was Crown Prince Axil?

"It is very nice to meet you, Isi." Axil turned, holding onto the hands of a tiny girl. The sight of such an enormous guy taking care with a part-Crakairian, part- human child essentially crushed her heart.

Evie chuckled. "I can't believe she's walking already. Isn't Alicia a big girl now?"

The baby cooed at Evie.

"She's sort of walking," a petite woman with long red hair and green eyes said, striding their way. Pausing beside Axil, she stroked his shoulder. "Alicia's only a few months old, but she loves when her daddy helps her walk." The woman held out her hand. "I'm Julia, by the way. And you're Isi, right? I've been looking forward to meeting you."

They shook and Isi stooped down to gush about the baby. "Alicia, you have such cute naanans." They floated around the baby's head, giving her a medusa-like appearance that was unbelievably cute topping a chubby baby face.

Lyel's hand glided along the back of Isi's neck, and her skin tingled. What would a baby they made look like? She couldn't wait to find out. She straightened as another couple joined them.

"I'm Thea, and this is my mate, Gaje." Lifting their clasped hands, she kissed his fingers. "So happy you could join us tonight. We get together about once a lunair, and each of us takes turns hosting. So, tag, you're it!" She grinned and tipped her head to other couples. "I just left our daughter, Stephanie, with Bane, and I'll introduce you later."

So many babies, but when Earth and Crakair set up matches, that was the goal.

While Jacob slept in Bane's lap, Stephanie clung to his neck like a monkey. He carefully plucked the girl off his shoulders and settled her on the ground. "No more of that, Stephanie. Good behavior is essential in the daughter of the kingdom's vizier."

"By the way she follows Bane around, you wouldn't

know Stephanie was ours," Thea said with a laugh. "But since she's occupied with Bane, I'm free for a few seconds and can hit the appetizer table. Babies. I love her to pieces but every now and then, it's nice to take a break from being mommy. Would you like to have a snack before you meet everyone else?" Thea linked her arm through Isi's.

"Sure." It was something Isi could do with her hands. She didn't know why she was still nervous, but there it was. Nothing she could do about it now but go with the flow and hope she loosened up soon.

With Lyel following, she went with Thea over to the table set up with a mix of Earth favorites and Crakairian specialties she recognized after eating with Lyel back home. Stuffed mushrooms! She snatched one up and popped it into her mouth, then wiggled, her eyes closing. "This is awesome," she said around the bite. She grabbed another and tugged Lyel close. "Try."

Reeling back, he narrowed his eyes. "One eats this?"

"It's yummy. Give it a chance. You'll like it."

"I like you," he said, his arm going around her waist to tug her near. "And if you enjoy this Earth delicacy, I am willing to try it." He opened his mouth, and she slid the treat in. After chewing for a moment, his eyes gleamed. "I like this almost as much as you, mate. What is it called?"

"Stuffed mushroom. A mushroom is a fungus. Back on Earth, they're grown in horse manure."

He gulped and swallowed. "Manure?"

"They wash it off."

"I see."

"They do!" She chuckled, and he joined in.

"I'm Lily," a woman said from beside Isi. She tugged a tall Crakairian close. "This is my mate, Jorg." Leaning into his side, she grinned. Her hand stroked her baby bump. "It's so nice to meet you. I want to hear about your adventures on Mara. Jorg and I had our own mishaps on Mia, the smallest moon. Those damn Al'kieern. But I hear you've taken care of that problem for good."

"Nothing made me happier than hearing the Crakairian government has formed a treaty with the new queen of Mara," Jorg said, his arm draped around Lily's lower back. "The Al'kieern kidnapping operation has been eliminated."

"What happened with Fedeema?" Isi asked.

"She is serving out her punishment on Mia in the sand mines."

"What does that entail?"

Grim satisfaction shone in Jorg's eyes. "Much physical labor."

A worthy punishment for the "queen".

"There are only a few more of us left to meet," Lily said. "And good news! There won't be a test later. But to round it out, the two couples dancing are Kral and Mila, and Taylor and Wulf. To help you tell who is who, Mila is the one with brown hair, and Tay's is black." She pointed. "Mila, Taylor, and I were on the same ship you stole aboard—a story I have to hear because holy shit that's amazing. We each had our own adventures, and we're eager to hear all about yours."

"I can't wait to talk about what happened," Isi said.

"Bryk is over by the entrance into the main building with my sister, Sadie. The youngling racing around is Bryk's son, Weld. He's smart and the sweetest kid you'll ever meet." She grinned. "And I think that wraps it up."

Bryk and Sadie were kissing, Sadie's pregnant belly jutting between them.

Isi laughed, feeling better all the time. The women shared a connection that couldn't be denied: they'd fallen in love with Crakairian males. And Isi wasn't an outsider after all; she was one of them. It made her eager to burst into song, but she'd hold back until she got to know everyone better.

With a happy nod to Lily, Isi drifted toward the dance floor and clapped along with Evie and Julia as the two couples swirled and dipped to the music.

Lyel wrapped his arms around her from behind. "Everything dokey okey, mate?" He kissed her neck.

"Dokey okey," she said, tipping her head back to meet his mouth for a kiss. "I'm not worried any longer."

"You are not?"

"Your friends are wonderful. And I'm one of them. I'm glad we came here tonight." Leaning into his embrace, she returned Taylor's wave. Mila grinned her way then stood on tiptoe to kiss her mate. Kral jokingly growled and swept Mila off her feet, spinning around while she laughed. Not to be outdone, Wulf twirled Taylor and then dipped her low to the floor. He kissed her neck, and her fingers wove into his naanans.

Could the night get any better?

"We're one big family," she whispered to Lyel.

His fingers linked with hers. "We are." Satisfaction rang out in his voice as Vork came over to stand beside him. "Finally."

Eight months ago, when Crakair's signal connected with Earth, no one could guess what might come from contact with these aliens.

But to Isi, the end result was perfectly clear.

They'd found love.

And there wasn't anything better than that.

~THE END~

Do you miss Isi & Lyel already?
Sign up for my newsletter & receive a FREE
"cut" bonus scene/epilogue. Lyel has a huge
surprise and, guess what? Isi has one, too.
Sign me up!

Ahhh. I have to admit, I'm teary-eyed.

This is the last book of the Mail-Order Brides of Crakair Series, and it's tugging at my heartstrings. I'm going to miss these characters!

But never fear. I love aliens and there are more stories inside me that have to come out.

Look for my Driegon warriors next. Aliens with dragon features who live in the mysterious, subterranean passages deep beneath the surface of Crakair? I'm in.

Turn the page to read Chapter 1 of Malac, Book 1 in the Brides of Driegon Series

After Driegons, I want to spend time with the Ferlaern, a warrior tribe living on the plains of a nearby planet. If you remember, they waged war with Crakair for many generations before forming a truce.

It seems they're also looking for Earthly brides…

If you enjoyed LYEL, would you
leave a review?

So few readers do.
I'll love you forever!!!
Here's a link.

Want to see what I'm working on next?
Sign up for my newsletter.

You can also find me on Facebook
in my reader group, Alienistas.

Twitter: @avarosswrites
Amazon

MAIL-ORDER BRIDES OF CRAKAIR

Vork

Bryk

Jorg

Kral

Wulf

Lyel

Axil, Gaje

(Companion novellas)

BRIDES OF DRIEGON

Malac

Drace

Rashe

Teran

Kruze, Allor, Skoar

(Companion novellas)

FATED MATES OF THE FERLAERN WARRIORS

Enticed by an Alien Warlord

Tamed by an Alien Warlord

Seduced by an Alien Warlord

Tempted by an Alien Warlord

Craved by an Alien Warlord

FATED MATES OF THE XILAN WARRIORS

Alien Commander's Mate

Alien Prince's Bride

Alien Hunter's Fate

Alien Pirate's Plunder

HOLIDAY WITH A CU'ZOD WARRIOR

Snowed in with an Alien

Falling for an Alien Elf

GALAXY GAMES

Alien Warrior Unleashed

Alien Warrior Untamed

Alien Warrior Unbeaten

Alien Warrior Unclaimed

You can find my books on Amazon.

MALAC

**An alien dragon king meets his
fated mate in a woman from Earth.
With conflict brewing in the kingdom,
will he be forced to make
a heart-breaking choice?**

Bella

When I came to the subterranean kingdom of Driegon as a mail-order bride, I didn't expect the dragon king to sweep me off my feet, take flight, and claim me as his mate. He says a mythical mating ritual called the Torrent proves we're fate. Yeah, sure. Then I find out he's almost engaged. He insists he'll find a way for us to be together, but I've fallen for pretty lies before, and I won't give my heart again easily.

Malac

To end a war among the factions of my Driegon people, I must marry the daughter of a rival warlord. I've accepted my fate. Until I meet Bella, one of three Earthlings brought to my kingdom as mail-order brides. One touch, and my blood roars through me—the first sign of the Torrent. We're fated and I ache to claim her, but I cannot betray my people. But the heart of a dragon will not be denied.

Malac is Book 1 in the Brides of Driegon Series. This standalone, full-length romance has on-the-page heat, aliens who look and act alien, a guaranteed happily ever after, no cheating, and no cliffhanger. Look for the rest of the series on <u>Amazon</u>.

Turn the page to read
Chapter 1 of *MALAC*...

Chapter 1

MALAC

"Then you agree to marry Cuzon Vouster's daughter?" my uncle asked, his thick, scaled brow shaft wedging inward. His slitted eyes remained focused on me, filled with a mixture of sympathy and resolve.

We sat in my office on the fourth floor of the Driegon castle, sipping glasses of whiskern. A cluster of spitzer bugs flickered in the upper corner of the ceiling, highlighting the bookcase below filled with ancient tombs my father had loved. Since his death, I hadn't touched them. I must clean them out someday, but I wasn't ready for the pain I'd feel packing them into boxes. Maybe I could do it next lunair. Or the lunair after that.

"I was not aware Brunjar had a sister," I said. Not that Brunjar and I spoke much about our personal lives, but he was a member of my elite guard. One would think he would've mentioned her to me in passing.

"That is not an answer to my question. And she is his half-sister. Her mother raised her at the family estate in the mountains. I only learned of her recently myself. I understand she is beautiful."

Her appearance truly did not matter. "I appreciate your effort on my behalf, Uncle," I said. After my parents died and I assumed the crown, he left his estates in the mountains and moved to the capital to give me guidance. There wasn't anyone I trusted more than him. "Yet… Marriage to someone I do not know."

"She will arrive in the city soon. Meet her. Talk with her. You will see. This will work very well for you. For the kingdom."

I heaved out a sigh. Leaning back in my chair, I clasped my durclaws together on my chest. My tail thudded on the floor behind me while I watched my uncle shift in his chair. This seemed so reasonable. Why did I hesitate? "My issue is not with the daughter. Assuming she agrees, she will do as well as any other bride. But I always hoped…"

"You wish for a love match through the Torrent," Uncle Grenik said. "And I well understand, having matched through the Torrent myself." He leaned forward. "You know the odds of that happening now are slim."

"There is still a chance."

"With only a handful of females left in the kingdom? Besides, the Torrent is for those without responsibility, not the leader of a vast kingdom. It is better for you to marry someone who brings an alliance."

It was not better. There was nothing wrong with wishing for love.

"My parents found each other through the Torrent and their match served the kingdom well," I said. "Her death devastated our people." She died of the plague that swept through my kingdom a yaro ago. My father died not long after, unable to go on without her, something common in Torrent matches.

As an adult, I should not feel abandoned. If only my

father had found a way to keep going after her death. For me, if not for himself

Grief creased my uncle's face. "So many lost lives, most of them our females. We are a people in mourning; a race with little hope for our future. You can give them that hope by agreeing to this match with the Zoad Clan. They offer a substantial dowry."

I'd never approved of the ancient tradition of buying a female a match. Everyone should be free to choose. "We have more dinars than we can spend in three lifetimes. What good is coin? A male cannot hold it in his arms. It will not bring him lasting joy."

If only I could feel the heartspire thrill of the Torrent, that aching need to be with one, special person. My chest tightened, and I wanted to gnash my teeth. Was I wrong to hold onto this scrap of hope for a full Torrent?

"You are our king. A new ruler who is still gathering the reins of responsibility. Trust me in this. Now is the time to solidify allies, to make agreements that will benefit the kingdom. Our truce with the Zoad Clan is shaky and could fall apart, plunging us back into a war that could destroy us all. Marry her and the Zoad insurgents will back down."

I wasn't sure a marriage between me and the cuzon's daughter would be enough to bring a halt to the conflict, but I held in my thoughts. My uncle was trying to be help-ful. He had worked hard to foster this arrangement for me. I should be grateful. I needed to put aside my own needs and focus on those of my kingdom. Peace was more important than love.

My uncle leaned forward, compressing his forearm aleern feathers on the arms of the chair. "I will tell the cuzon you have agreed?"

For some reason, I could not force a yes past my mouth. Why did I hesitate? I had met almost every surviving female in the kingdom and a Torrent spark had not been lit. It did not matter if I loved this Zoad match or not, though I would do my best to care for her and treat her kindly.

I could find a way to be happy.

"I must tell the cuzon your decision soon." Uncle Grenik shook his head and sorrow creased the paling scales on his face. His shoulder impaler spikes had taken on a gray tinge since my father's death as well. He'd aged during the past lunairs, as had we all. "Your father—"

"If he were here, he would encourage me to find love through the Torrent."

"He would ask you to do what was needed to secure the kingdom."

Would he? Or would he give me the freedom to make my own decision? The head healer said his heart gave out, overcome with grief. But after the recent attempt on my life, I wondered…

Someone knocked on the door, and Drace, the lead cuzon of my elite guard, poked his head through the opening. His sever spikes rippled from his forehead, across the middle of his scaled head, and down the back of his neck, as sign of agitation.

"They will arrive within minars," Drace said, his voice filled with gruff eagerness. He *would* be excited, since he was one of the twenty males chosen to meet and potentially create a Torrent match with the Earthling females. If this group formed marriages, Earth would send more women. It was a chance for our species to thrive once again.

When the disease decimated my kingdom, it also struck Earth, killing most of their males. Rumors of Earth-Crakairian matches reached us, and when I heard the females could form full matebonds, I approached the

Crakairian government to arrange an introduction to Earth. We formed an alliance and the first group of females were traveling through the subterranean passages beneath the surface of Crakair this minar.

"Thank you," I said, and Drace shut the door. "I need to go," I told my uncle, standing.

He peered up at me through his dark slitted eyes. "The cuzon's daughter?"

Say yes.

I could not. Not yet. "Give me a few daelas to decide."

"But—"

I held up my hand. "The cuzon can wait." The entire Zoad Clan could wait. A few daelas would not make a difference.

My father once called me a dreamer. Said I winged too high and wanted too much, that I needed to ground myself in my future role as heir to the kingdom. Perhaps he was right. I had dreamed too long about what could not be. It was time to accept the duties that came with the crown I now wore. This included marrying the Cuzon's daughter.

Love found through the Torrent was for other males. Not me.

My uncle followed me down the stairs to the second floor, but we split on the landing overlooking the main entrance hall, him continuing to his quarters. I paused to peer over the balcony. Below, the marble floor gleamed. The fritzen staff had outdone themselves, polishing and cleaning, and filling pots with dark-blooming flowers. Their sweet essence perfumed the air.

It wasn't often I saw my home as an outsider might, and I was proud of how this ancient building presented itself. The materials used to construct the castle had been painstakingly crafted ages ago from stone harvested deep within the fiery Caverns of Blithe, where it was said our people originated, cast from the very flames themselves.

The front door opened, and a battalion of guards preceded a group of emissaries, a few males, and five women. The battalion bowed en masse to the group and filed back out through the front door, one of them shutting it behind him.

The Crakairians had warned us Earthlings might be frightened by our reptilian features. To present a less intimidating appearance, I arranged for a Zoad with a more human-like form to greet our guests.

Flendor, a signet male with shorter horns, nubby sever spikes on his spine, and lacking the majestic wings many of us took pride in, strode forward and bowed. His tail flicked back and forth and one of the Earthlings released a squeak much like a youngling asptral. The others fluttered around her, peering at everything within sight. Would they see the beauty of the Driegon world?

"Welcome," Flendor said. "I hope your journey was pleasant." I was grateful he remembered the correct greeting.

The images the Crakairians sent did not compare to seeing an Earthling in person. They…amazed me, from the fluff on their heads to their limbs coated with a smooth, unscaled surface in varying shades of tan and brown.

One of the females stepped forward and bowed, her gown swishing across her calves. "I'm Ambassador Smythe." The stately appearing elder fingered her necklace and spread her lips wide, revealing blunted white teeth.

Flendor jerked backward at the implied threat but quickly recovered. We were told Earthlings enjoyed making this teeth-baring gesture, that it meant goodwill. Still, it would take time to feel comfortable with it.

"It is nice to meet you," Flendor said, using the appropriate Earth reply to an introduction. "I am Signet Flendor Ja'dir Albirt Trundesk, an emissary of the Driegon races."

"A pleasure." The Ambassador looked around and smoothed the gray bands bound in a knot at the nape of her neck. So strange not to see spikes on a person's head. And how could she maintain her balance without a tail? The Ambassador gestured to a male standing at her side. I assumed it was a male as it did not possess the two chest accessories I heard distinguished Earthling males from females. "Allow me to introduce Justin Albright, a senior representative of Earth's government."

Justin Albright stepped forward, holding out his hand. When Flendor stared at the appendage, Justin Albright grabbed Flendor's hand and pumped it. "Nice to meet you, Flen. All right to call you that—Flen?" While Flendor blinked slowly, the male peered around. "Fantastic. This is an awesome place you've got here."

"Oh, I do not live here, Emissary Albright," Flendor said. "This is the main palace. I have quarters within the city."

"You know what I mean. And no need to be formal. Call me Justin," Justin Albright—*Joostenn*, it sounded like—said, releasing Flindor's hand and smacking him on the shoulder.

The guards standing on either side of the door hissed and their aleern feathers, the spikes on their lower arms, lifted, secreting toxin.

I waved for them to stand down. These beings were our guests. The motion on Joostenn's part must be a gesture of friendship. I noted it for future use.

As if he sensed the threat, Joostenn spun to face the guards but shrugged and turned forward again when they stared at him blankly.

"Our photographer, Clara Devenshore," the Ambassador said, tipping her head to a female holding a silver box close to her face. She moved around the vast lobby, depressing a tiny button on the side of the box. "Ladies?" She turned to the women fluttering behind her. "Step forward for introductions, if you will."

One of them stepped forward, and I studied the golden fluff on this being's—*her*—head, and marveled again at the smooth material covering the exposed parts of her frame. We were told to expect no scales, but I could not believe this pale, speckled material would protect her in battle. And the fluff was called...hair.

Our healers had traveled to the surface of Crakair and after much persuasion, examined a female mated to a Crakairian. Upon their return, the healers assured us this species was physically and genetically compatible with Driegons. We could mate with them and they would not die birthing a clech of drieglings.

Thankfully, the healers warned us of their peculiar appearance.

"Emmaline Jones," the Ambassador said, gesturing to the golden-haired female.

"Indie," Emmaline said, flashing her teeth.

"Excuse me, dear?"

"Remember? I'm Emmaline *Indie* Jones. I love archaeology, so it fits, right?"

"Yes, yes, of course." Ambassador Smythe blinked as if she needed to gather her wits. "And here we have Bella Loring." Her hand flicked to her left, to a female with fiery hair hanging in waves below her shoulders. Outfitted in a formal Driegon day dress, she was so short, the hem skimmed her shoes instead of lying along her knees, as was usual with Driegon females.

I studied her tiny form. How would a Driegon or Zoad

warrior avoid crushing her during sex? Even the slightest Driegon female would tower over her. *I* would tower over her.

Why did I picture myself lifting her up so our mouths could meet? My heart pounded, a furious beat in my ears. My chest tightened, and I gripped the railing, my fingers biting into the wood.

"Last, but not least," the Ambassador said. Unable to take my gaze off Bella Loring, I only vaguely heard the next introduction. "Aria Gagnon." She tugged on Aria Gagnon's arm, dragging her forward. "Come now, dear. Don't be shy. Say hello to the…Signet, was it?"

Flendor nodded and bowed again. "Signet Flendor Ja'dir Albirt Trundesk. I hope your journey was pleasant."

"Yes," Aria said. She gulped and shot a panic-stricken glance toward Bella Loring. "Thank you."

Joostenn strolled around the perimeter of the large room, and the female with the silver box followed him. He stopped in the double doorway leading to one of the many parlors. "All right to check it out, Flen?" he called out.

"Yes, yes, of course," Flendor said.

Joostenn walked into the room with the box-woman.

My gaze returned to Bella Loring, and my sever spikes prickled. My horns…

I must've made a sound because she looked up. Since I stood in the shadows, she could not see me, but I swore she sensed my presence. I knew this as well as I knew the scaling pattern on the backs of my hands.

My horns twitched, and I reached up to touch them but my hand dropped after making contact. Wonder filled me. My horns had grown. Straightened. And gone rigid.

This…was not possible.

As Bella continued to stare in my direction, the realization roared through me. I was experiencing the first phase

of the Torrent, and this tiny Earthling had made it
happen.

She was my fated mate.

You can find MALAC, Book 1 of the
Brides of Driegon Series
on <u>Amazon</u>

Would you like to read, Kruze,
a novella set in my
Brides of Driegon world?

I've included Chapter 1 here…

KRUZE

**An arrogant, dragon-like alien insists
I'm his fated mate.
I plan to return to Earth.
Unless he can convince me to stay...**

Clara

A hot alien dragonish dude is convinced I'm his mate. No way! Sure, I came to the Driegon kingdom with the wannabe brides, but I was hired to take pictures, not get lured into a secret matebonding ceremony called the Torrent. But when my skin ignites like a sparkler during the reception—seriously need to see a doctor about that—Kruze takes flight with me as his intended bride. He says he'll release me after three days if he can't prove we're fated. If only his touch didn't set my veins on fire.

Kruze

As a warrior and elite member of the Driegon King's Guard, I take what I need. When Clara's skin responds to the Torrent, and my horns flare, it's clear she's my fated mate. Following traditions laid out eons ago in Driegon, I take her deep within the subterranean passages of Driegon for a pairing. I'll release her if I cannot convince her to stay. With my heart at risk, there's nothing I won't do to prove she's mine.

Kruze is a prequel novella in the Brides of Driegon Series. Look for Malac, Drace, Rashe, and Teran, on Amazon.

Turn the page to read Chapter 1…

Chapter 1

CLARA

The Driegonian castle had a living, breathing dungeon. Okay, it wasn't living or breathing as far as I could tell, but it was grimy, cobwebby, and full of secrets I was dying to explore. If finding a dungeon wasn't enough, it was located in the recesses of an *alien* castle deep below the surface of the planet Crakair. How could I resist checking it out?

Sure, I promised myself when I left Earth I'd behave, and I had so far. But when I snuck out of the opening speech of the Driegon bride match reception to use the bathroom, I accidentally took a left instead of a right when I exited the room. Discombobulated as I often was, I somehow found my way to the kitchen, upsetting four hip-high, skeletal alien cooks feverishly preparing food for the celebration that would follow the Matchmaking Torrent.

I'd yet to learn what the "Torrent" entailed…

While the kitchen crew fluttered their sinew-connected bony arms, and squealed in a language my implanted translator did not comprehend, I gulped and gave them a curtsy. They curtsied back, the head cook's solitary horn nearly gouging me in the belly. Since he didn't rush forward and impale me, I must be on to something with the bobbing.

"I'm really sorry," I said, curtsying again for good measure. I backed up, hitting a row of pans hanging from hooks. A few—okay, all of them—slipped off their pegs and dropped to the stone floor. The clatter would wake the dead, which was not a good thought to have while creeping around in an enormous, gloomy, alien castle.

Bones clattering together and their bleached white heads dipping, the cooks scuttled around me to pick up the pans. When they didn't call for guards to arrest me, I sagged against a wall that was fortunately free of hanging pans.

As if that settled it, the cooks returned to work. Phew. For a minute there, I thought they'd… Who knows what? Throw me in the dungeon? That would be awesome. Please.

I rushed across the room, spying a door that I hoped would take me back to the reception hall. Yanking it open, I scurried out onto a landing, finding a set of rickety stairs plunging downward.

"Oh, freakin' cool," I whispered, and my voice echoed back at me. The door closed, hitting my butt and urging me forward.

It was dark down there, but how could I keep myself from seeing where the stairs led? This wouldn't take long. I could snap a few pictures and zip back upstairs before the matchmaking started. Assuming I could find the hall. No one would miss me regardless. Tonight was all about them, the first Earth women meeting their potential Driegon grooms, not the hired Earth crew.

Tiptoeing to the bottom, I slunk out into a long hall.

The decorator used stone liberally. Oh, and metal bars, but this *was* a dungeon.

Since I never—okay, rarely—jumped into things without assessing the situation first, I stopped and peered around before moving forward. No sounds reached me, and the cells appeared empty. Cobwebs networking the corners suggested no one had used the prison—dungeon— in years.

Evenly spaced on the walls, small cages filled with winking lights shot murky beams across the passage, and I paused to peer into one of the fixtures. Creatures the size of my palm flung themselves around inside, slamming against the wooden bars. They stilled while I watched, giving me the impression I was being spied on, too.

Talk about creeping me out. My skin prickled with gooseflesh, and I hurried forward, taking pictures as I passed more empty cells and steering clear of cages filled with fat, sparkly bugs.

As the team's photographer, I wasn't required to take pictures in places like this; I was hired to record every moment of the upcoming, "blessed" event. Tonight, three Earth women would be introduced to a fleet—the Driegonian word, not mine—of bachelor males. Like a TV dating show, they'd chat, stroll through the gardens, dance, and if any of them hit it off with Driegons, they'd participate in the highly secret "Torrent". If heartstrings were not plucked, the women had two choices. They could return to Earth or be transported to the surface, where they could participate in a meet and greet with a different species, the Crakairians. More aliens to get to know, but maybe that group would produce a better fit.

Who would've thought Earth women would arrange matches with aliens?

After a mysterious disease swept through our galaxy,

killing almost all of Earth's male population, the options for having a family were grim. Until a ping reached Earth. Yes, Virginia, there were aliens in outer space, and since they lost females to the disease, they were eager to meet human women. Contact was established and at first, it was a one-way information street with Earth receiving the boatload of tech needed to drag us forward a few centuries. Then one of the alien races made a bold suggestion. As each planet had a mismatch of women to men, why not set up marriages? The doctors did their thing, making sure everyone was genetically compatible, and mail-order bride arrangements were made, first with the Crakairians and now, with Driegonians, a species with dragon-like features.

You'd think Earth women would run in the opposite direction at the thought of meeting aliens, but…

Dragons!

Sort of. We were told they didn't shift; they had dragon body parts, including retractable wings, scales, tails, and… who knew what else? No one had met a Driegon, and the introductory brochure was vague in the description department.

Everyone loves a mystery, right?

Thousands of Earth women begged to be chosen, and a lottery was set up.

Today, the women and Earth dignitaries had arrived on Crakair and were whisked to the subterranean caverns far below the planet's surface, where we were greeted by a Driegon emissary who mostly appeared human—if you ignored his tail and stubby horns. Tonight, we'd meet the potential Driegon mates.

A quick glance at my watch told me I had a few minutes before the meet and greet ceremony started.

"Just one peek," I whispered. "I mean, an alien

dungeon! I'll never get a chance to see something like this again."

While the weirdo lights hissed and banged against their cages behind me, I creaked open a heavy barred door and stepped inside a cell, my heels click-click-clicking on the rough stone floor and my skirt swishing around my ankles. On eager feet, I approached the back of the room and stood staring at the chains with…manacles? hanging from steel spikes embedded in the back wall. Dark stains coated the stone surface, and I reached out to touch—

"You should not be here." The harsh words echoed around me, making my heart stop. Gulping, I spun. My heel wedged between two stones, making me lumber forward, my arms spiraling. I smacked against something solid and surprisingly cool. Wings—freakin' dark blue, webbed wings—wrapped around me, holding me upright. A scratchy-smooth tail coiled around him to tease my calf.

I tipped my head back, looking up, up, up.

"Damn, you're tall," popped out of me.

He dipped his head forward, and I swore his dusky blue horns curled toward me and grew in length, though I must've been mistaken. About ten inches long, they were as thick as my wrist at the base and tapered to a rounded end, but they couldn't move independently, could they?

He grunted. "*You* are not tall."

"You noticed that, huh? I'm five-feet-two, and you're, um, at least seven-feet."

"I do not understand these…fives and sevens."

"I'm talking about height but no worries. Without a tape measure, we can guesstimate."

"You are…different than I envisioned." His teal blue, elongated eyes like a reptile's, drifted across my face, making me feel wound up and squirrelly. "I accept your wingless state, but your lack of scales is a problem."

"Why?"

"How will you protect yourself?"

"With a swift knee to the groin?"

He said nothing.

"It was a joke."

He still said nothing, but his lips twitched.

"I take it you're a Driegon?" My gaze dropped from his penetrating gaze, studying the iridescent scales covering his face. Sharp spikes shot up off his shoulders—his *naked* shoulders—and I had to wonder why he needed body weapons in a peaceful castle. Maybe the spikes were an evolutionary holdout. Larger scales covered his chest and rippled across his taut abs. Black pants hung low on his hips, and a good tug would make them… Don't go there. His scales were made up of a full palette of blues, reminding me of a turbulent sea. His glorious wings trapped me, but I had no urge to back away.

"They're retractable. So I heard," I said.

"What are re…tract…able?"

"Your wings. They somehow recess into your back when you don't need them."

"One could say this."

Oh, one could, could they?

His tail was also scaled but in darker blues with a split on the end. The tip teased across my lower leg. Should I nudge it away? It wrapped around and coiled up to my knee.

"Um, um…" Why did I find the touch of his tail arousing? I shouldn't be thinking about what it might do if it snuck beneath my dress.

"You need to return to the reception hall, brideling," he said. His gaze shot past my shoulder to the stained wall, and his tail whipped away, coiling behind him. "I will join you soon."

"Oh, I'm not a bride. Well, a potential bride, if that's what you mean. I'm here with the staff."

"Yet you feel the early phase of the Torrent?"

His deep, gravelly voice stirred something inside me, like a slumbering part of me rolled over and opened its eyes.

What an odd thought. Totally out of place in this situation. Within days, I'd be back on the ship, returning to Earth. The kingdom of Driegon and this hot alien dragon dude would be a memory. Plus, a steamy, late-night fantasy.

"I'm not sure what you mean by feeling a…Torrent, but perhaps it doesn't matter." I lifted my camera. "I'm the photographer, here to record the event. Nothing else." I backed up, bumping into his wings. They parted, and I scooted through the narrow gap, avoiding the claws spiking from the top of the webbing at regular intervals. The spikes curled forward and the tips glided across the bare skin of my arms as I passed.

"Deadly," I whispered.

"*You* have made *me* defenseless."

"How?"

Silence echoed around us.

"You're not defenseless." My gaze dropped to his hands. His curved thumb claws had to be four-inches long. What would they feel like caressing my body? There was something sexy about a weapon being used for pleasure.

I definitely needed to run, before I asked him to test out my theory.

"You should be careful with your claws. They could pop an eye out." I blurted the words. So much for diplomacy. The ancillary staff had been counseled to behave at all times. Don't make waves and no insulting the Driegons.

Leave it to me to fail during my first meeting. But, jeez, I was talking to a sort of dragon!

"You have nothing to fear, brideling," he said.

"I told you, I'm not a bride."

"Are you sure?"

"Of course I'm sure." My hands fidgeted, and I resisted the urge to step back inside the shelter of his wings.

What was wrong with me? I wasn't the kind of woman who flung herself at a guy during our first meeting.

Before I did something foolish, I scooted around him and darted out into the hall. As I hurried toward the stairs, I glanced back.

The brooding Driegon stood in the open cell doorway, watching me.

When our eyes met, he swept out his wings and bowed.

Look for the Brides of Driegon Series
on Amazon

About the Author

Ava Ross fell for men with unusual features when she first watched Star Wars, where alien creatures have gone mainstream. She lives in New England with her husband (who is sadly not an alien, though he is still cute in his own way), her kids, and a few assorted pets.

www.ingramcontent.com/pod-product-compliance
Lightning Source LLC
Chambersburg PA
CBHW032010150726
47990CB00005B/1910